THE JESUS DNA

A NOVEL

THE ZACH DORSEY SERIES: VOLUME ONE

MARC MOUTON

THE JESUS DNA
THE ZACH DORSEY SERIES:
Volume One

The cataloging-in-publication data ™ is on file with the Library of Congress.

Copyright © 2022 by Marc Mouton

Print ISBN: 978-1-66784-453-4
eBook ISBN: 978-1-66784-454-1

To my family:
Cabell, Skyler, *and* **Sarah,**
for your love and devotion has inspired me.

To my fabulous editor Anne Evans and my creative soundboard Roxanne Marchand, your contributions were invaluable and appreciated.

And to all who have believed in me and my abilities, whose trust and faith in me will be richly rewarded.

"In the End, the Truth will be told"

Jesus Christ

FACT:

- The Roman Emperor Titus, who seized Jerusalem and the Holy Land by force, destroyed all known eyewitness testimonials of the life of Jesus Christ and his apostles in 70 AD. It was not until 80-85 AD, that the second and third generation disciples of the apostle Mark rewrote the first stories, upon which the entire New Testament was based. All Christian writings in the Bible have been rewritten, edited, and translated over the centuries.

- The oldest original Canonical Gospel currently available dates to the 5th century.

- From 70-325 AD, Rome jailed and put to death many Christians as heretics for writing and teaching the historical, but forbidden messages of John the Baptist and Mary Magdalene.

- The Fleur-de-lis is a secret emblem created by French King Clovis I in the 5th century. The symbol represents the divine Royal Blood ancestral lineage of Jesus Christ and his heirs.

- The *Sangreal Documents,* which portray the legendary genealogy of Jesus and Mary Magdalene, are protected by an underground network of faithful guardians from the Jesus of Nazareth Church.

- *"It has served us well, this myth of Christ."* - Pope Leo X, 16th Century

- In 1718, a joint undertaking from two French Kingships, the House of Orleans, and the House of Bourbon, claimed a new crescent shaped river port for France and officially named it New Orleans.

- French Capuchin Father Dogobert de Longuery arrived in the colony of New Orleans in 1743 and served as headmaster of the St. Louis Cathedral until his mysterious death in 1776.

- The Illuminati are a secret society, founded in 1776. Its members pledge absolute obedience to the *New World Order* and have been linked to the Freemasons. The Illuminati ultimately intend to establish a world government through assassination, bribery, blackmail, infiltration of governments, control over banking institutions and other financial powers. It is known that they had a hand in the French Revolution and American Civil War and wielded the power and money behind Napoleon Bonaparte and Adolf Hitler. It is believed that the United States' founding fathers, many of whom were Freemasons, were corrupted by the Illuminati, as witnessed by their official seal on the back of the dollar bill: an Egyptian pyramid with all-seeing eye.

- The Brothers of the Sacred Heart is a religious congregation founded in Lyon, France in 1821. Their mission is the evangelization of young people, especially through their ministry of education, physical and mental excellence, and tiered mentorship.

- In 2022, many around the World believe the End of Days has now begun.

- *"Am I therefore become your enemy because I tell you the Truth? -* Galatians 4:16

PROLOGUE

The dense fog rolling off Lake Pontchartrain held visibility to a minimum in the humid night air. In the affluent Lakeview subdivision, the city's elite occupied the pristine houses with manicured lawns. One of the safest and most esteemed neighborhoods in New Orleans, Lakeview was not usually the target of violent crimes.

However, this night was different.

The overcast night skies obscured the heavens from view. Under the cover of ominous darkness, a trained predator scouted the exterior of the Ratcliffe home, scanning for weaknesses. Noticing that the rear of the structure provided the best chance for an undetected entry, the attacker identified a small inlet alcove with the façade of a secured entrance. Using an eighteenth century locksmith's device to release the deadbolt, he easily gained entry through the rear door.

No alarm was set tonight.

The assailant quickly evaluated the floor plan and situation. He surveyed every room on the first floor, but didn't spot his intended targets.

Quietly climbing the masterfully crafted oak stairs, the intruder focused on a large upstairs bedroom, where he discovered that Holden Ratcliffe, and his young pregnant wife, Evelyn, were sound asleep. The humming of the air-conditioning unit silenced his entry into the bedroom. He paused, mentally preparing for the task at hand.

Relishing in his assignment, the infidel leaned down and snapped the neck of Holden Ratcliffe. The God-awful sound of the skull breaking from vertebrae awakened Evelyn.

She sat up and screamed.

The shrewd assassin reached into his dark brown cassock. He pulled out a chrome- plated pistol from his cincture as Evelyn begged for the life of her unborn children, as she was pregnant with twins. The man leveled the pistol at her chest.

The terrified woman asked, "Who are you, and what do you want?"

"I am the bringer of eternal light," answered the man, "If you want your child to enter this world alive, tell me what I need to know. Where have you hidden the Sangreal?"

"Sangreal? I don't know what you are talking about. You must believe me," Evelyn pleaded. "Please, this is my first pregnancy, and I am only twenty-eight years old."

"I will ask one more time, and I suggest you reconsider your answer. Where is the Sangreal?"

"I swear, I know not what you are seeking. If it is a matter of money, I am willing to help …"

It was of no use, the man was remorseless, harboring a deep seed of resentment for those who tested his patience. He quickly shot the woman in the chest, then directly into her bulging stomach. She collapsed back onto the bed.

The residual smoke from the pistol drifted into the air and faded away.

The hired gun observed his handiwork for almost ten seconds before taking a Polaroid picture for verification. With his mission completed, the assassin successfully departed.

Less than a minute later, Evelyn Ratcliffe's eyes fluttered open. She sat up and started to cough. A small stream of blood ran down her chin. Now conscious, but in shock from her gunshot wounds, she pieced together what just happened. Her husband and soul mate's lifeless body lay next to her. She placed her left hand on his forehead and made the sign of the cross with her right.

Knowing that she herself did not have long to live, she struggled to reach into the nightstand drawer next to the bed. Evelyn pulled out an ancient, heterodox wooden crucifix and a brass-plated device. She pushed a small black button located on the top of the brass electronic apparatus. A distinctive red light on the device began to blink periodically as she dropped it to the floor. With her remaining strength, Evelyn placed the cross around her neck and gently laid it on her blood-soaked chest. She gathered her hands and started to rub them together in a rapid motion until a magical, heavenly light illuminated from her palms.

The intense light was warm and inviting.

She placed her hands on both sides of her enlarged and hemorrhaging stomach and began to pray in Latin: "*Non omnis moriar. Dei gratia, fata viam invenient. Amor vincit omnia. Vis medicatrix custos, alea jacta est in aeternum.*" (*I shall not wholly die. By the grace of God, the fates will find a way. Love conquers all things. The healing power of the guardian, the die is cast forever.*)

Within ten seconds, it was over. Evelyn fell lifeless, and the house became eerily quiet.

CHAPTER 1

Friday, 8:46 AM - Uptown, New Orleans - 2021

The blaring car horn jolted Zach back into reality. He quickly realized that, again, his mind had been somewhere else. Glancing down at the clock, he accelerated his battered, 2006 silver Honda Accord across the intersection. He had just fourteen minutes left to make it to the Tulane's University Theater Hall, where he was set to partake in a much-anticipated lecture by his idol.

Zachary Dorsey's friends considered him an all-American guy, featured with stone brown eyes, chiseled good looks, and a slim, athletic frame. He would take a ribbing because he bore a virtual resemblance to a youthful Robert Redford in preppy clothes. Most considered him a spiritual academic, resourcefully intelligent, but with the impetuousness of youth. Zach always strived to learn more about himself, his spirituality, and his place in the world. If he had a true negative, those closest to him would say he was naïve to the real world: always willing to help and joke at every turn, willing to forgive, and willing to look the other way to be accepted by the masses.

As Zach pulled in a parking spot next to the main campus center, he reached for the inside pocket of his worn tweed sport coat to collect his carefully worded introduction of his mentor, Brother Guiden. Even though he had been blessed with an unabashed confidence in his eidetic memory and raw public speaking abilities, today was the final step towards receiving his hard-earned degree in theology and acceptance from his peers, especially from Brother Guiden. Guiden, the popular leader of the Brothers of the Sacred Heart, housed at the Notre Dame Seminary on Carrollton Avenue, was the only true father figure that Zach had since he was taken in as an infant after his parents' death. This man, whose hair now exhibited streaks of gray from his many years of experience, had sternly and lovingly mentored young Zach in the traditional ways of the world as well as some of the mystical experiences of the disciplined monastic life. As a young child, Zach was reading by age two, writing text by age four, a published poet by age seven, and, by age ten, could speak six languages fluently.

Zach ran a hand through his still damp, sandy brown hair as he reviewed every detail of his introduction one more time in his head. He took a second to close his eyes and take a deep breath, trying to relax. He made sure to say a short prayer. A tremendous calm engulfed him, and a breath of fresh air blew away all doubt about his calling. Just then, his cell phone rang. It was Sam.

Samantha DelaCroix, smart and pretty, with watchful brown eyes, long, flowing black hair and beautifully tan skin, was one of Zach's most trusted comrades. They had known each other since the beginning of his studies at Tulane University. Although always uniquely attracted to one another, for whatever reason, dating never seemed in the cards for Sam and Zach.

She called to find out where he was and to personally inform him of the standing-room only crowd. Zach smiled to himself. Sam was always his biggest fan. Zach checked the time again - eight minutes left. He scrambled out of his car and grabbed his notes, then made his way into the bustling arena.

Tulane's main auditorium, nestled on tree-lined Saint Charles Avenue in New Orleans, was still under repair from damage suffered by the floodwaters of Hurricane Katrina. Upon entry, the conspicuous smell of fresh plaster and paint prickled Zach's nose. The university had refurbished all of the wonderful, hand-crafted, marble statues and colorful hand-painted symbols dating back to 16th Century France in the arena. It replaced all of the theater chairs with plush royal-red movie-style stadium seating that could hold up to 500 guests. On this day, hundreds of religious scholars and priests occupied the main seating area. Miscellaneous guests and a sprinkling of students filled the remaining space to capacity. A large, separate projection screen, podium, and microphone stood on the intimidating main stage. In a theater of this size, a distinct echo could be heard. Zack shook at the thought of hearing every word he said reverberated back at him a half-of-second later.

As Zach entered the theater, Professor Earl Lindrum, Chairman of the Tulane Theology department and Zach's academic advisor approached him.

"Dorsey, where have you been?"

"Don't worry sir," Zach replied. "I'm ready to go. How do I look?"

"Fine." Professor Lindrum looked him over. "You're the last of the honor graduates to introduce a featured speaker. Do you realize that Vatican TV will be broadcasting this specific lecture live back to Rome?" Professor Lindrum nervously fiddled with a crucifix strung around his neck. "Brother Werner from the Vatican's media department stated earlier this is the first time that a sitting pontiff has ever made such a request. It is quite an honor."

"Relax, Dr. Lindrum," Zach answered with a smile. "I won't let you down, I have my notes right here." He patted the pocket of his sport coat.

"Let me see those." Zach handed over his notes. "The good brother has switched the main title of his discussion. I'll write it down for you." Dr. Lindrum made a few corrections and handed the paper back to Zach. Meanwhile, Brother Guiden distributed reports covering his findings and introduced himself to certain scholars and priests throughout the room.

When it was time, Zach nervously approached the podium as the audience quieted. He looked out into the vast sea of humanity. With the lights shining brightly upon him, Zach began, "I am proud to announce that the last lecturer of this week's series on *Religion in Today's Society*, is my personal mentor and teacher. Please welcome Brother Jeremiah Guiden, recipient of a 1979 doctorate in Ancient Theological Studies from Tulane University and Headmaster of the world-renowned Notre Dame Seminary located right here in New Orleans."

Zach paused momentarily before continuing, "Brother Guiden will be presenting the widely discussed and highly controversial subject of…" He glanced briefly at his corrected notes, "*The Jesus Unknown*." Confused, Zach abruptly ended, "Sir, the floor is yours."

Brother Jeremiah Guiden approached the podium and graciously responded to the audience, "Thank you Mr. Dorsey, my peers, esteemed colleagues, and the viewing audience of Vatican City in Rome." A proud and astute man, Brother Jerimiah was formally dressed in a silver cassock bound by a royal purple rope band. He spoke slowly, specifically emphasizing the words projected on the overhead screen behind him, "*Legends are born when the truth is too dangerous to write.*" He took a second to scan the audience, "I want all of you to think about that for just an instant." Brother Guiden gave the appearance of making eye contact with every person in attendance. This attention to detail always made his lectures legendary.

"If you are present today, it means that you, too, have questions in search of answers," Brother Guiden continued. "I will take it for granted that human nature forces society to always ask what, when, how, and why. I will suggest now that absolute truth in religion is a powerful and well-guarded subject, one that has piqued the interest of all Muslims, Jews and Christians in the twenty-first century." Brother Guiden paused briefly, "You know, there is a rumor going around that to be a good Christian and get into heaven, you need only do three things, over and over again: *Pray - Pay - and Obey.*"

An unintended laugh surmised from the crowd.

"It is my opinion; a good Christian is not that at all. A good Christian is a person who models themselves after Jesus Christ, a true revolutionary. Someone not afraid or ashamed to get up and speak the truth."

Gentle applause erupted.

"Remember, in all the written materials, there is only one instance that caused Jesus to become angry: when he traveled to the Temple Church and witnessed what a travesty humanity made of religion. Since I became a Christian all those decades ago, there is one thing I have yet to figure out." Brother Guiden displayed the following question on the projector screen: "Specifically, why has the Roman Catholic religion been so popular, and might I add, profitable, in recorded history?"

He paused to let this question sink in. "Over the last two-thousand years, the Roman Catholic Church has relied exclusively on the faith of its followers. As the head of the Brothers of the Sacred Heart, I'm not bound by Church canon like Catholic hierarchy, so I do not defer to certain traditions or code of conduct. Because of this, I feel it is my solemn duty as a historian and a man of God, to share with all my brothers and sisters what I have learned about the *true Christian history*. So, let's continue. What is religious faith? Faith, in stunning simplicity, is absolute conviction without confirmation. Essentially, belief without proof. Does a religion really have to be based just on faith without any scientific explanation or evidence?"

The audience murmured amongst themselves.

"The Church has been unsuccessful in its many attempts to provide evidence other than the Canonical Gospels (Matthew, Mark, Luke and John), which have been proven to have been edited by the church itself. For example, Bishop Clement of Alexandria, in 195 AD, made the first known change to the Gospels. On his influential authority alone, the Bishop completely deleted a substantial section from the Gospel of Mark, and justified his exploits in an ancient codex that is still preserved today. He stated: '*For even if they [the apostles] should say something true, one who loves the truth should not agree with them - for not all true things are to be said to all men.*'

Brother Guiden leaned over the podium, his excitement for the topic building in his voice, "As a matter of record, over the last several centuries, the Church has had to defend itself numerous times in the wake of new and recent scientific and historical discoveries like that of the Gnostic Gospels in 1945. For over two-thousand years, the Church has forbidden any Christian to question the validity of scriptures related to the life of Jesus Christ. In 1965, the Second Vatican Council reversed centuries of intellectual repression with the publishing of *The*

Church in the Modern World. With this publication, freedom of inquiry and discussion was finally encouraged by the Church."

"In 1985," he continued with enthusiasm, "I was part of a group of distinguished scholars that met in Berkeley, California, called *The Jesus Seminar.* Our job was to discuss the New Testament as it relates specifically to Jesus and his historical life. Our goal was to determine, once-and-for-all, what was fact, and what was fiction among the scriptures. This pursuit took several years of pain-staking academic study and analysis. Today, I am ready to reveal to you, what one-hundred and fifty of the greatest religious minds on the planet contemplated."

Brother Guiden realized that he was starting to preach instead of teach, so he took a moment to lighten up. "Is anyone familiar with the old French word *Sangreal?*" He asked the audience as he displayed the word on the overhead screen.

A handful of clergymen yelled out, "The Holy Grail."

"Well, sir, you are partially correct, according to thousands of years of history, anyway. In the old French dialect, *San Greal* has the literal meaning 'Holy Grail.' Most people think of that term as the cup or chalice that Jesus drank from during the Last Supper. But I am going to ask you to do what I have asked my own colleagues to do many times: Think outside the box. Open your mind and take a closer look. Sometimes the truth is right in front of us all."

The Brother took out his black pen and started to write on a clear transparency for the overhead projector. "While *San Greal* means 'Holy Grail,' a slightly altered interpretation, S-A-N-G / R-E-A-L is strictly translated from Old French as **Royal Blood**. Hmmm. Does that raise any red flags for anyone out there?" He scanned the audience as its members whispered to each other.

"So, is the *Sangreal* the Divine Chalice that Christ used at the Last Supper? Or is it the being or vessel that actually passed *down* the Royal Blood of Jesus Christ, the Son of God?"

His audience started to lean forward in their seats, and their frowns and scowls told Brother Guiden they were fascinated, if not repelled, by his indoctrination of the life and meaning of Jesus Christ.

"After his resurrection from the dead, Jesus told Mary Magdalene that 'In the End, the Truth will Be Told.' Many religious leaders believe that we are currently living in the precursor to the End of Days, or the Apocalypse. Look around you: Catastrophic natural disasters like Hurricane Katrina, constant war in the Middle East, and terrorist attacks like September 11th. If this is really the beginning of the end, is God trying to correct history as we know it?

"I have investigated many philosophical theories to secure a logical basis for my Christian faith. I believe that Jesus was a human man. Spiritually divine, but human. He ate, drank, loved, and suffered just like every human. I also believe that expressing love and affection is what makes a person truly human. The Church needs us to believe that Jesus chose a life of celibacy. The evidence I plan to present today indicates not only that he was married, but produced ... a *Royal Blood offspring*."

CHAPTER 2

Friday, 3:07 PM - Vatican City Suites in Rome

Accompanied by a stunning female companion, a man known only as the *Holy Seer* watched the live closed-circuit telecast from his luxury accommodations in the Vatican Suites. The man picked up the phone and dialed a series of thirteen numbers. The call was immediately answered by his assistant, Tiberius.

"How may I serve?" Tiberius asked.

"Tiberius, are you in position?"

"As instructed, I am outside of the boy's home awaiting your orders."

"The target is vacant. Proceed with your duties," the Holy Seer confirmed.

"Understood." Tiberius, a toned, dark skinned manservant, had worked professionally for the Holy Seer for many years. Master made sure from the tone of his voice, that this by far, was his most important mission.

The Holy Seer's attention was now engrossed by the beautiful and mysterious Cara Lesem. Cara was the first female victor of the ancient tournament for the order-for-hire assassin cult called the *Punarjanam*, Islamic for Rebirth. The Punarjanam order and its origins could be traced back twenty-five hundred years, to the religious descendent warriors of the Persian Army, once, the greatest army who roamed the Earth. Cara, with her short brown hair and smokey green eyes, wore a flattering, low cut, beige blouse with a white, seamless silk skirt. She meandered out to the balcony area in her high heel pumps. Here she could see the entire layout of Vatican City first hand. Her gaze swept over St. Peter's square, the green-gold tinted domes of the museum and cathedral, and the orange rooftops. The sun sat on the apex of the horizon. She sighed at its luminous beauty. As a master of the martial arts, Cara was now employed by the Holy Seer as his personal body guard and protector. She was his trusted sounding board as well as the occasional mistress to his sick and perverted sexual fantasies.

#

Minutes later, at the Carrollton Apartments in New Orleans, a popular haven for many Tulane students, Tiberius knocked on the door of apartment number seventeen. Confirming that no one was home, he picked the simple door lock and gained entrance to the small, one-bedroom apartment. Tiberius, avoiding a few weeks worth of dirty clothes spread along the floor, immediately headed straight for the computer, and inserted a thumb drive. Within seconds, he began to copy all of the existing stored computer files. While he waited, he rummaged through the physical belongings in search of something. Something of grave importance.

CHAPTER 3

Friday, 9:19 AM - Tulane University, New Orleans

Brother Guiden could see that Zach, now seated, quietly conversed with the man he had met earlier,

Brother Saul Werner, Director of Media Services at the Vatican. Brother Werner was a delicate looking man in his fifties, an intellectual whose reddish hair was probably cause for much teasing in his youth.

Brother Guiden continued, "With so many convincing links and recent discoveries over the past century of this prominent story, I decided to take my research to the beginning, all the way back to the time of Jesus and the Apostles. It is a proven scientific fact, that the Bible, as we know it today, is at least five linguistic removes from the original scribe. Since there are no first-hand testimonies that can be diligently researched, my main focus was one of an academic collaboration of all of the historical works written about Jesus Christ. I took into account both the Canonical and Gnostic versions, plus looked at the legends that were born in the main populous of that era. The laws of probability state that we will be able to form a pretty solid representation of the fundamental truths about the real life of Jesus Christ."

Brother Guiden took a brief moment. "I have learned that only two different people are named in the New Testament as having officiated major rites in Jesus' life: John the Baptist, who baptized Jesus in 30 AD, and Mary Magdalene, who witnessed his crucifixion and anointed him at the end. Yet the Canonical Gospel writers marginalized both people, and only included them because what they did was far too important to leave out. Both the Baptism and Anointing imply authority on the part of those who officiated. Perhaps it is no coincidence that the Roman Church was founded by Saint Peter, who emerges from the newly recovered Gnostic Gospels as a man with little patience and who was slow to firmly understand Jesus' teachings. Peter's documented jealousy and hatred of Mary Magdalene, whose life he actually threatened, and also his disdain for the entire female race, suited Roman needs. From all my research, it is clear that Mary Magdalene was one of Jesus' favorite and most loyal disciples."

Guiden paused, trying to swallow against a dry throat. "Please raise your hand if you were taught in Sunday school that Mary Magdalene was a prostitute."

Almost everyone in the audience raised their hand.

"Was Mary a prostitute? Absolutely not. Such an idea is rubbish! Mary was made a prostitute in history by the Church, and that biblical manipulation lasted over 1500 years until the Vatican was finally forced to issue a little-known reversal decree in 1969. What the Canonical Gospels do not mention is that Mary Magdalene was a woman of means who actually assisted in the bankrolling in the ministry of Jesus and his disciples. Mary Magdalene has been called the most indefinable person in the New Testament. She is the only woman in the Gospels to be identified entirely as her own individual and is always depicted in history as wearing red, an iconography for her queenly stature in Nazarene tradition. I have also noted that nowhere in the New Testament does it state that Jesus was celibate. I believe that on the night of the Last Supper, Mary Magdalene, as well as John the Baptist, were both present with the other apostles for the celebration of the Eucharist."

Brother Guiden could feel the current tension growing in the audience as his verbal assault exposed thousands of years of the Church's weaving of a tangled web of half-truths and outright lies. He placed a new slide on the overhead projection screen for all to view. The iconic images filled the screen with what appeared to be Egyptian hieroglyphs, cartouches, and cuneiform engravings: line after line of mysterious symbols distinctly drawn with the remnants of color shading.

"This historical passage was discovered in 2007 inside the great pyramid in Giza. It is a tale not spoken about in public until today. A rough translation is as follows." Brother Guiden placed a pair of bifocal glasses onto the tip of his nose. "On the eve of darkness, in the Garden of Gethsemane, when the original apostles were spellbound and asleep, Christ beseeched the heavenly father for physical and emotional strength. As the wind whipped the grassy knolls, Mary Magdalene and John the Baptist arrived in the presence of Jesus. And it is understood: God has sent Mary and John to Jesus to be his physical and emotional strength. Jesus, knowing where his fate lies, asked John to perform the proud tradition of Holy Matrimony. And as it was commanded by the heavens, man and woman are joined as one. Duality becoming unity, love begat love. Once the sacred ritual was completed, Jesus and Mary were left alone in the misty garden hue. It was at this time that they consummated their love, marriage, and commitment to one another, and the seed was planted to the greater glory of God's will. The apostles awakened, not knowing what had transpired, and Jesus, with his new strength and conviction, was taken into Roman custody. At this time, the Lord spoke, *'Father, if this is your will, then it shall be done.'* That night, a new star was bequeathed by God himself, became visible to the eye of the beholder, and was known as the *'One Star Rising,'* a vital symbol that changed humanity for all eternity."

The audience murmured to each other as they took in this news. Unfazed, Brother Guiden continued, "The next day, Jesus made the torturous half-mile gauntlet carrying the cross through Jerusalem, was crucified, died for our sins, and was buried. On the third day, he was resurrected from the dead. It was to Mary Magdalene that he bore witness and gave instruction to, not Peter. Apart from the Virgin Mary, Mary Magdalene is the only woman reported, specifically by her individual name, in all recorded gospels, and her significant value is suggested by the fact that, almost without exception, her name comes first whenever a list is given of Jesus' female followers, ahead of even the Mother Mary. She was present at the Anointing, Crucifixion and Resurrection, and it is her testimony alone on which all of the gospel writers rely for their information. The church initially recognized her utmost importance to Jesus by granting her the title in the religious hierarchy of *Apostola Apostolorum* or the Apostle to the Apostles / The First Apostle. But the Church elders, for whatever reason, would soon deny this important revelation.

"After the Resurrection, Peter, Paul, and the rest of the apostles preached the word of God that was acceptable to the Romans of the time. The Romans knew that simply by removing Jesus' image from the front lines and denying any possible bloodline, the popes and cardinals could reign supreme and be adequately controlled. The only way for the Roman Church to restrain the heirs of Jesus and Mary Magdalene was to discredit Mary herself and deny any marital relationship with Jesus. Mary was then portrayed unjustly as a whore and sinner in history. For her own safety after the crucifixion, Joseph of Arimathea, James who was presumed to be Jesus' brother, and John brought Mary Magdalene, now pregnant, to Alexandria, Egypt. There they settled in a nondescript, growing Jewish community and planned for the future."

Brother Guiden displayed the image of an ancient map including Israel, Egypt and France on the projector. "Presumably, this schism left Peter and Paul in control of the Roman Church hierarchy and cleared the way for Peter to become the first pontiff on record in contemporary history. So Mary Magdalene, Joseph, and John, together with Mary, mother of Jesus, Mary Jacobi and Mary Salome, Jesus' aunts, Philip, Thomas, Mary Magdalene's brother Lazarus and sister Martha, formed the *Nazarene Church of Jesus*, and passed the true message of God down through the divine blood generations.

"By the end of 33 AD, the year Jesus was crucified, Mary Magdalene had given birth to a Daughter in Egypt and named her Sarah, which means Princess in the Jewish natural tongue of Hebrew. It is said that within three years, The Nazarene Church of Jesus had over ten thousand followers in Egypt alone. It was in 37 AD that the divine leader of the New Christian faith, Mary Magdalene, met an Egyptian sage named Ormus, who converted to Christianity and was baptized by John. Ormus was the key to the rapid expansion of Christianity in all of Egypt, since he was well-respected and his position was one of honor and truth. Ormus pledged to Mary Magdalene and the Christian fellowship his life in service.

"In 42 AD, Mary Magdalene and her daughter Sarah, along with the new Christian hierarchy, traveled to the South of France by a boat with no oars, and landed on the Coast of Roussillon, at a place still called *Mas de la Madeleine*. Mary and her disciples settled in

Languedoc. It was at this time when King Herod Antipas, now exiled in Southern France, heard of the return of John the Baptist and had him arrested, then beheaded, with what little power he had left. Knowing that Christians would repeatedly be hunted and persecuted for their beliefs, Ormus recruited an arcane, underground organization of powerful individuals who were committed to the Christian cause, and in 46 AD, he named this organization the Order of Sion. The Order of Sion was formally charged with the awesome responsibility of protecting the Holy Bloodline. A strict code of Nazarene law governed the Order's business. The true brilliance of Ormus languished and ultimately vanished in history unappreciated."

Brother Guidan looked intently at his audience, making eye-contact with those who would meet his gaze. "All of what I have learned about this journey through historical fact cannot just be construed or justified as coincidence when, actually, it points to the beginning foundation of the greatest cover-up ever told in history."

CHAPTER 4

Friday, 3:32 PM - St. Peter's Basilica, Vatican City

In the mystical, shimmering gold of St. Peter's Basilica lay the executive hideaway for the holy of holies, a man so enriched with power that he was the undisputed leader of the largest organization in the modern world. This sacred man was bejeweled in an elegant, long, white silk robe adorned by a single purple drape and was comfortably viewing a closed-circuit feed on his digital, high-definition plasma screen. He was easily identified by his priceless gold, ruby, and diamond-encrusted ring. His oversized wooden crucifix, bound to a singular leather strip, lay at his waist. Pope Aloysius watched the live telecast of Brother Guiden's controversial lecture on Vatican TV.

Realizing the potential fallout of such information being released, the pope smiled and gently whispered to himself in amazement, "Quid pro quo, Brother ... quid pro quo. I will see you soon, my friend."

CHAPTER 5

Friday, 1:51 PM - Tulane University, New Orleans

Reaching the climax of his speech, Brother Guiden refused to hold back as he continued his controversial and mesmerizing dissertation on the *Unknown Jesus.*

"In the following years, as Mary Magdalene's teachings took root and spread, Sarah began a family of her own. Within seven years, Sarah produced three male heirs to the Holy Bloodline, better known by today's scholars as "The Trinity" or "Fisher Kings." Mary tutored all of her grandsons using her profound first-hand knowledge of the teachings of Jesus Christ. Each of the boys were assigned a devoted apostle of the faith from the Nazarene Church of Jesus and granted a lifetime guardian from the Order of Sion. The names and Gospels of these three remarkable men were recorded and stored in a secret burial vault, yet to be found by modern archeologists. Legends say that the Trinity or Fisher King Gospels contain the still undiscovered parchments of the inspirational words of Jesus himself, written in his own hand, intended for Mary Magdalene to use in the *Original Bible.*"

You could have heard a pin drop in the auditorium as the good brother continued with his lecture.

"The heirs of the Royal Blood openly appealed to their followers, and were deemed more credible than Peter's ministries because they were blessed with a unique gift: they could heal the sick, just as their grandfather Jesus had done. Stories, passed verbally through the years, state that a true heir of Jesus would have the flow of magnetic energy or life-force that radiates from the body. It was also believed that an heir of Jesus had the power to read minds and communicate with nature. The heirs could also telecommunicate with one another. Needless to say, after the sudden popularity and notoriety that the Trinity generated, especially from the Romans of the day, the Order of Sion, for their safety, brought Royal Blood heirs underground. Out of the public eye, they flourished for many centuries.

"Roman history states that the Roman Emperor Titus, who seized the Holy Land of Jerusalem by force, destroyed all known eye-witness testimonials of the life of Jesus Christ and his apostles in 70 AD. It wasn't until 80-85 AD that the second and third generation disciples of the Apostle Mark rewrote the first stories, upon which the entire New Testament was based. The Bible as it is published today, has been rewritten, edited and translated over the centuries, not just by the Romans, but by the Catholic Church itself.

"In 1945, the Gnostic Gospels were discovered in some mountainous caves by a poor, local man at Nag Hammadi in Egypt. This man, not understanding the value of his discovery, put the remaining collection of writings (that were not used for fueling his home fire) up for sale in the local marketplace for the equivalent today of a mere thirty dollars. The surviving documents span over fifty authentic Christian texts and scrolls, some from the same time as the Canonical Gospels, and include versions of the Gospel of Mary Magdalene, the Gospel of

Thomas, the Gospel of Philip and the Gospel of Sofia. Today, many scholars genuinely believe that the Gnostic Gospels contain as much historical information as those of Matthew, Mark, Luke and John.

"Saint John the Divine wrote the *Book of Revelations* in the 3rd century. Many biblical scholars consider it a coded connivance Gospel of the continuing story of Jesus, Mary Magdalene, and the Holy Blood heirs. The book refers to Mary Magdalene's pregnant state at the time of her exile and persecution by the Romans, and it refers to the future of Christianity with the foundation of The Trinity's growing ministries.

"The Roman Catholic Church never wanted its followers to know about the marital relationship between Jesus and Mary Magdalene. This knowledge would erode the Church's enormous power and negatively affect financial offerings, which is why the Gnostic Gospels were not included in the New Testament. The original exclusion of these Gospels was officiated at the Council of Nicaea in 325 AD. The bishops in attendance acted out of self preservation, for the power of the true Christian tradition was now too eminent among the people for the Church hierarchy to control."

Guiden paused momentarily. "Now let's discuss in further detail the *Sangreal Documents,* or what I like to call *The Jesus DNA*." Brother Guiden displayed the list of genealogies on the computer screen.

The Jesus DNA (33-131)

Jesus & Mary Magdalene

|

Sarah

/ | \

The Holy Trinity

"The *Royal Bloodline* were separated to France, England, and Egypt to be raised independently. Over the years, the Royal Blood heirs have been in constant danger. There have been thousands of assassinations of the heirs, first from the Roman Church, then from numerous royal family factions, and finally from the Illuminati and other secret religious societies. It is believed that if the Royal Blood heirs can be exterminated, the Roman Catholic Church and the existing monarchies will forever hold their monopoly on religion and sovereign power. However, in the 21st century, the will of religious sovereignty, universal education, the Internet, and the media, are in the process of changing this theory completely."

Guiden paused for some water before landing the big fish to close out his speech. The water smoothed his parched throat, bringing the sudden realization that he was as much "a fisher of souls" as Christ had been.

"Just as interesting and impressive as the Royal Blood heirs are the members of the Order of Sion, who were responsible for the safety and well-being of all Royal Blood heirs and their descendents. Historians believe that the Order of Sion is the longest tenured secret organization in history, with almost two millennia of clandestine protection of the true blood heirs of Christ. Little is still known today about their identities and explicit functions, but history does confirm that they do exist and are considered the backbone of the Nazarene Church of Jesus. The thing I find most interesting is that the Order of Sion knew the fundamental truth of what the Canonical Gospels and Roman Catholic Church have adamantly refused to admit to the general public for over two-thousand years. There are actually Royal Blood descendents of Jesus and Mary Magdalene alive today."

Brother Guiden placed the last of his overhead slides on the screen, a synopsis of his presentation.

"I have offered each of you a compelling array of information that reveals an alternative and very feasible version of the true Christian story. Take of it what you will. But for me, there remains only one uncertainty: Where are these Royal Blood descendents today?"

Guiden concluded, "I thank you for your attention and now open the floor to any questions you may have."

The shocked audience unleashed a barrage of questions, so frantic, that none could be heard or articulated. Amongst all the ruckus, Professor Lindrum finally stood up from his seat in the seventh row and began to applaud. Within seconds, everyone else in the auditorium joined him. The buzz about Brother Guiden's lecture rapidly became the talk of the university, not to mention the Vatican hierarchy.

#

Brother Werner's cell phone began to ring, and he excused himself from the company of Brother Guiden. Caller ID told him it was the Vatican Suites. He felt a horrific knot grow in his stomach.

"Yes, your Holiness, how can I be of assistance?" Brother Werner asked.

"I want that Dorsey kid brought back with you to the Vatican tonight!" he answered. "He is the key. Do you understand?"

CHAPTER 6

Friday, 2:37 PM - Uptown, New Orleans

Zach walked out the back door of the auditorium through the throngs of congratulations for his mentor from the Tulane staff. He caught a glimpse of Sam in the parking lot.

"Hey, Sam. Wait up!"

As Zach tried to get closer to Sam, a daily newspaper reporter with notebook in hand caught up with him.

"Mr. Dorsey ... Mr. Dorsey, my name is Joel Brown, beat-writer for the Times Picayune. Can I ask you a quick question before you leave?"

"Sure, as long as you walk with me."

"How long did Brother Guiden research to come up with that Royal Blood theory?"

"I don't know. But he has been studying various religious writings and scriptures on the subject for as long as I can remember."

"And you have to tell me ... is it all true?" the reporter questioned.

"I believe it's true. For me, it's true. Let's hope that the modern religious leaders will take both a factual and analytical look at all the evidence and theories presented today and open up a serious dialogue." Zach grinned and turned away. The reporter smiled as he scribbled notes before leaving.

Zach approached Sam, and they exchanged hugs. "What did you think of the speech?" he asked.

"It was mesmerizing, and you were so good." She smiled up at him. "Are you officially a college grad now?"

"I hope so, or else all those nights of studying alone in the library were for naught. Zach continued cautiously, "What are you doing for the rest of the afternoon?"

"Why? You have a proposal for me, grad?"

"I'm kind of pumped, and was thinking about heading over to Cooter Brown's for a celebration beer or two. Would you like to keep me company?" Zach couldn't bear to look at Sam until she answered.

"If you're buying, I'm in," answered a blushing Sam.

"Great. We can take my car, but I have to stop at my apartment to get out of this monkey suit."

"I thought you appeared quite dashing in your coat and tie. Real dignified and professional."

"I can be dignified in a nice pair of jeans, thank you very much."

Meanwhile, a young priest in a conventional, white linen cassock urgently approached them in the courtyard.

"Excuse me, Mr. Dorsey? My name is Father Christian Rose from the Vatican, and I was wondering if I could have a minute of your time, sir."

Zach turned his attention to the young priest, puzzled, he answered, "Of course Father, how can I be of assistance?" The priest directed Zach away from Sam for a moment of privacy. He slipped a small golden device into the outer right pocket of Zach's jacket undetected.

"I wanted to congratulate you on the exemplary thought and labor process put into your educational learning to date. You must keep it up," the young priest said.

"Well, thank you, Father. I would have thought that a Catholic church representative would have some unsympathetic words in response to Brother Guiden's lecture."

"On the contrary, Mr. Dorsey. Some of us find it refreshing that the next generation of society, like you and I, have delved into the history and true meaning of Christ and his disciples with such vigor. I won't hold you up any longer, but I wanted to share my personal email address with you, so you may keep me up-to-date with any new progress on your mentor's theories. It was an honor and pleasure meeting you, sir." The priest shook Zach's hand, then briskly walked away.

Zach experienced a dèjá vu moment, feeling a certain connection with the young priest. He glanced down at the plain black and white card that read: <u>christian-rose@vatican.org</u>.

"What was all that about?" Sam asked, joining Zach.

"The first active member of my fan club," Zach admitted, placing the priest's card into his wallet. Sam grinned, and they walked side by side to Zach's Accord.

It was a sunny Friday afternoon, and Uptown New Orleans bustled with students from both Tulane and Loyola universities preparing for a wild weekend. On Broadway Avenue, Zach and Sam passed fraternity row, and saw that the 'keggers' were already in full swing. Sam was lost in her thoughts. She worked up the courage to confront Zach with a question that had unnerved her all day.

"Are you still seeing that girl, Donna, from the Theater department?"

"No, that ended a few weeks back," Zach answered. "I didn't tell you?"

"No, you didn't. If you would pick up the phone every once in a while, and not be a hermit in your apartment and the library, I would know these things." Sam playfully slapped the top of Zach's head.

"I'll try to keep you better informed next time." Zach smiled.

They pulled up to Zach's apartment on Carrollton Avenue. "I'll be right back." Zach jumped out and left the car and air running. His building was a mundane complex with eighteen one-bedroom apartments that were occupied primarily by cash-strapped college kids. The cement cracks were overrun with weeds. The weathered fence line was littered with empty Dixie beer cans.

Zach had a certain spring in his step while walking towards his apartment door. He was relieved that the finals were over, and that his appearance at the lecture seemed to have been a big success. Moreover, he was happy to celebrate the occasion with a great girl like Sam. Zach eagerly slid his key in the lock and turned it. The door opened slightly, but was obstructed. When Zach entered, he saw a pair of wooden drawers removed from a desk and strewn on the vinyl flooring. Zach's heart began to pound. As he came closer to the kitchen, Zach realized his whole apartment had been trashed. An alarming expression of fear froze on his face.

Zach fought to draw a breath; he blinked several times to refocus his vision. He scanned the rest of the apartment, which had been searched and ransacked. He wondered, "What have they taken?"

With dread, Zach sensed a separate, distinct presence in the room. When he turned to investigate, he was grabbed from behind and his arms pinned behind his back.

"Ready to sleep?" a menacing voice whispered in his ear.

Feeling the assassin's warm breath on his neck, Zach instinctively maneuvered his right arm free, cocked his right elbow, and fired it back into the assassin's abdomen, causing his sudden release.

Now face-to-face with his stunned assailant, Zach attempted to throw a right hook, but the assassin caught his fist in mid-air. With the assassin's left arm completely extended and exposed, the sight of a memorable tattoo of a pyramid and Arabic script on his wrist emblazoned itself in Zach's mind. The assassin then twisted Zach around, picked him up, and hurled him over the computer table area. Zach staggered to his feet. The assassin pulled out a ten-inch blade, and moved directly towards him. Looking for anything he could use to defend himself, Zach spotted a souvenir wooden bat from a New Orleans Zephyrs baseball game. He picked it up, closed his eyes and swung with everything he had. He heard a giant thud as the bat made contact with the assassin's shoulder, temporarily knocking him off his feet. Zach, knowing that he was fighting a losing battle, vaulted over the computer table, and raced past the assassin's fallen body and out of the apartment.

Running down the apartment alley, Zach yelled to Sam: "Drive the car, Sam! Drive the Car!" Bewildered by Zach's sprinting and yelling, Sam slid over to the driver's seat and gunned the battered Honda's engine, "Now go … go!" Zach barked.

Sam started to pull away from the apartment while Zach chased the car. The unidentified assassin, now back on his feet, raced out the door. He pulled out a pistol with a silencer and fired round after round at Zach and the fleeing car. Sam ducked as bullets hit the exterior of the Accord and burst through the drivers' side rear window. Zach recklessly launched himself through it, and landed in the back seat of the car.

The assassin, now at the paved street, continued firing, and shot out the back windshield of the car as it sped down South Carrollton Avenue.

"What the hell was that?" Sam yelled, looking in the rearview mirror. "Why is there a monk shooting at us?"

Zach, trying to catch his breath, shook shards of glass from his hair. "I don't know, but he was waiting for me and trashed my apartment looking for something."

"Looking for what?"

"I assume something he didn't find because he was still lurking there."

"Did this have something to do with that speech today?"

"Of course! The speech," Zach answered. "A fanatical monk didn't like my involvement with the lecture or the true story of Christ, so he came after me?"

"Maybe the Church sent him," Sam chimed in jokily.

"The Church ... sending a hit man." Zach actually thought of the possibility, but confusion had the market on his sensibilities. "I need to call Brother Guiden, and ask his advice. He'll know what to do. We need to get off the road and compose ourselves. When you get to it, pull into the Olde College Inn, and park in the back, out of sight."

Zach dialed his cell phone. "Yes, I need to speak with Brother Guiden immediately, please. Tell him it's Zachary."

While waiting for Brother Guiden to answer his page, Zach carefully scanned the surrounding area.

"Zachary, my boy, what a lovely introduction today, congratulations ..."

Zach cut off Brother Guiden's greeting with a rant of helplessness. "I'm sorry Brother, but I need you. Some fanatical man in a brown robe just tried to kill Sam and me at my apartment!

"Are you and Sam okay, my son?"

"Yes, we're fine now, but what should I do?"

"Have you ever seen this man before?" Brother Guiden quickly replied.

"No, but he was of European or Middle Eastern descent, I think. And he was well trained," Zach said.

"Well, come home to Notre Dame, and we'll figure this thing out together. But I need to inform you that Brother Werner from the Vatican media department is here at the seminary. He has a special papal invitation for both of us directly from Pope Aloysius himself. But I don't want you to worry yourself about this now. I will handle it."

"A formal invitation from the Pope? For what reason?"

"I don't know. He probably just wants to read me the riot act of a crazy man's theories, that's all. Just come on over as soon as you can. I will try to stall him until you arrive."

"We'll try to get there as soon as possible, but I have to get some questions answered first."

"Let me send Brother Martin to help you ..."

"No," Zach said. "I'll call and let you know when I'm on my way."

Zach hung up the phone and exhaled in disbelief of the events that had occurred. He took off his sport coat and dispersed the myriad of glass shards off of his body. He realized that he was getting one hell of a headache and the day wasn't even half over.

"Well, where to now?" Sam asked.

"New Orleans Museum of Art in City Park," Zach said.

CHAPTER 7

Friday, 3:12 PM - City Park, New Orleans

Perfect rows of live oak trees adorned the entrance to the New Orleans Museum of Art in City Park. The distinctive sculpture garden featured fifty-five life-size statues of important historical figures from the diverse city. The exhibit featured in the museum this day was: *Mysteries of Egypt - Age of the Pharaoh: Sex, Religion, and the Pyramid.*

Sam and Zach approached the long marble stairway to the museum.

"Should we call the police about your apartment?" Sam asked.

"They're probably at the complex by now," Zach said. "I'm sure they're looking to question me."

"Well, what should we do? I keep seeing it in my head, that man shooting at us."

Zach throws his arms around Sam in a reassuring gesture. "I know, Sam. Let's just try to keep it together and find out why this is happening, okay?"

"Okay," Sam said. "Now, why again are we at the Museum of Art?"

"Research."

"Research on the crazy killer monk in the brown robe?"

"Close. Research on the crazy killer monk's tattoo. I know I've seen it before, and I'm hoping that the collage of symbolic Egyptian images will jog my memory."

As they entered the museum, something immediately jumped out at Zach: a giant sized diagram of the "Valley of the Kings" graced the back wall of the first floor. Zach smiled, thinking of the time long ago when Brother Guiden brought him to the museum to see the King Tut Exhibit when he was a child.

"Now, Zach, what did this tattoo look like?" Sam asked.

Lost in his memories and not hearing Sam, Zach replied, "I'm sorry, what did you say?"

"What did this tattoo on the monk's arm look like?"

Zach tried to describe it. "It was like a three-quarter pyramid made up of small bricks, and, on top, it had the *Eye of Providence*. Underneath, I think it read in Arabic, *Discipline* and *Sacrifice is Eternal Salvation*."

"Wow, you can read Arabic? What is the Eye of Providence?"

"The Eye of Providence or the all-seeing eye is the Egyptian symbol that is surrounded or encased in rays of light or immaculate glory. It is commonly interpreted as representing the eye of God Himself, keeping eternal watch over humanity."

Nodding at the clerk, Zach said, "Sam, I need you to use your charm on this high school kid, so we can take a quick look at the Ancient Book of Symbols. Maybe what we need is part of the main collection."

They advanced to the museum's special reference section help desk.

"Well hi there, young man, and what's your name?" Sam drawled in her very best southern damsel in distress voice.

"My name? Um, it's Steve," the scrawny teenager answered.

"Well, Steve, I have this horrible book report due next week on abstract Egyptian symbology, and I was wondering if I could take a look at that *Ancient Book of Symbols*. If you could fetch that for me, I would be real appreciative."

The young man dashed off without wavering. He returned moments later with a large book. "Here you go, miss. Is there anything else I can get for you?"

"No, Steve. I think that will do it," Sam said.

Now in possession of the book, Zach flipped through page after page, seeking a match without any luck. Then it came to him. It wasn't in a book, it was printed on U.S. currency.

"Sam, do you have a dollar bill?"

"Sure, but why?"

"Just let me see the dollar, please!"

Sam fished through her purse, producing a crumpled bill.

Zach flipped the dollar towards the backside. "That's it!"

"What's it?" Sam asked, confused.

He pointed out the two seals on the back of the one dollar bill.

Zach showed her excitedly. "See, here on the left side is the pyramid with the Eye of Providence. That's the international symbol for the *Illuminati*, or the *New World Order*."

37

"The Illum-a-what-ee?" Sam asked.

"The Illuminati," Zach repeated. "It is a real secret society founded in 1776. Their members pledged absolute obedience to the "New World Order," and their superiors have been linked to the Freemasons. They say the Illuminati intend to establish a world government through assassination, bribery, blackmail, etc. It's rumored that they were the power behind Hitler and World War II. It's suggested that the founding fathers, many of whom were Freemasons, were corrupted by the Illuminati."

"And these people are after you?"

"I'm not sure. There was also another symbol on his arm, a simple cartouche of an Ankh."

"What is an Ankh?" Sam asked.

"In Latin, the Ankh is *crux ansata,* cross with a handle or the Egyptian cross. In Egyptian hieroglyphics, the cartouche stood for everlasting life. If I remember correctly, the Ankh was the primitive representation of human genitalia in Egyptian culture."

"Human genitalia? Oh, gross. You may stop explaining now."

"No, really, it is quite interesting. Look here in the book at this Ankh.

"The "O" shaped part on top symbolized the female vulva. And the "T" shaped part symbolized the male penis and testicles. The symbol secretly identifies the union of these parts in intercourse, thus under-scoring the method of the giving of new life by the ancient Gods."

"Okay, that is a little too much information. Didn't you say that this Illuminati cult was the source of power behind Hitler and World War II?" Sam asked. "So, if they are that powerful, how difficult would it be to control a few killer monks?"

Zach shook his head, and a sliver of glass hit the page. "If we know that the pyramid and Eye of Providence represents the Illuminati Order and the Ankh represents the continuation of the life cycle by the Gods, then we have our answer. But why do the Illuminati want me dead? I'm no threat to them."

"Brother Guiden's speech, Einstein. They know you helped dis-cover the truth about Jesus and the Royal Bloodline; and you could expose the Church and its leaders in the greatest cover up in history!"

"The Illuminati have control of the Roman Catholic Church?" Zach whispered. "Can that be possible? Brother Guiden just men-tioned on the phone that the pope had a special invitation for me. Then is the pope an Illuminati leader, clandestinely controlling this whole situation?"

"I think we're in way over our heads," Sam said. "We have to tell someone."

"Who do you tell? The Pope is one of the most powerful men in the modern world, backed by the Vatican, which is a multi-billion dollar business enterprise. Who would listen to us? Think, Zach," he told himself. "Follow your gut."

Zach's gut led him back downstairs to the first floor and into the main foyer of the museum. He ran the whole scenario in his head from start to finish, and still could not figure out any common denom-inators. Then he looked up, and, again, saw the detailed map of the

Valley of the Kings. He noticed the continuous pattern of the Egyptian Pharaohs and their elaborate burial chambers. But what was he missing? Zach thought to himself, "What do my eyes see?" He studied the images more closely.

Bingo! The natural progression of the way the tombs were distinctly laid out over thousands of years made a definite pattern. An arrow, in fact. In this museum, an arrow that was simply pointing upward towards a small gallery opening on the third floor. Zach started climbing the stairs towards the third floor. He was taught by Brother Guiden that when a good man is in his greatest need, God always sends a sign. Could this pattern have been his sign? When he reached the third level, he saw the inscription on the wall: *New Orleans History Exhibit*, a permanent display. Zach went around the wall and saw an illuminated picture at the exact point where the arrow indicated. It was a small painting by Austrian master, Erasme Humbrecht, titled, *Capuchin Father Dagobert de Longuory*. The caption read that the French Father Dagobert arrived in New Orleans and was appointed the head priest at the newly-founded Saint Louis Roman Catholic Cathedral.

Zach thought to himself, "Dagobert … Dagobert … it couldn't be possible." He wrote down all the information about the painting on the back of a business card.

Sam slunk up behind him. "What the hell, Zach? Why did you run away?"

"It's amazing, Sam. Do you remember in Brother Guiden's speech earlier when he mentioned the different French Royal Blood Dynasty's, the true and pure descendents of Jesus and Mary Magdalene?"

"I recall parts of it."

"Well, the last King of the first dynasty was assassinated in 681 AD, allegedly by the Church itself," Zach said. "That man was King Dagobert II. He was theoretically the last remaining King with pure royal DNA intact. When he was assassinated, it was assumed that the rest of the Bloodline of Christ was less than pure. Understand?"

"You're saying this Dagobert, was the last pure descendent of Jesus and Mary Magdalene?"

"Right! It was thought that the Royal Bloodline was diluted after that event. Call me over zealous, but I believe fate brought us here today, not to find out about the Illuminati and the connection with the Ankh, but to find him." Zach pointed to the painting that hung eloquently before them.

"To Father Dagobert … ah … and King Dagobert … both from France," Sam said. "Oh, I understand now. So how can we prove any connection between the two? What's our next step?"

"We need to find out as much as possible about the background of young Father Dagobert. We have to go to Saint Louis Cathedral in the French Quarter."

CHAPTER 8

Friday, 3:15 PM - Uptown, New Orleans

Mitchell Begg, an experienced homicide detective from the New Orleans Police Department, Mid City Division, arrived on the scene at Carrollton Street case number 76019. From the official statement of the witness who called 911, the tenant, one Zachary Dorsey of apartment 17, ran down the pathway screaming hysterically, followed by a man in a brown robe running after him firing a gun. Once they left, she went to investigate what all the fuss was about. She came upon Mr. Dorsey's apartment in shambles.

Thibodeaux, the first officer on the scene, waved Begg over. "Detective, I have the apartment manager right over there if you would like to interview her."

"Thank you," he said as he made his way over.

She was in her thirties, a brassy blond smoking a cigarette with a shaking hand. "Ms. Marie Domangue, my name is Detective Begg with the NOPD. I was wondering if you could answer a few questions for me?"

The woman nodded her head.

"Great. Now, what can you tell me about the tenant who resides in apartment 17?" Begg asked.

The woman nervously bit her bottom lip before answering. "He's some sort of genius. Very religious. I think he was going for his degree at Tulane. Nice fellow. He would never hurt a fly."

"And the other man, who you stated was wearing a brown robe. Have you ever seen him before?"

"No … never seen him, but he looked foreign, like one of those rebels on CNN in Iraq a while back. You know, tan."

"You say the tanned man looked like a militant from Iraq?"

"Yes, that's what he reminded me of."

"Did you see the tanned man shoot at Mr. Dorsey?"

"No. I didn't see it because I was afraid … but I heard it. It sounded like one of those air-pressured guns, like paintball."

Detective Begg knew right away that the witness was talking about a gun silencer. "To your knowledge, has Mr. Dorsey ever had a drug or gambling problem?"

"Oh, no. Not this boy, he was not the type."

"What about girlfriend problems? Maybe a jealous father?"

"It's very rare I see anyone but him coming or going from that apartment."

"OK, thank you for your help, Ms. Domangue. Make sure the officer has your information." He walked away.

When Begg entered the apartment and examined the contents of the home, he had even more questions about what actually happened than he had answers. He discovered no apparent motive or sensible reason for the crime. Long "married to his job," Detective Begg knew that if the initial motive wasn't evident in the first examination of a crime scene, then either the investigation would be long with many twists and surprises, or the answer was overly simple, hovering just under his nose. He didn't want to overcomplicate matters, so he retraced his steps through the apartments, searching carefully for anything he might have missed. He looked out the window and watched as CSI members worked just outside the door collecting bullet casings from the alley that led from the apartment to the street. Begg called to them, "Anything unusual from the casings?"

"The weapon was a 9-millimeter pistol but the casing is strange. The serial ID codes have been sanded off of each individual bullet. I've never seen anything like it before," the CSI man commented. "I'll still send them to the lab for analysis, but I wouldn't hold my breath."

"Thanks for your help." Begg left the apartment and walked down the alley, "Thibodeaux!"

"Right here, sir."

"Find out everything you can about this guy, Zachary Dorsey. I especially need to know who his friends are, where he hangs out, if he has a girlfriend, and so on. And have it on my desk within the hour."

"Yes, sir."

CHAPTER 9

Friday, 3:17 PM - French Quarter, New Orleans

There is a sign that hangs on the exterior of the great St. Louis Cathedral that reads: *"And thou, O tower of the flock, the stronghold of the daughter of Zion, unto thee shall it come, even the first dominion, the Kingdom shall come to the Daughter of Jerusalem."* Micah 4:8

#

Sam and Zach raced through the park in front of the St. Louis Cathedral after parking near the Moonwalk along the edge of the French Quarter. Since it was a beautiful Friday afternoon, most of the action was centered west towards Bourbon Street, so the Church was free of visitors. When they entered the massive structure, an overwhelming sense of struggle and past oppressions suddenly coursed through Zach's veins. He noticed all of the historic writings engraved on the marble pillar stones - eclectic clues left by holy men over one-hundred and eighty years ago. As he studied them, Sam called to him from the other corridor.

Zach moved to the side foyer of the church by Sam. Directly in front of them hung a gold, illuminated plaque that listed the past hierarchy of the cathedral rectors. Sure enough, near the top of the list dated from 1749 to 1776 was a Dagobert de Longuory, O.M.Cap.

"I can't believe it," Zach whispered, tracing the outline of the plaque with his index finger. "He was real. Father Dagobert lived right here in New Orleans."

Zach and Sam continued to study all of the rich history and eloquently painted murals of the Cathedral. Soon, a rather feminine older man leisurely strolled up to them and said, "May I help you?" Zach and Sam looked up. "My name is René, and I am the Official Guide of this remarkable and holy place, and you are …"

"Samantha, and this is my good friend, Zach. We're curious about the history of the cathedral and a man who once worked here. His name was Father Dagobert de Longuory. Do you know anything about him?"

René puffed his cheeks, preparing his speech. "Capuchin Pere Dagobert, of course, my dear. He was a legend in this surrounding area in the 18th century. Anything in particular you would like to know?"

"If you can tell us everything you know about the Capuchin and the history of the cathedral, we would appreciate it."

"Come right this way, and have a seat," René said. Sam and Zach entered the cathedral and admired the many symbolic flag ensembles that were hanging down from the upper decks of the church. At least two dozen decorated the walls, each marking a period of occupation by the French or Spanish.

"Now let me know if I run off at the mouth too much for your liking," the guide commented.

"First of all, the Saint Louis Cathedral, originally built in 1720, is the oldest Catholic cathedral in continual use in the United States today. The church has welcomed many distinguished visitors over the years, including General Andrew Jackson, General Zachary Taylor and the Marquis de Lafayette. More recently, on December 9th, 1964, Pope Paul VI elevated the St. Louis Cathedral to the religious status of basilica. Basilica honors are rare and conferred only to certain Catholic churches because of their antiquity, historical importance, or as a significant place of worship. Why this cathedral was deemed worthy of basilica status is unknown, but it is rumored that the port of New Orleans became such an important site in the New World, the Vatican had many of their prized religious relics shipped and stored right here in the bowels of this cathedral."

"What type of relics?" Zach asked.

"Some say it was Vatican gold bullion, others say it was precious art from the master collection, and some even theorized that the Church hid the Holy Grail itself right here for safe keeping."

"The Church had possession of the Holy Grail?"

René answered, "Ah, the Grail. Young man, it's believed that the grail is not an object to possess; rather it is a symbol or legend that is shared by all of God's followers. It shows us the divine path that we all must take to holy redemption."

Zach, blowing past the guide's explanation asked, "So, if I understand correctly, what you're saying is that there have been rumors or legends that the Holy Grail was housed in this very building?"

"Yes," René confirmed, "but any evidence or writings of it was supposedly lost in the Good Friday fire."

"Good Friday fire?" Sam inquired.

The guide continued, "In 1788, the first of two devastating fires broke out on Good Friday. Eighty percent of all the structures in New Orleans were completely destroyed, including St. Louis Cathedral. The church itself was rebuilt upon the ruins of the previous structure, and the Holy Grail was never recovered or spoken about again among the lay community. The fire actually destroyed many of the early church's sacramental registers, creating a major gap in reconstructing early family histories of the original French immigrants in New Orleans." After a long pause, he continued. "I'm proud to mention that I was here when Pope John Paul II visited the historic St. Louis Cathedral basilica on September 12th, 1987, in his second visit ever to the United States. I officially transported the papal copies of the early lost church documents to the vault in our achieves department."

"So the Vatican had in its possession a second handwritten copy of these original records and replaced the documents that were lost some two hundred years ago?" Zach questioned.

"Well … yes. I never thought of it in that way before," René said, slightly defensive.

"And what about Father Dagobert? What can you tell us about him?" Sam asked.

"Capuchin Father Dagobert de Longuory arrived in New Orleans in 1743. For the next thirty-three years, he labored in the province, working in the parish until his mysterious death on May 31st, 1776. Father Dagobert became a New Orleans mainstay, known as a patron of children, the baptizer of all who were devoted, a positive force during difficult times and one of the first champions of Christian rights in Louisiana.

"There is a legend that in September of 1764, France announced the colony of New Orleans had been given to Spain in a treaty. The

French families of the colony petitioned the King of France not to cede New Orleans to Spain, but the petition failed. In March of 1766, Don Antonio de Ulloa, the first Spanish Governor of Louisiana, arrived in New Orleans. His new and unjust policies were summarily rejected by the French masses, and the locals devised a plan to overthrow the Spanish regime. The local ring leaders, all close friends of Father Dagobert, were the wealthiest and most prominent men of New Orleans. The political rebellion was deemed a success when, by December 1768, the Spanish had fled the region.

"It is said that Spain's government was furious and sent a military detachment of twenty-four ships and ten-thousand soldiers in response. In early 1769, the local rebellion was easily overtaken, and the courageous leaders arrested. On October 24, 1769, the rebel leaders, Lafreniere, Marquis, Villere, Noyan, and Milhet, were executed by a Spanish firing squad. The brave locals were cruelly killed, but Spanish leaders refused to grant them a proper burial. Their corpses were said to have been lined up on Decatur Street and left to decay in public view. The bodies were placed under the watchful eye of the local Spanish garrison.

"Father Dagobert summoned all of the family members of the slain men to the St. Louis church that very night. To their disbelief, all their loved ones were present, cleaned up and dressed respectfully in scented robes. An elaborate funeral mass in the Catholic faith was held for them at midnight, and then they were properly buried on church property by candlelight. This deed was never forgotten by the city's French contingent, and just how Father Dagobert negotiated the return of the bodies from the Spanish soldiers remains a mystery to this day."

"Wow," Sam said. "Did Dagobert have any flaws?"

"Well, there was one legend that was bandied about. It said that Father Dagobert fancied one of his female parishioners, Madeline Rothschild, a woman of means from the famous European Rothschild family. It is said that Madeline was the muse from whom Father Dagobert drew strength. He painted her portrait in the church gardens, and it was rumored that they spent many years together in friendship."

"Whatever happened to Madeline?" Sam asked.

"She married a wealthy businessman named Peyton Ratcliffe in 1776. Soon after, she became pregnant with a baby girl they named Monica. After her marriage, Father Dagobert became introverted, and grew mysteriously ill. He passed away shortly afterwards."

"What became of the baby, Monica?" Zach questioned.

"If I remember correctly, she traveled to France for her studies and got married. I believe that her husband was arrested by Napoleon and sentenced to death. Well, I know she eventually made it back to New Orleans with her three children and devoted herself to God. It was rumored that she had miraculous healing powers, and, upon her death, her vast fortune went to establish the Ursuline Convent right here in New Orleans. I believe that the Vatican ultimately even made her a saint."

Zach nodded. "Very interesting. I noticed the many prominent flags perched upon the balconies. Most of them seem to have the *fleur-de-lis* symbol depicted. Do you know how the *fleur-de-lis* began in New Orleans culture?"

"Good question, sir," the guide noted, "but I do have an answer for you. In 1727, when the first St. Louis Church was built in New Orleans, the King of France, Louis XV, from the House of Bourbon, declared that the new French colony should bear the holy symbol of his ancestor, King Clovis I. The *fleur-de-lis* symbolizes the blood of Jesus Christ which is shared in the Catholic Eucharist."

"It seems that everything in New Orleans has a *fleur-de-lis* attached to it," said Zach. "Even the current pro-football team, the Saints, uses the symbol."

The guide saw a large group entering the cathedral, "Excuse me. I see I have another tour to conduct. Any further questions?"

"Thank you so much, René," Sam replied. "You have been very informative."

René took a step toward the group before calling back over his shoulder. "Oh, by the way, if you would like more information on Father Dagobert, I would try the local Archdiocese archives to see if they have any recorded history on him."

Upon leaving, Zach asked, "Sam, do you know the true meaning of the *fleur-de-lis?* René was right in that it's the French symbol chosen by King Clovis I of France in the 5th century, but it's my understanding that it's also the special emblem worn by the secret royal family line, a symbolic icon of the pure blood of Christ carried by the Royal Blood Kings themselves."

"It's the symbol for the descendants of Jesus Christ?" Sam asked.

"Yes and no," Zach replied. "Remember about King Dagobert being of pure royal DNA?"

"Yes, I recall."

"I believe King Clovis created the *fleur-de-lis* symbol to signify the pure royal bloodline heirs from heirs whose blood has been diluted throughout the centuries."

"But that doesn't answer why the *fleur-de-lis* is so prevalent in New Orleans," Sam said.

"It doesn't?" Zach asked. "Let's think about it for a second: We know that the *fleur-de-lis* was created in the 5th century by King Clovis. We know that King Dagobert, who was the last of the pure descendants, was allegedly assassinated in 681 by the church. But what you might not remember is the fable that his son, Sigebert IV, was secretly brought to Rennes-le-Chateau, France, where he continued the pure Royal Family Bloodline. If the *fleur-de-lis* is the pure descendant symbol, why can't New Orleans be the place where those heirs have chosen to live? When Napoleon took over France, the country was in the middle of all kinds of Christian upheaval where hundreds of thousands were persecuted with even the slightest hint of religious heresy, right? So if the French Father Dagobert, a Roman Catholic priest, was formally assigned to go to the New World, wouldn't it make perfect sense for him to go there?"

"Yes, it would make sense, but you have yet to convince me how King Dagobert and Father Dagobert are tied together through eleven hundred years."

"You're right Sam, it is a reach … but if you are game, let's keep searching for the truth."

"I'm with you. Where does the adventure lead us next?"

"The Archdiocese of New Orleans Archives."

CHAPTER 10

Friday, 9:47 PM - Royal London Hospital, London

Dr. Sofia Boudreaux, a sophisticated twenty-one year old OB/GYN resident intern with dirty blond hair, a shapely petite frame with well-defined legs, had just signed in for the night shift of emergency room duty in an renowned Royal London teaching hospital by the Thames River. Although born in Southern France, Sofia was raised in London as a well-to-do prep school prodigy by her father, a famous Archeologist. Ever since she could remember, she had always been a healer, especially of the young and helpless. Sofia was a natural, home schooled by professors. She chose OB/GYN because she was able to witness God's greatest miracle, the miracle of life -- animated in her presence.

The head ER nurse on duty glanced up from filling out a form at the main desk. "Good evening, Doctor Boudreaux."

"Good evening to you, too, Agnes," Sofia replied. "How is the board going tonight?"

"Rather slow for a weekend night."

"Good, let's keep it that way. I'll be in my office checking messages and patient files if anyone needs me."

Dr. Boudreaux entered a well-lit, cramped office behind the nurses station with a mountain of files on the desk. She clicked on the computer and whispered, "Let's see what wonders God has sent me tonight."

As she went through the computer files, no cases really excited her, so she glanced across to a framed photograph of a scrawny teenage girl with her father at a Swiss ski lodge. It was a photo of a young Sofia. She was mesmerized by the many happy thoughts of her youth. Then she lifted up a picture of a golden retriever sitting proudly. "At least I have Max to keep me company," she said.

The main phone in the emergency rang. After noticing Agnes was not there to answer, Sofia picked up the receiver from her extension. Immediately, she began to call out codes to fellow staff, and the hospital personnel started bustling around the rotunda.

The doors of the ER were flung open by an out-of-breath paramedic. A pregnant woman bled on a gurney.

"Code One! Code One!" the paramedic yelled.

Sofia ran to investigate. "What do you have?"

The EMT talked while he hurried the gurney to the exam room. "Caucasian, pregnant female, approximately thirty years old, early third trimester. Side swiped by a drunk driver. The amniotic sac may be ruptured, and she's hemorrhaging from the uterine wall. Blood pressure is 170/90, pupils dilated, possible rib fractures, and she has lost about a liter of blood. We've given saline with a bag of O-negative and have her on compressions. Patient is stabilized, but critical."

Sofia put on surgical gloves and took over the portable bag compressions on the patient. "I got her. Page the attending doctor on call and get the pediatric team down here, STAT. We are going into OR One."

Within seconds, Agnes joined Sofia in the operating room.

"Who's on call?" Sofia asked.

"Dr. Carmichael is until eleven, then Dr. Wooldridge is set to relieve," Agnes answered.

Sofia checked the patient's pupils and airways with a penlight. "We can't wait. She has a crushed larynx, and is bleeding internally. We have to intubate her, and stop the bleeding now."

"Okay, I need a type-two surgical tray up here, pronto!" Sofia said while putting on an OR gown.

Sofia used a scalpel and made a straight line surgical incision across the throat of the patient, who was still partially conscious, and gasped out the air and blood that had been trapped since the accident.

"Tube, please."

As she inserted the clear breathing tube, gurgling sounds of fluid meeting a new positive airway arose. Sofia capped the end of the tube with her thumb.

"Somebody grab the purse under the gurney and find out this woman's name," she insisted.

"Pelham Richardson," the nurse shouted.

"Okay, Pelham, I need you to look at me and listen - do you understand?" Sofia said.

The frightened woman nodded her head.

"I will let the end of the tube go, and fresh air will flow through, but I can't have you panicking. You must slowly breathe in, then out. Okay, let's do it." Sofia removed her thumb and instantly, a toe curling sound was emitted from the tube as Pelham took in her first unobscured breath in at least twenty minutes. "Now relax, breathe in, now out. Very good, Pelham. Keep it up."

Sofia turned to Agnes. "Get Dr. Carmichael or Dr. Wooldridge down here now, or you and I will be forced to deliver this baby ourselves. Let's get an ultrasound machine in here and see what's going on. Get me another bag of O-negative slung and hung, please." Sophia started to feel more in her comfort zone; she reminded herself to breathe. Her heart was racing a hundred beats per a minute in all the excitement.

#

At Sofia's apartment in downtown Paris, a familiar shadowy figure emerged from a small car parked adjacent to the building. The assassin pulled out a satellite phone and dialed.

He got the machine. "You have reached Sofia. Max and I are not at home, so please leave us a message, and we'll call you back as soon as we can." The man hung up and got comfortably situated back in the vehicle, knowing it would be a long night.

#

The ultrasound machine finally arrived in the ER. Sofia pointed to the patient. "Pull it over here, and run a quick diagnostic. Let me know when it's ready."

Agnes re-entered the room. "I have some bad news. Dr. Carmichael is already officially off call, and is not answering his cell. Dr. Wooldridge answered his cell, but was detained after stopping to help out on an auto accident victim. The main hospital wing will be sending down a surgeon to help out but until then, it looks like it's up to you and me, kid."

"Doctor, the ultrasound machine is ready to go," someone in the room said.

Sofia tried to clear her mind. "We can do this," she told herself.

As she used the machine's wand to pass over the stomach, both she and Agnes did not like what they saw.

"No movement, no visible heartbeat, possible stillborn situation," Agnes assessed.

"We won't know that until we get the child out," Sofia said.

"It's your call, Doctor." Agnes commented in a discerning voice.

Within a split second, it seemed all actions were frozen in time. In Sofia's mind, the OR room became misty with blissful white clouds. Sofia's consciousness was transported out of her body, and hovered above her physical being, still mindful of the surroundings, but in a dream-like state. The last statement was replayed in slow motion, "It's your call, Doctor." Sofia was reminded of every wrong decision she had made in her life, all in one instant. Insecurity and doubt seeped ominously into her mind. Overcome by these emotions, Sofia felt compelled to just relax in the moment.

Agnes looked at Sofia in real time and urgently said, "We need a call, doctor."

Still in her trance-like state, the images swiftly turned into an abyss of darkness. Out of the darkness, she heard the voice of her father, faded, as if from a distance: "Sofia, it is time. Time to become what you were born to be; what you have been pursuing your whole life. This Madonna and her child need your help. You must help them. God has granted you the talent to heal from the heart, so pull out of the darkness, go back to the light, and save these innocent souls."

Sofia thought about what her father said and snapped back into reality. Without pause, Sofia firmly ordered, "Let's prep for an emergency C-section. I need a shot of epidural up here, STAT!"

The haze of doubt was now gone.

This procedure would be the first major operation Dr. Sofia Boudreaux would perform without assistance, and everyone in that operating room was aware of it except Pelham and her dying baby. This moment was what she had prepared for her entire life: to be the deciding factor in life and death situations.

As Sofia mentally prepared, she whispered a brief prayer to the heavens, and all her remaining nerves and anxiety were soothed. She was ready.

"Any sign of Carmichael or Wooldridge?" Sofia asked.

Agnes replied, "No."

Sofia then turned to the mother, "Calm down, Pelham. I've got to go in and get your baby." Sofia rolled Pelham onto her side and took a deep breath as she positioned the needle. This was her first time to administer an epidural, and she knew she had to insert the extra long needle at the exact position into her spinal cord or the drug wouldn't be effective. With steady hands, Sofia inserted the needle and then the plastic tube that administered the anesthetic. As she lifted the needle out, she knew she had succeeded.

She repositioned Pelham in the stirrups as the epidural took effect. "Okay, team, are we ready?" Sofia asked with renewed confidence. "Scalpel, and stand by on the suction." Sofia made the standard incision two inches below the belly button and eight inches across in length.

"Now suction. I need gauze over here."

"There's a lot of amniotic fluid draining, and the sac has been ruptured," Sofia said. "This baby is a code blue. CODE BLUE people, let's look alive. Bring the incubator with the pediatric crash kit in here now!"

She placed her hands inside the incision directly into the uterine lining.

"I can feel the head," she gladly exclaimed. "How are her vitals?"

"Holding steady," a nurse confirmed from beside.

Sofia spent several minutes positioning the baby for birth. "I need suction." Sofia gently nudged the infant's head through the incision opening. Mucus and blood were pushed through the opening.

"The head is out," Sofia said.

"My God, the baby is already blue," Agnes stated.

"No time for commentary. Can you help me get this baby out?"

"I ... I ... think I can. Move a little to your right."

"I get the shoulders. You keep the head aligned. On the count of three, pull," Sofia ordered.

"One ... Two ... Three ... Go!"

As the two women pulled, the baby and the bloody amniotic sac were expelled from the abdomen.

"We did it!" Sofia thought for a moment.

"Doctor, the baby's vitals are descending rapidly."

"Clamp," Agnes ordered.

"No! Do not clamp the baby off until we can revive her and stabilize the mother," Sofia called out.

"But the mother is losing too much blood!"

"You resuscitate the baby. I'll handle the mother."

"Doctor, we're losing both of them," the nurse confirmed.

"Get me 20ccs of epinephrine and prepare a 50cc shot of pure adrenaline," Sofia ordered.

"Get me the pediatric crash kit," Agnes shouted.

Sofia injected the epinephrine into Pelham's drip as Agnes prepared to use the miniature shock paddles on the baby's chest.

A monitor wailed. "We have a flat line on the mother," the nurse exclaimed.

"Beginning CPR," Sofia yelled, as beads of sweat started to drip from under her light blue cap.

"Clear," Agnes shouted, as a small thud was heard when she shocked the heart of the tiny infant.

"No pulse on the mother or child," a nurse confirmed.

"Come on, Pelham, don't you die on me. This baby needs her mother's strength!"

"Up it to two hundred … clear!" Agnes tried to resuscitate the baby again.

"Fight, Pelham, fight!" Sofia shouted in desperation.

"No pulse on the mother or child," the nurse reported.

The distinct smell of stale blood and amniotic fluid permeated throughout the room. Agnes looked at Sofia, who performed CPR.

"Don't you give up yet, Agnes. I can feel that the baby's soul is strong. Try her again."

"Give me three hundred … clear." The thud of the little baby's body hitting the bloody mat was disheartening to witness. The rest of the nursing staff were now reticent and started to pull back.

"Where's the shot of adrenaline?"

"Here it is, Doctor." The nurse gave her the syringe.

"Still no heartbeat from the baby," Agnes said.

She thrust the medical syringe directly into Pelham's heart. "Keep giving CPR. I have an idea."

"What are you doing, Doctor?" Agnes asked, her brown eyes wide with concern.

"I know what I am doing; just do your job!" Sofia said defensively.

Another nurse entered the fray. "Still no pulse on the mother or child."

"Dr. Boudreaux, you have to call it," Agnes said somberly.

"Quiet!" Sofia shouted. Everyone stopped what they were doing. Sofia wiped the sweat from her brow and closed her eyes as the tired staff gazed at her.

"One last attempt, and then I'll call it. Everyone down on your knees, eyes closed, head tilted down."

"What the hell …" one of the nurses muttered to Agnes.

"Just do it … now!" Sofia ordered. The staff complied.

"Now, I need you to pray. Pray for this innocent child who never had a chance, and pray for this mother who is willing to die for her baby. I want you to pray the Hail Mary and ask for strength and power. I need you to bow down now and close your eyes and pray like you've never prayed before. Understand me?"

As the staff members were down on their knees, praying to the heavens, Sofia carefully placed the lifeless infant on her mother's chest. She then laid one of her hands on the infant and the other over the heart of the mother, and prayed: "Oh, Mary, eternal mother of us all. Please send us a tower of your strength, so these two innocent souls may be reborn and elevated to greatness in the magnificent glory of Jesus Christ."

Just then, Sofia's precise, surgical hands became illuminated beacons of light. The whole operating room was blasted with a stream of warming, maternal light. The supreme power of Mary was transmitted through Sofia to breathe new life into these souls, and, in the greatness of God, it was done.

The room fell completely silent.

"Everyone may now rise and continue in your duties," Sofia said.

"I have a pulse on the mother and the child."

"The baby's color is returning," Agnes exclaimed. "What did you do?

The nurses witnessed the greatest miracle of all: the power of the Holy Spirit and the will of life.

With a relieved smile on her face, Sofia finally relaxed, and said, "Ladies, never underestimate the power of teamwork and the divine intervention of prayer."

CHAPTER 11

Friday, 4:01 PM - Archdiocese Archives, New Orleans

The Archdiocese Archives stored nearly two hundred and eighty years worth of first-hand religious history of the colony/city of New Orleans. Under the meticulous care of Dr. Angel Deykin and the Archdiocese of New Orleans staff, the historic collections of sacramental records, parish writings, and personal journals provided a wealth of crucial information about the past. Although open to the public, many researchers never even considered the Church as a viable source of historical data, yet Zach thought differently.

Sam and Zach pulled into the archdiocese archive office parking lot at the intersection of St. Bernard and Paris Avenue. The office would be closing at four-thirty so they would have to act quickly. They entered the office and stopped at the front desk. A petite young woman glanced up from her gossip magazine.

"Good afternoon, my name is Zachary Dorsey. Brother Werner, a Vatican guest at the Notre Dame Seminary, sent me over to conduct some quick research in the archives on the creation of the St. Louis Cathedral and the priests who ministered to the colony."

"You do know we will be closing in a few minutes?" the administrator noted.

"Yes, I realize that, and I apologize. Maybe we can narrow our search to a cleric named Dagobert de Longuory. Are you familiar with him?"

"Why, yes. Père Dagobert was a very popular figure in the early religious movement in New Orleans. Let me see what I can dig up for you. You and your friend are certainly welcome to wait in the conference room."

"Great. We really appreciate your assistance."

As Zach and Sam waited for the records, Sam asked, "Zach, what do you hope to find?"

"Anything that can confirm or elaborate on what the cathedral guide discussed with us."

"Do you suppose that Father Dagobert had some sort of inappropriate relationship with Madeline Rothschild or one of the other members of the congregation?"

"I'll wait for all of the facts, but I have a gut feeling that our saintly priest was smitten with the young Miss Rothschild."

"It must have broken his heart when she married someone else and began a family, but what a remarkable story about her daughter, Monica, who was widowed after her husband was put to death during the French Revolution," Sam said. "I wonder why, after having children, she returned to New Orleans and devoted the rest of her life to serving God?"

"I'm not sure, but there is more here than meets the eye," Zach replied.

The door to the conference room opened and the administrator leisurely walked in holding a small, numbered steel box.

"Is that all the information you could find?" Sam blurted out.

Zach shot her a look. "Anything you have for us to look at is beyond expectation," Zach said, appreciatively to the clerk.

"Well, I know it's not much, but there was a fire that utterly destroyed most of the official church records, and much of the existing archives were either lost or damaged by Hurricane Katrina. I was able to locate Père's personal journal marking his last years of life. That should give your guest from the Vatican a little better insight on Father Dagobert." The assistant handed Zach a brown leather satchel containing the priest's journal.

"This is terrific! Do you have a copy machine available?" Zach asked.

"We sure do," the assistant answered. "It's twenty-five cents per copy and is right across the hall," she pointed in the direction. "Feel free to go through the box, but we'll be closing in fifteen minutes." The young administrator smiled and returned to her duties at the front desk.

"Sam, you take the box and sort through it, looking for anything relating to Father Dagobert's relationships outside of the church, and I'll take his personal journal. Anything you consider relevant, just make a copy and we will go through it later, okay?"

"Sure thing."

Both Zach and Sam feverishly worked their way through the materials, gathering every bit of evidence they could. Zach was enthralled by every page of the priest's detailed personal diary.

"Amazing. These pages tell a true Romeo and Juliet story," he said.

"Oh my gosh," Sam grabbed Zach's arm. "I think I just found something big!"

"What is it?" Zach looked over her shoulder. Her dark hair smelled of melon and citrus.

"I believe it's a receipt of the purchase of a cemetery plot for Madeline Rothschild, evidently paid in full by Father Dagobert in 1776," Sam said. "But I don't understand these strange markings."

"Let me take a look."

Sam held the document out so Zach could see. "What do you suppose it means?"

"I don't know yet, but make a copy of it," Zach said and dove back into the journal entries.

"Five minutes left!" the assistant called from the front desk.

The journal contained direct knowledge of the secrets of Father Dagobert. Knowing that the journal was the key, Zach stored the book in the back waistband of his pants and proceeded on with the remaining articles in the box.

"Sam, is there anything left in the box to be examined?"

"No, I think that's about it. But you owe me $8.75 for the thirty-five copies I made," she winked.

Back in the French Quarter on Decatur Street, the pair spotted the traditional green and white stripes of the Café Du Monde, a centerpiece of the local New Orleans culture for over a century -- from the old style black and white waiter attire, to the breezy courtyards filled with patrons sipping their café au lait. They decided to take a break and discuss what they learned over some French Market coffee and beignets. They sat at an outside table in the shade of the Mississippi riverfront oak trees. Nearby, pigeons pecked at the crumbs on the ground.

"So, have you gathered any new insights?" Sam asked, smelling her steaming cafe au lait.

Zach ripped off a chunk of beignet and dipped it in his coffee. "Get this," he answered, "According to Father Dagobert, in his own hand, he claims to have had a whirlwind love affair with Madeline Rothschild from 1774 until his sudden death in 1776."

"But what about her husband? Didn't she get married in 1776 before Dagobert passed?"

"It appears that Madeline accepted the marriage proposal from the gentleman Ratcliffe only after her parents threatened to disinherit her from the family fortune when she became pregnant."

Sam sipped her coffee. "Wait, I'm confused. Was the baby a Ratcliffe or a Dagobert?"

"Ah ... that is the million dollar question. It's hard to tell because the journal shows that Father Dagobert and Madeline Rothschild had, it appears, an intimate and emotional love affair. It never speaks of a child or a future together, only examples of the deep despair that Dagobert felt in the end. Read this entry." He pushed the journal toward her and took another bite of his beignet.

20 January, 1776
To my love, Madeline,

As I reflect on the past and the decisions I have made,
I have only one regret: all of the wasted decades that I

should have shared with you. If only our paths had crossed sooner! Why has God denied me this blessing and weighted me with this curse? I gave him an entire life of service and He burdens me with the only temptation He knows I can't deny. Why? I was content to live a life of altruism as a man of the cloth without any expectations of glory, until I met you. The Holy Father sent Mary Magdalene to Jesus in his last hours, and I fear he has done the same with you, my love. I am told that I have an illness no medicine can cure. God has the benevolence to grant me your goodness as my only lifeblood. With trepidation, I move forward, not knowing where our destinies lie. I will just live in this moment, marvel at your beauty, and pray for forgiveness. Oh, how I will miss the smell of your hair and the tenderness of your soul. Why was I so honored? My love and my trust are the only possessions I can give to you. I will always love you, now and for all eternity.

Forever yours,
Dagobert

"Wow," Sam remarked. "Dagobert certainly had a way with words. Was there any response?"

"No, not that I can see," Zach said. "Pass me those copies that you made from the archives. Let's see if we can piece together more of the mystery."

As Zach intently studied the copies, looking for any connection, Sam savored a powder-sugared beignet chased with coffee. Zach's lack of patience caused him to tap a pen in a rhythmic fashion on the pages.

"It appeared that Father Dagobert presided over thousands of Catholic rituals in the New Orleans region," Zach observed. "His tedious record keeping was quite impressive. Just the remnants of the church logs would have taken months, if not years to transcribe."

Zach continued to flip through the pages, and came upon a design hand drawn by Father Dagobert. At first, it appeared to be a wooden cross with a royal purple velvet wrap hung over the horizontal beams. This depiction of a basic Christian symbol left Zach feeling strange. He slid the picture over to Sam. "Why would Father Dagobert draw this heterodoxy of the crucifix? What does it symbolize?"

Sam studied the image thoughtfully. Zach continued through the copies and came back to the receipt that Sam had pointed out earlier. Upon inspection, it appeared that Father Dagobert did indeed purchase the plot of where his true love would be laid to rest. But what were those symbols … LON29*N59/LAT90*W15? Zach asked Sam to retrieve the laptop from the car. Once online, Zach ran an Internet search on the inscription. Suddenly, the answer was clear. The markings were a simple longitude and latitude position in New Orleans. Moreover, they pointed to a specific location in downtown New Orleans: Saint Monica's Church.

CHAPTER 12

Friday, 4:09 PM - Mid City, New Orleans

At the bustling New Orleans Police Department's Mid City station, Detective Mitchell Begg sat at his desk trying to assess the details of the Zach Dorsey case. He kept asking himself, why would someone want to kill a religious, twenty-two year old college student? What could this young man possess worth killing? Who was this pistol-whipping monk in the brown robe and what was this mysterious man seeking in this apartment? His long years on the force had taught him to be patient and to keep asking questions. Mysteries often revealed themselves in a series of small steps.

"Sir, I have that report that you requested," Thibodeaux approached.

"Thank you, I'll take it here," Begg reached out his hand.

Thibodeaux hesitated, glancing at the clock.

"What? Give me the report already," Begg said impatiently.

"Can you promise me you won't work through dinner and all hours of the night?"

Begg let out an exasperated sigh. "Now you're worried, too?"

"We all know how hard you work and how good you are at your job. Just remember you need your rest, too."

"I know, Doctor's orders. I promise to eat a healthy supper with lots of vegetables and get plenty of sleep."

Thibodeaux smiled and handed the file over. It was no secret at the department that Begg had seen a cardiologist after feeling some chest pain while chasing a perpetrator the week before. The doctor had recommended some "lifestyle" changes. Begg had dedicated his life to the force - his style was to dive wholeheartedly into a case, working overtime until it was solved. He couldn't fathom working any other way. This passion and commitment to justice earned him many honors and accolades, but had cost him his marriage, and now it seemed might be threatening his health.

"The shell casings are still at the lab, but were identified as coming from a distributor in the Middle East," Thibodeaux explained.

"Thanks. Let me know what else they find out."

"Yes sir," Thibodeaux nodded and left the office.

The meager report contained Zach's high school transcript, a drivers' license photo, college grades, graduation cap and gown photo, a few of his published articles in the Tulane newspaper, some W-2 tax statements, and a single arrest report for disturbing the peace during a pro-life / anti-abortion rally on St. Charles Avenue. The middle-aged detective focused on the color graduation photo of his star witness.

"Not much to go on," Begg thought, as he examined the evidence. "Let's take a closer look at this arrest back in 2019." Using the police computer, he pulled up the complete file from the arrest number. "Looks like young Mr. Dorsey spent a night in central lock-up, and was bailed out of jail by one Jeremiah Guiden of 2901 S. Carrollton Avenue in New Orleans," Begg said out loud, "Why don't we give Mr. Guiden a visit to see if he knows where the wayward Zachary could be hiding."

#

In Uptown New Orleans, Detective Begg did a double take as he realized that 2901 South Carrollton was actually the Notre Dame Seminary, one of the most illustrious religious institutions in the city, and a political ally of the mayor's office. He realized he had to tread lightly on this one. Begg walked through the main gates to the front entranceway and rang the doorbell.

"Can I help you, my son?" a nondescript man in an ivory-colored robe asked.

"Yes, I was looking for a Jeremiah Guiden. Is he here?"

"Why, yes, Brother Guiden is in audience. If you would like to come in, you may wait in the chapel area," the brother motioned to a nearby door.

"Sure, that would be great," Begg wondered who this important guest from the Vatican might be. He entered the chapel and felt drawn to the marble statues of a woman positioned along the walls.

After a few minutes' wait, Brother Guiden entered the chapel. "Oh, I must apologize, I was expecting someone else. My name is Brother Guiden, how may I help you?"

"I was admiring these beautiful female statues in your chapel," Begg looked up. "Who do they represent?"

"And you are?" Brother Guiden asked pointedly.

"I'm sorry, my name is Mitchell Begg, I am a Detective with the New Orleans Police Department. It is a pleasure to meet you, Brother." He held out his hand as the Brother turned his back on Begg for a disdain of the current enforcement of the law in society today.

"To answer your question, the statues are devoted to the patron Saint Mary Magdalene. Did you know that in some parts of the world today, she is more revered than even Jesus Christ?" Begg's light brown eyes widened as he gazed at the Brother in amazement. "Now how can I help you, detective?"

"Right to business, I see. That accent - what is it, Scottish? I am actually looking for someone whom you're familiar with. Zachary Dorsey, a student from Tulane University. Do you happen to know where he is right now?" Begg handed the graduation photo of Zach to the Brother.

"I'm Irish, and why do you seek Mr. Dorsey?" Brother Guiden shot back, distinctly staring at the photo.

"It's an official police matter, sir, with all due respect," Begg was starting to feel like the Brother was engaging him in some sort of superior mind game.

"Is Mr. Dorsey in trouble?"

"Well, no, not exactly. We have a few questions that need to be clarified."

"Oh, a terrible thing, isn't it? The attempted assassination of such a young and promising soul." Guiden nonchalantly handed the photo back to the stunned detective.

"What do you know of the incident?" Begg asked.

Brother Guiden scanned the detective like a father sizing up his daughter's first date. "Come here, my son. Let me see your hand."

"What?" a confused Begg asked.

"Let me see your hand. I need to know if your heart is good and your soul is kind."

Begg felt strangely compelled to comply. Brother Guiden took control of the Detective's hand and closed his eyes, entering a semi-trance like state. After feeling each grove of the palm, he opened his eyes. "You are a firm believer, I see. Let me ask you, are you a trustworthy man … an honorable man?"

"I believe I'm a good cop and a decent Christian, if that's what you're asking," Begg replied.

"Do you have spiritual questions in need of answers?"

"I would say most Christians do, in one form or another."

"If you could save the world from evil, would you embrace a hero's role?"

"I would do what I felt was right and just."

"Do you believe in *good and evil*?"

"You mean like Yin and Yang? I suppose that there is a law in the universe that for every good or positive action, there is an evil or negative reaction."

"Do you believe in God, detective?"

"I believe that there is a superior being, something greater than myself in the universe."

"And final question. Are you willing to die for your moral convictions?"

"Yes," Detective Begg affirmed to himself as he said it outloud, "I believe I would."

"Then come this way, you and I have much to discuss," Brother Guiden said.

CHAPTER 13

Friday 4:55 PM - Downtown, New Orleans

Zach and Sam imputed the GPS coordinates of longitude and latitude of St. Monica's into his laptop. When they arrived near the location, they remembered this neigborhood near downtown was hit hard by the severe severe floods of Hurricane Katrina. In this part of the city, they'd been told, water rose over eight feet high on most of the surviving structures. Zach wove the Accord down the pot-holed streets.

"Zach, take a right up here," Sam said. "It should be midway down the street."

Upon taking the turn, the vision of a spectacular gothic cathedral rose into view. Stone masonry on the archway read *The Holy Catholic Church of Saint Monica*. Zach and Sam were amazed by the detailed design and expert craftsmanship of the cathedral. The steep arches of the limestone and granite framed beautiful French hand-blown stained glass windows that depicted the life of Monica.

"Wow, I don't remember any churches of this scale in New Orleans other than St. Louis Cathedral," Zach remarked. "Where has this been hiding all these years?"

"Well, this isn't in one of the tourist neighborhoods," Sam said as she gazed up at the spires.

"This church doesn't seem adversely affected at all by Hurricane Katrina, or else it has undergone one amazing renovation."

Sam grinned. "Well, come on, Einstein, let's see why Dagobert listed these coordinates on our boundless tour of this great city."

Zach and Sam exited the vehicle to seek out new clues. They first noticed an aging brass dedication plaque secured on the front of the church. It read: *The Holy Catholic Church of Saint Monica, Est. 1891, by the Brotherhood of the Sacred Heart, is a monument to the strength, teachings, healing powers and memory of the beloved Monica Ratcliffe Dorsey (1776-1858), Founder and Headmistress of the Ursuline Convent in New Orleans.*

"Do you see what I see Zach?" Sam touched his arm. "Amazing."

"Yes, I do." Zach blinked as he reread Monica's full name.

"Is she related to you and your family?"

"I don't know," he confessed. Zach's thoughts became an inconceivable mixture of fear and excitement. He pulled out his cell phone and dialed the Notre Dame Seminary. "Ah, good afternoon Brother Carl, this is Zachary Dorsey. It's imperative that I speak with Brother Guiden at once. Can you track him down for me, please? Thank you." Zach contemplated several strategies to get all of his questions answered.

Brother Guiden's voice came over the phone. Zach could hear the strain in his words. "Zachary, where are you? I expected you over an hour ago."

"We'll be coming in just a few minutes, but I have a question for you that needs a direct and honest answer," Zach said.

"When have I ever been less than frank with you, my boy?" Brother Guiden answered.

Zach continued. "Point blank: am I related to Monica Ratcliffe Dorsey?"

After a long hesitation the Brother replied, "Why do you ask such a question, Zachary?"

"Because I am currently standing at St. Monica Church after a difficult day that included a dissident monk shooting at me and discovering things that I couldn't have even imagined twenty-four hours ago," Zach said. "I need answers and I need them now."

"So, you've found the gravesite. How did you get there?"

"What gravesite? What are you talking about? Answer the question, is Monica Dorsey a relative of mine?"

#

After much thought, Brother Guiden disclosed that Monica Ratcliffe Dorsey was indeed Zach's great-great grandmother, with the complete reliance that Zach would understand why his heritage and past had to remain secret for so long.

"Zach, I need you to come home so we can sit down and talk this out. There's much to discuss that I can't get into over the phone. I promise I'll tell you about your parents and the special traits that have been passed down to you, as I sense you're beginning to understand. The time has come, my beloved son, for you to know the whole truth."

There was silence on the line. "I'll need a few minutes to sit and digest this whole thing."

"I understand. But be aware, there are forces out there that you have yet to encounter. Please come to the seminary as soon as possible."

After brief consideration and in no mood to argue, Zach said, "I can be there in about thirty minutes."

Zach sat on the front steps leading up to the church entrance. The ever confident young man rubbed his temples in bewilderment. Sensing his whole life had a distinct purpose in the eyes of God, Zach now realized that his mere existence has been a sham -- a complete lie. He felt like a fool. Like someone has just conned him out of his last ten cents. All of those evenings learning the scriptures of truth, only to be stabbed in the back by the only father he has known. Where was the honor among men, and the love of family and friends? And most importantly - God?

"Are you okay?" Sam touched his shoulder and looked at him with her watchful, kind eyes.

"I will be. I just feel so lost right now."

Sam sat down and put her arm around him so that he could smell her citrus hair. "You know, they say God acts in mysterious ways, so maybe today is a significant turning point in your life. I mean, it is your last day of school. Time to enter the real world and all. No one ever said that life was going to be easy. I have known you for, what? Seven years now? And I, for one, have always known you were destined for some greater purpose in life." She gently rubbed his back as she talked. "You're special, Zach. You always have been. I've never told you this before. When I'm around you, there is a serenity that graces the innermost part of my soul. A peace within myself that is warm and safe. Let me hold you tight and give back some of that tranquility that you have graciously and unconditionally shared with me many times over."

Sam placed Zach's head against her bosom and held him tight, like a mother consoling her child. Surprising to her, Zach wrapped his arms around her. She slowly pulled away from him to look into his eyes. As she witnessed a single tear fall from his cheek, she gently leaned over and slowly kissed him delicately on the lips, like a raindrop on a sunny day hitting the lavish petals of a beautiful rose in full bloom.

Zach felt whole again. The mythical magic of a kiss had healed his wounds.

After this resilient display of passion, Sam pulled away, stood up and said, "So come on, stand up, dust off your pants, and tell me exactly what Brother Guiden told you."

"Thank you, Sam." Zach reached out and took both her hands in his. "Not just for who you are, but for being such an important and vital part of my life." He gave her hands a gentle squeeze.

Sam smiled and squeezed back.

Zach released her hands and stood up. "Brother Guiden did say that Monica Dorsey was a direct blood relative of mine. My great-great Grandmother in fact. After I told him that we were led to Saint Monica's Church, he assumed we found some sort of gravesite, and that's why we were calling."

"Whose gravesite?"

Zach shook his head. "He didn't say, but this site holds some answers we need to find. Let's get back to work. I promised Brother that we would be heading over there soon."

Zach and Sam checked every possible opening to the church, but couldn't find access. As they strolled to the back of the property, towards the rectory, they came upon an old, small secluded cemetery. The individual, centuries old, above-ground plots with their haunting rows of marble and granite tombstones were distinctive, even for New Orleans. Surprising to Zach, he noticed inside that something felt eerily familiar about this place, like he was drawn there, predisposed by some external force that seemed beyond his control.

Fate perhaps?

"This must be the area that Brother Guiden spoke about." Zach remarked. "If we spread out, we'll cover more ground."

As the two of them began reading the headstones of the numerous graves, Zach discovered something to his left that made the hair on the back of his neck stand up.

"Sam, over here."

Sam approached the two isolated tombstones closest to the rear of the church, and the pieces of the puzzle started coming together. The first tomb on the left read:

Here lie the blessed remains of

Madeline Rothschild Ratcliffe

1751-1812

Devoted wife of Payton and mother of Monica,

whose financial contributions and **good** deeds

helped establish the local Ursuline Convent

in her adopted hometown of New Orleans.

May God absolve her of her earthly sins.

Then the second tomb, immediately to its right, read:

80

Here lie the saintly **remains of**

Monica **Ratcliffe Dorsey**

Holy Patron Saint of Healing

1776-1858

Mother of three beloved **children**,

Founder and **head** mistress of the

Ursuline Convent in New Orleans.

Anointed into Sainthoo**d** in 1923

by the Vatican and Pope Pius XI.

Both Zach and Sam stared in awe at this finding, realizing that these were the same Madeline and Monica that René spoke about at St. Louis Cathedral.

"Sam, please go back to the car and get the camera out of the glove box. We need to record this."

While Sam ran off, Zach tried to figure out what didn't seem right about these headstones. If Father Dagobert purchased this tomb in 1776, he must have left some sort of clue or sign for *people to see.*

As Zach continued to study both of the explicitly engraved, solid granite headstones, a realization came to him. Sam came back with the camera. Zach asked, "Sam, when you look at the lettering on both of these headstones, what sticks out to you?"

Sam took a hard, long look at both headstones, and finally caught the clue. "On both headstones, a few of the letters are slightly larger and etched deeper, which sets them apart from the regular letters."

"Yes, Sam, I see it, too. I think Dagobert left us an encoded message." He looked at the headstone on the left, and selected each special letter in specific order: **D-A-G-O-B-E-R-T-S**. "Sam, can you believe it? It actually spells out Dagoberts."

Now for the other: **R-O-Y-A-L-C-H-I-L-D**.

"That's it! *Dagobert's Royal Child!*"

"So does this mean that baby Monica was the biological child of Madeline Rothschild and Father Dagobert?" Sam asked with an excited edge to her voice.

"Not only that, but the headstone declares that Monica was of Royal Blood. Did you see the italics on Madeline's headstone where it asks that God absolve her of her earthly sins and on Monica's that had her first name singled out in script? Madeline must have known that Monica was Dagobert's child. When her parents dealt her that ultimatum, and he was suffering with illness, she had no other alternative but to marry Ratcliffe and raise Monica as his daughter. In hindsight, that decision saved this entire family tree from harm's way."

"If Monica is your great-great grandmother, then that makes you a direct blood descendant to Father Dagobert and, in turn, possibly to King Dagobert of the Merovingian Royal Bloodline of Christ!"

Anticipation and excitement suddenly turned to confusion and anxiety for young Zach.

"We need to go meet with Brother Guiden," Zach said, wondering if the good Brother had any prior knowledge of this information. What news did Guiden have to share about his parents and this new-found family secret history?

CHAPTER 14

Friday 11:09 PM - London, England

It was past eleven in London, and the assassin grew restless waiting outside of his intended target's high rise building. With no apparent sign of activity in the suite, he decided to investigate the residence. He pulled up the hood of his traditional long brown robe, and with umbrella in hand, the assassin made his way through the stormy weather to the rear access entry of the establishment. The door was left ajar by the last resident who discarded their trash, so he had an easy entrance.

Dr. Sofia R. Boudreaux had lived in suite number three-eleven for the past eighteen months with her golden retriever, Max. Although a classic beauty in every sense of the word, Sofia was a workaholic with very little social life. Her idea of a hot Friday night was curling up with Max, a chilled bottle of Chardonnay, and a good thriller novel. With very few pounds to spare due to repayment of medical school loans and a desire for designer label clothes, Sofia lived in a modest one-bedroom suite in the quaint downtown art district. Being only a second year resident, she was forced to work nights at the hospital until she graduated from the advanced internship program.

The assassin made his way up the back stairwell to the third floor and opened the door. Suite three-eleven was all the way down the main corridor and to the left. Using a specialty locksmith's device, he easily gained entry through the deadbolt lock and slipped into Sofia's residence. Max, half asleep, came to investigate, thinking his mistress had returned home. Once the canine realized that this was an intruder, he began to growl and bark uncontrollably. The assassin hissed back, took out his pistol, and shot the dog dead. He removed the personalized leather collar from the dog as a souvenir. The assassin then proceeded into the bedroom and grabbed a framed photograph of Sofia from the dresser. He began going through various personal items in the drawers. Her undergarment drawer was of great interest. The direct invasion of his target's privacy aroused him. He then lay on Sofia's bed, and could smell the lingering scent of her perfume on the pillow. What a waste the elimination of this target would be, he thought.

#

Sofia tried to relax in the ER break room after the heart pounding excitement of her first solo surgery. While sipping on her Coke Light, Nurse Agnes came in with her trademark, smiley-face tea cup.

"You know, that was brilliant work that you did tonight," Agnes said.

"Thank you, but I don't think I would have gotten through it if you weren't by my side," Sofia admitted.

"Well, you're welcome. Hopefully, we won't have to do that again in the near future. Are you going to tell me what *really happened* in there tonight?"

"Maybe one day," Sofia said, "But for now, you just need to believe in the divine intervention of prayer."

"Uh-huh, prayer. Oh, by the way, Dr. Wooldridge is looking for you. I'm sure you have now inherited all of his paperwork from this surgery as well. I believe he's in his office." Agnes strolled out of the room with a hot cup of tea with honey.

#

The assassin, now back to business, searched various papers located in a writing desk in the den. It wasn't long before he found an old wage receipt from the hospital. He picked up the phone and dialed the main phone number on the statement.

"Good evening. May I speak to Sofia R. Boudreaux, please?" He waited for a response. "Thank you, no need to ring her. If she's at work, I'll come to her."

He strolled to the kitchen, pulled out a croissant and a bottle of strawberry flavored water from the refrigerator, and temporarily made himself at home while he considered his next move.

CHAPTER 15

Friday, 5:22 PM - I-10 Interstate, New Orleans

As Zach and Sam drove back to Notre Dame Seminary, Interstate-10 was jammed with rush hour traffic. Citizens of New Orleans, eager to begin their holiday weekend, rushed to get home. Zach kept replaying the newly-conceived idea in his mind that his whole life had been a lie. Brother Guiden knew all along who his biological family was, and had kept it secret from him. But why? Why would he keep such important knowledge from him?

Sam's words broke into his thoughts, "Well, you still owe me a beer, mister, but I would settle right now for a piece of gum or a Lifesaver. Do you have any?"

Zach, half-heartedly listening to her, reached into the inside pocket of his tweed coat, now showing the wear of the day's activities. No luck. As he felt the exterior of the other pockets, he noticed an awkward, oblong-shaped object in his right coat pocket. Zach pulled the object out into the open. It was gold and wrapped in a small parchment adorned with rare colorful jewels and embellished with various mystical symbols.

"Where did you get that from?" Sam asked.

"I don't know, I've never seen it before," Zach answered.

"It's so beautiful," Sam whispered. "Let me take a look before you get us in a wreck."

Zach handed the strange item to Sam while he eagerly scanned for a safe place to pull the Accord off the interstate. She carefully unwrapped the attached parchment and examined it.

"What does the parchment say?" Zach asked.

"It's a riddle," Sam answered, proceeding to show Zach a glimpse of the black, hand-written calligraphy. She went on to read from the text:

'To find the three that you seek,
Blood and honor must be true,
Only the strong, not the weak,
Will the answer be awarded to.'

'For the singular task at hand,
Is to solve the end game,
The riddle will answer the land,
Lives will never be the same.'

'Stored up in the skies,
Is the beating of one's heart,
This test does not allow lies,

So make sure you act smart.'

'Thirteen will be the key,
To fight the rising tide,
To find the fishing three,
The answer will be your guide.'

Zach pulled the car over in the emergency lane of the interstate, and put on the hazard lights so he could take a closer look at the object.

"Have you ever seen anything like it?" Sam asked.

"No. It's definitely hand crafted - a one-of-a-kind piece, but modern, I would say," Zach said.

Unaware of what he was doing, Zach touched something that activated a mechanism within the object. On one panel of the device, an electronic window opened, revealing a small LCD screen. A miniature computer keyboard was directly beneath the screen.

"What did you do, Zach?"

"I didn't do anything. It just opened on its own."

Zach and Sam continued to marvel at the intricate and futuristic design of the miraculously small device.

"I assume that the riddle in the parchment is a key," Zach said. "If we solve the riddle, then type in the answer, the device may reveal something of importance to us."

"But where did it come from? How did you get it?"

He shook his head. It had to be after the lecture, but he'd talked to so many people, he couldn't be sure who'd slipped it into his coat pocket. "Let's bring it to Brother Guiden to see what he thinks."

CHAPTER 16

Friday, 5:42 PM - Uptown, New Orleans

The majestic site of the Notre Dame Seminary had graced the uptown streets of New Orleans for nearly one hundred years. Built in the decorative style of a medieval castle in Southern France, few outside of the Church had seen the internal structure. The practical purpose of the seminary was to produce the next generation of qualified and committed brothers and priests to serve the local Catholic Archdiocese. The Brotherhood of the Sacred Heart, led by Brother Guiden inhabited the entire west wing of the seminary. A religious congregation founded in Lyon, France in 1821, The Brothers of the Sacred Heart's mission was the evangelization of young people, especially through the powerful ministry of education.

Zach and Sam parked the car around the rear of the complex and walked along the south wall on the cobblestone path towards the main entrance. Zach still ran the clues from the riddle through his mind:

'To find the three that you seek,

Blood and honor must be true.'

The doorbell was programmed to play the "Bells of St. Mary," a favorite of Brother Guiden's from his youth. Upon entry, they were asked to wait in the library until Brother Guiden could properly greet them.

"So, this is where you grew up?" Sam asked.

"Yeah. It wasn't so bad. Everything I ever needed, the brothers provided."

"Look at all these old books. Where did the seminary get all these?"

"Most of them were purchased or donated over the years from the well-off families in France or from the New World."

"The New World?"

Zach nodded. "That is what France called the colony provinces back in the 18th century."

"And what about these numerous scrolls?" Sam persisted.

"Some of those ancient scrolls date back to the ninth century. They're Christian writings from all over the world: Tibet, Egypt, Gaza, and the Holy Land."

"Neat. Have you read any of them?"

"Actually, I have read some of them. Those on the left are written in Latin, the middle ones are in Hebrew, and these over here are in Aramaic, Coptic, Greek, etc. It's really fascinating to see how many different cultures reflect upon the life of Jesus Christ and his moral teachings …"

"Zachary! You had me so worried." Brother Guiden entered the room and embraced the young man.

"Brother, this is Samantha DelaCroix. Sam, this is Brother Jeremiah Guiden, my friend and mentor."

"Zachary, you didn't tell me Ms. DelaCroix had the looks of an angel and skin as soft as a dove," Brother Guiden joked while kissing Sam's hand. "It is my pleasure to make your acquaintance."

"Why, thank you, sir. Zach talks about you all the time."

"Disregard anything he tells you. Whatever it was, I did it for his own good."

"All right … now stop it," Zach chimed in.

"Can't an old man have a little fun once in a while?"

"Let's get to the task at hand, Brother. Have you ever seen an object like this?" Zach held out the device he found in his pocket. "And what do you know about my parents?"

"Where did you get this?" Brother Guiden asked. "These are very rare, kind of like an original Faberge egg done by the master Faberge himself. It's called a *CompuZen*. As far as I know, only seven of these devices exist in the world today. I never thought I would actually see one."

"But what does it do?" Zach asked.

Brother Guiden carefully took the object from Zach and studied it before answering.

"Theoretically, it electronically stores data that is impregnable without the required encoded password. It is said to store a small counting device that when activated, gives the recipient a certain amount of time to solve the clues to the riddle and unlock the information before it is lost forever."

Brother Guiden pressed a series of buttons and a digital timer appeared on the screen that read: 21.28:52 and counting downward.

Quite fascinating. It appears we have a little over twenty-one hours to solve the riddle in order to learn the information that was secretly stored into its memory. But for the next few minutes, we can't worry about that because I have two guests that have been waiting for your arrival. We'll have to deal with this later." He handed the CompuZen back to Zach. "Please, let's join them in the conference room. Right this way, my lady. And Zachary, keep the CompuZen a secret for now - understand?"

Situated in the conference room, both Detective Begg and Brother Werner were engrossed in separate conversations on their cell phones at opposite ends of the room. Zach and Sam took seats at the wooden oval table, waiting patiently for some direction from Brother Guiden, who whispered with Brother Martin, obviously about some urgent matter given his facial expression. Brother Guiden signaled to the gentlemen on the phones that the meeting was set to begin.

"Not everyone at this table knows one another; but let me assure you that, as of this moment, you will need to work together if you *want to survive another day in this world*," Brother Guiden said.

In that instant, each person looked around the room, then at Brother Guiden, in disbelief at the statement he had just made.

"We have precious little time, and so much information to relay, that I would appreciate you withholding all questions until I am finished with this briefing. I believe everyone here, with the exception of Detective Begg, was present at my lecture on the Jesus DNA earlier this afternoon. I am here to say that 90% of what I stated is undeniably true."

"I knew it," Zach said.

"Let me first go around the room and give a brief synopsis of why you are seated here in this very critical moment in history. First, Brother Werner: as the Director of the Vatican Media, you were responsible for the telecast to the Vatican, which understandably, caused quite a stir from the ideological traditionalists of the Catholic faith. I believe you are under orders to bring me and Zachary back to the Vatican tonight, is that correct?"

"Yes, it is," Brother Werner responded.

Brother Guiden continued. "For your information, Pope Aloysius has graciously invited all of us to join him tonight in Rome via the personal Vatican jet. It is waiting for us to disembark as we speak."

"My security advisor, Brother Martin, just notified me that a group of mercenaries, believed to be the Illuminati, have launched an extensive covert worldwide operation to eradicate any man, woman, or child that had suspected ties to the Sangreal."

Brother Martin rubbed his chin. "Just like the Friday the 13th, 1307 attacks on the Knights Templar that destroyed an entire monk order in three countries. That date has been forever cursed."

"Wait a second; who are the Illuminati and what is the Sangreal?" Detective Begg asked.

"The Illuminati are a secret religious sect. Their sole purpose is to create whatever disturbance necessary - war, political assassination, sex, blackmail, banking scandals, etc. - to move their own people in higher positions in the political and religious hierarchy. Unfortunately, these acts of terror have been very successful to date, and very few Sangreals, or for Detective Begg, Royal Blood descendents, have survived the onslaught. Because of this fact, I must now disclose that I'm not just a Brother of the Sacred Heart, I'm also a member of the Fraternal Order of Sion, a sworn protector of the Blood Royals. Zachary, the assassin you encountered earlier was sent to kill you because of what you were born to be. Stand up and remove your shirt, please. It is time."

Zach removed his shirt and revealed a black *fleur-de-lis* birthmark, magically trimmed in gold, on his chest, right above the heart.

"The *fleur-de-lis* legend is true ... the holy mark," Brother Werner gasped.

"But how did you know?" Zach asked Brother Guiden. "You've never seen it before. It didn't appear until after my 21st birthday. I have never shown this mark to anyone, including you."

"Zachary, I have known your entire life who you are and what you are meant to do," Brother Guiden revealed, now in a much more serene mood. "Back in the Winter of 2000 after over sixty years of peaceful existence among the blood royals, the Illuminati launched a worldwide attack, similar to the one today. Your family was hit hard. Your father was brutally murdered, and your mother, eight months pregnant, was shot multiple times. By nature, the baby should have died in her womb. But your mother, she was a fighter, a brave soldier of God. Evelyn signaled the Order of Sion in distress, and Brother Martin and I immediately responded. When we arrived at your home, there was nothing we could do for your parents, but amazingly, a faint heartbeat was detected in your mother's womb. It's my personal belief that once the assassin left, your dying mother used every last bit of her strength to heal her unborn child. That child was you, Zachary. Your brave mother saved your life. I was there for your miraculous birth at Charity Hospital, where they removed you from the womb in an emergency C-section. Brother Martin and I brought you home from the pediatric ward and raised you as our own.

"But what happened to my family?" Zach asked.

"The Order of Sion buried your family in a discreetly marked tomb at Greenwood Cemetery, along with other Blood Royals."

"Why didn't you tell me the truth before today?"

"Knowledge is power. I didn't realize that you had the capabilities to research all of that material and figure out the truth for yourself. Most Blood Royals are told of their destiny at the age of thirty so that the minimum maturation process can take place naturally, without divine pressure." Guiden said with stern conviction in his voice, "Today, I believe that you are the 'One' who was foretold in the prophecies of Mary Magdalene herself."

"What prophecies?" Begg asked.

"It is written in the Gospel of Mary Magdalene that a Blood Royal will rise up at the beginning of the End of Days, after the second coming of Jesus, and he should be revered in the battle of good versus evil."

"You're saying this kid is the precursor to the rebirth of Jesus Christ?" Begg nodded at Zach.

"Jesus has already been reborn," Brother Guiden firmly stated. "He entered our world at the exact turn of the millennium, in New York City in the year of my Lord *MM* (01/01/00), as predicted by former Order of Sion member, Michel Nostradamus, in 1566. I've come to the realization today that young Zachary must be the supreme Royal Blood warrior foretold in the prophecy. The struggle between good and evil and the balance of power has yet to be decided."

"So, you claim that the Blood Royals, and the second coming of Jesus, represent the good side; and that the Illuminati, and the Pope of the Catholic Church, represent evil?" Brother Werner surmised.

"I'm not sure about the Pope," Brother Guiden answered, "but the Antichrist himself, born somewhere in Europe on 06/06/06 to set up the future Final Battle of Armageddon in the Valley of Megiddo."

CHAPTER 17

Friday, 5:59 PM - Uptown, New Orleans

"Both Jesus and the Antichrist are alive in the modern world today?" Sam questioned.

Brother Guiden held his hands wide. "Yes, my dear, I'm afraid that's a fact. We are living in a precious time that will be written about for thousands of years to come, if the human race survives."

Under the oval table, Zach held the CompuZen in the palm of his hand, still reeling from the stunning revelations disclosed by Brother Guiden. He wondered what the device's purpose truly was.

"I have a question," Detective Begg admitted. "If what you're saying is all true, and I'm not saying that I buy into any of this, what would be accomplished by going to the Vatican and having council with the Pope?"

"To be frank, we need to determine if the Pope is an antagonist, or worse, part of the Illuminati itself," Brother Guiden admitted.

"But what about the other Blood Royals?" Zach asked. "Who's helping them? There's no way that I'm the only survivor of these attacks.

Can you contact the Sion headquarters and demand more viable information? This should be our first priority. The Blood Royals must not become extinct at any cost."

"I readily agree with you, Zach. Brother Martin has been working on this problem all day, since the first reports started coming through. If there is anything we can do, rest assured that it will become our main objective."

"Wait a second," Brother Werner interjected. "You said that you would be returning with me to the Vatican. I'm not authorized to be flying around trying to save every man, woman and child who needs help!"

Guiden responded, "Brother, what would Jesus do in this situation? His first concern was always the aid of his people, not some scheduled secular meeting. I will tell you now: you will do as you are told, or we will not be coming to Rome at all."

"I agree with Brother Guiden," Zach added.

"How would we know if other Blood Royals survived and now need help?" Sam asked.

Brother Martin directly answered, "Each Blood Royal has his or her own guardian assigned by the Order of Sion. Brother Guiden and I have been Zach's protectors since the day he was born. I have informed Sion of our situation and requested a detailed list of other survivors and their current locations, so we may assist."

Suddenly, a tremendous explosion outside the Notre Dame seminary rocked the conference room and startled everyone.

"What in God's name was that?" Brother Guiden gasped.

"It sounded like a bomb exploding near the South Carrollton entrance," Brother Martin said. "Whatever it was, it can only be bad news. Everyone should evacuate immediately."

"Detective, you and Brother Martin go investigate the explosion. I'll bring Zach, Sam, and Brother Werner to the rear and leave from the seminary back parking lot. If we get separated, meet us at the large hanger at the rear of the Lakefront Airport as soon as you can. I'm sure the Vatican Concorde is unmistakable."

The sound of an automatic machine gun firing rapidly in the distance along with cries for help filled the room. Chaos ensued as smoke started to infiltrate the complex. Before he was whisked away, Zach noticed Brother Martin attaching a large belt over his robe. It looked like an antique and bore the symbol of a gold cross draped with purple cloth - the same design that Father Dagobert had drawn in his journal. The brown leather belt contained a set of nine medieval knives in varying sizes. Detective Begg pulled out his standard, police-issue Glock 9-millimeter, and followed intently behind the Brother. Another explosion shook the room, this one much closer in range.

#

"Was that a hand grenade I just heard?" Begg asked.

"I believe it's the Punarjanam, the legendary order of the assassins," Brother Martin responded.

"What do they want?"

"They want to destroy everything that the Order of Sion has protected for thousands of years. Detective, we cannot let that happen … no matter what. Do you understand the gravity of the situation?"

"I'm with you," Begg said, as he cocked the trigger of his gun.

They heard the assassin questioning one of the other Brothers about the whereabouts of Zachary Dorsey. The Brother rightly claimed not to know, and the assassin put a gun to the back of his head and fired. Blood and pieces of human debris splattered the nearest wall.

"Let's split up and surround him," Brother Martin whispered. Brother Martin moved left and Begg snuck right.

The assassin grabbed an elderly secretary and repeated the question. Her frail body shivered with fear, but she couldn't produce the correct response either. The assassin picked her up by her neck and with one violent wrist thrust, disposed of the woman like a rag doll.

Begg could now see the silhouette of the assassin and moved in, inching closer from the rear. The room was dark from the massive blast, and the dust still settled in the air. As he approached, he inadvertently stepped on a broken piece of glass giving away his position. The assassin turned swiftly before the detective could fire his weapon. He grabbed Begg by the throat, and knocked away his gun. Begg could now see the insidious assassin in full view, and the brown robe was evidence that this was the same man that had fired upon Zach Dorsey earlier that day. His pulse grew rapid as the assassin tightened his grip.

The wanted assassin spoke in accented English: "You have ten seconds to tell me where you are hiding the boy, or I will kill you where you stand."

Begg scowled, knowing that the man's immense strength gave him little chance to break away. His whole life flashed in front of him as he contemplated his options. Brother Martin's simple words from just moments earlier sounded in his mind: *We cannot let the assassin get to Zach, no matter what.* Looking for any avenue of hope, he found himself beginning to pray: "As I travel through the valley of death, I fear no evil, because the Lord is with me." At that moment, Brother Martin hurled one of his knives into the shoulder blade of the assassin's arm used to restrain Begg. This action instantaneously caused the killer to release Begg and sharply drew his attention to Brother Martin. The assassin turned and faced his opponent.

"My name is Brother Rodney Martin, devoted member of the Order of Sion and protector of the man you seek. If you want Zachary Dorsey, you will have to go through me first."

The assassin smiled, pulled the embedded knife from his shoulder and rapidly fired it in the direction of the Brother, narrowly missing his head.

"It will be my immense pleasure. My name is Tiberius, member of the Punarjanam, and the man who will cause your painful death."

Brother Martin glanced at the now recovering Begg lying on the floor, and signaled for him to join the others. The two warriors began to fight in an ancient martial arts style taught by their elders. This fight had taken place between the Sion and Punarjanam countless times over the past millennium. Both men proved to be extremely skilled warriors. The physical strength of the assassin, Tiberius, versus the quickness and fluidity of Brother Martin made for an intriguing match-up. Begg, now on his feet, thoroughly searched for his weapon, but could not locate it. Slowly but surely, he backed away from the action, and went towards the front of the building, which now had a big opening from the initial explosion. Begg felt guilty about leaving the Brother to defend himself, but the memory of his recent helplessness was still fresh in his mind. He had never faced a perpetrator such as a professional assassin before. Recalling that the task at hand was to maintain the safety of young Zachary, Begg left the premises to join the others.

#

Brother Guiden, Brother Werner, Zach, and Sam were now all safe in the elegant confines of Brother Guiden's 2020 Cadillac, and driving to Lakefront Airport. Zach continued to ponder the riddle clues:

'Only the strong, not the weak,
Will the answer be awarded to.'

#

Brother Martin, with his many years of training, held his own against the assassin. Every time one adversary had a slight advantage, the tables turned. The violent action was non-stop and appeared to be a test of physical and mental endurance. Both competitors used the seminary grounds as an arena in battle. Brother Martin used a fire poker like a skilled knight with his medieval sword. Tiberius wielded a letter opener like a blade of death, slashing at the Brother in defense. Both men battled for their lives.

Tiberius restrained Brother Martin in his specialty hold, the Eastern-style Bear Hug. He crushed Martin's neck, cutting off his air supply. The Brother, on the verge of losing consciousness, countered this enormous amount of brute strength with a head butt, followed by a roundhouse kick square in Tiberius' jaw. Just when it appeared that Brother Martin had seized the upper hand, Tiberius opened a secret compartment in his Punarjanam ring. The small container held a white, powdery substance. At the first viable opportunity, Tiberius blew the powder into the Brother's eyes, blinding him. Without his sense of sight, Brother Martin looked bewildered, and swung his fists wildly in the air, screaming in pain. Tiberius struck him in the back of the head with a broken wooden chair, thus rendering the Brother temporarily unconscious.

After a few minutes of much-needed rest, Tiberius tied the Brother to a cement column and opened a homemade liquid opium packet, the Punarjanam version of smelling salts. He held it under Brother Martin's nose, and the very distinct and strong odor revived the Brother instantly. When the prisoner came to his senses, he struggled against the ropes binding his wrists and ankles. Tiberius positioned himself directly in front of the bound Brother to question him.

With the belt of knives in his possession, he asked, "Where is Zachary Dorsey?"

"You should just kill me now because I'm never going to tell you," the Brother responded.

Tiberius picked up a tattered stone and one of the smaller knives. He used the stone like a hammer, pounding the knife into the Brother's left foot. The Brother screamed in pain.

"I will ask you again. Where is Zachary Dorsey?"

The Brother adamantly refused to answer, so Tiberius kept repeating the process of impaling nonessential body parts until he was down to the last two knives, the biggest in the antique prized collection.

"Very good, Brother. I do not believe that I have ever seen a person sustain so much personal pain and anguish without succumbing to the pain. Six knives stuck in one's body must cause an enormous amount of doubt. There are two knives left, and I plan to use them to slice open your belly and cut out your heart. Where is Zachary Dorsey?" Again, he received no response. Frustrated, Tiberius, an experienced virtuoso in torture, resigned himself to the simple fact that the answer was not forthcoming.

After shaking his head in disdain, Tiberius took one of the remaining knives and made a deep and gruesome, six-inch incision, straight down the Brother's abdomen. He then reached inside and forcefully pulled out intestines, placing them in view of the dying Brother, now with the curse of restored sight. Brother Martin hollered in pain. Then, sensing a small moral victory, he began to laugh in the face of the assassin. With blood now freely flowing from his mouth, he spat in the assassin's face, and continued his laughter. Now incensed with rage, Tiberius shoved the last knife into Brother Martin's heart, ending the vicious torture session for the first time in his history without getting the answers he sought.

CHAPTER 18

Friday, 6:37 PM - Lakefront Airport, New Orleans

New Orleans Lakefront Airport thankfully afforded private jets a secret haven, away from the prying eyes of the common folk. Presidents, movie stars, and rock & roll icons had all flown into town unnoticed to enjoy time in the Big Easy. Nestled on the shores of Lake Pontchartrain, this private oasis was once run like a small military base. Since Hurricane Katrina, however, the FAA had disbanded all Federal air traffic control officials, so many of the hundreds of weekly flights were now unregulated by the proper aviation authorities. Several small Cessna-type aircraft were used as runners for cheap labor from Mexico and the import of drugs from South America.

The sleek and impressive Vatican Boeing Concorde that taxied out of hanger seventeen was one of the last Concordes remaining in private service. It could travel about six times faster than conventional commercial airliners, and could cross an ocean in about the time it takes to watch a movie. The Concorde was protected by a small attachment of Swiss Guards located around its perimeter. Brother Werner called ahead and confirmed status with the pilot to prepare for an immediate departure upon arrival. Brother Guiden continued his attempts to reach Brother Martin and Detective Begg via cell phone to no avail.

"Brother Werner, what type of communications equipment do you have on board?" Zach asked.

"The Concorde is equipped with a state-of-the-art communications system that incorporates satellite phones, satellite cards for internet, television and fax reception, and laptop computers with access to the Vatican's private information servers - the works."

"Good. Brother Martin will be able to link up with the Order of Sion database and see exactly how bad the damage done by the Illuminati was, and if there are any Blood Royals who could use our help." He caught Sam's eye. "Sam, how're you holding up?"

"I suppose I'm okay, but I have to admit that a day spent with you is never boring." She grinned.

"You know, you don't have to continue on this quest. I'm sure the bad guys have no idea who you are. When we reach the airport, you can take a taxi and go home."

Sam laughed. "And miss a ride to Rome on a Concorde and an international audience with the Pope? I don't think so! If you want out of this date, you'll have to come up with something better than that."

"So this is a date?" Zach asked.

"I'll let you know…but it's looking good so far," Sam said as she gave Zach a kiss on the lips. "Besides, you need my woman's intuition to help solve the riddle for the CompuZen."

The CompuZen. Zach's mind went back to the words:

'For the singular task at hand,
Is to solve the end game."

The Cadillac pulled into the hanger and parked adjacent to a huge jet fuel tanker. Several Swiss guards approached the vehicle and requested to conduct a search of each person who would be boarding.

Brother Guiden expressed his concern about the welfare of Brother Martin and Detective Begg back at the seminary. He hated being forced to leave them and not knowing how they had fared.

"Are you ready to board Brother Guiden?" Brother Werner asked.

"No, not yet. Please notify the pilot that we will be leaving in fifteen minutes, so we can give Brother Martin and Detective Begg a fair chance to catch up. Can you show Zach and Samantha the communications center on board? I know the lad is raring to go. Thank you." Brother Guiden checked his watch and scanned for any incoming traffic.

#

Detective Begg hailed a cab and directed it to the Lakefront Airport. His outward appearance was disheveled, and there was major bruising on his neck from the strong grip of the assassin. Traces of blood remained on his face and parts of his white, long-sleeve polo shirt. Debating if he should report his current situation to his superiors, or to anyone for that matter, he felt Brother Guiden's rough hands on his palm and heard his question in his head, "Are you willing to die for your moral convictions?" He felt deep in his inner being how spiritually significant this mission was and how important to keep it secret. Thinking back to the rush of emotions he had felt when he prayed just minutes ago, he decided to continue this journey without telling anyone. Besides, who would believe his story?

#

"Sam, turn on the TV to CNN, please. Let's see if any of these assassi-nations have made the world news yet," Zach said.

Sam found CNN, but no one was reporting their story.

"Wow, check out this laptop," Zach said. "Brother, it appears that I need your thumb print and an eleven-digit access code to get online."

"Here you go, young man, and today's access code is *crucifixion*," Brother Werner said.

"Naturally."

Zach typed in a phrase from the riddle into a search engine, seeking any help whatsoever:

'The riddle will answer the land,
Lives will never be the same.'

#

Brother Guiden waited at the end of the jet stairway, and noticed a marked cab approaching from the west frontage road. Seeing only one person in the back seat, the Brother prepared for anything, handling two hidden knives positioned up the sleeves of his ivory robe. As the cab drew closer, the figure joyfully began to wave. The Brother was relieved to find that the man seated inside was Detective Begg.

"Where's Brother Martin?" Brother Guiden asked.

"He's still at the seminary," Begg said. "He saved my life. The explosions you heard were caused by a Punarjanam assassin called Tiberius. He brutally killed several of the people there who wouldn't tell him where Zach was."

"You weren't followed, were you?"

"I don't believe so. I was on foot for over half a mile before finding the cab."

"Are you okay? You look terrible."

"Well, it's good to see you, too, Brother. I'll be fine."

"We'll wait five more minutes to see if Brother Martin shows or not. Come aboard the jet, and get yourself cleaned up."

After ten minutes had elapsed, and there was no sight of Brother Martin, Brother Guiden sadly feared the worst. He ordered the Concorde to take off for Rome.

CHAPTER 19

Friday, 7:21 PM - Onboard The Concorde Jet

The aerodynamics of the one hundred-fifty million dollar Concorde provided for a smooth ride while cruising at sixty thousand feet. A virtual five-star hotel in the sky, the now, near extinct Concorde was a marvel of modern air transportation. Since Brother Martin was unavailable, Zach used a little of his computer skills and a lot of luck to successfully decipher Brother Martin's password for his personal computer files: *Les Miserables*, his favorite Broadway musical. Once logged into his account, Zach sent an urgent request to the Order of Sion. He attached Brother Guiden's emergency code and requested current Royal Blood information. Still searching for clues to the answer of the riddle, Zach did a search on another verse:

'Stored up in the skies,
Is the beating of one's heart.'

Now there was nothing to do but wait. Brother Guiden and Zach both found it interesting that none of the national news outlets had yet broadcast confirmation of any assassinations of some of the most powerful and respected people in the modern world. The only reasons why they knew that the select killings had actually taken place were the attempt on Zach's life and the verbal conformations from some of Brother Guiden's Sion connections. Zach and Brother Guiden were now alone in the communications center at the rear of the plane.

Zach could feel the exhaustion of the day leaking out his body. "Brother Guiden, I sent the priority message to the Order of Sion as you asked me to do. Is there anything else I can do?"

"Patience, young Zachary, patience. Try to get some rest, if you can. I have the feeling it's going to be a long night."

"You know I can't rest at a time like this. There are so many thoughts running through my head. I need to stay active. What else can I be doing or researching to help with our current situation?"

After a long pause, sensing that this was the perfect opportunity, Brother Guiden said, "Have I ever shared my profound knowledge of sacred geometry with you? Every entity that is frequently perceived as holy or mythical, theoretically, has some sort of sacred geometry involved. For example, take the geometric layout of Washington, D.C., our nation's capital. Did you know that Washington has its main landmarks perfectly aligned in the Masonic symbol of a compass and square? The Masonic compass is easily confused with the protractor device that is commonly used in schools, and the Masonic square is nothing more than a perfect ninety-degree angle or half of a square. Now imagine this, the head of the compass represents the U.S. Capitol Building in the east. One axis of the compass goes northwest to the White House. The other axis, of equal length, goes southwest to the Jefferson Memorial.

"The center of the square is the Lincoln Memorial in the west. One ninety-degree angle goes directly to the White House in the north. The other ninety-degree angle, of equal distance and length, goes to the Jefferson Memorial in the east. A perfect geometric Masonic compass and square design. Was that just sheer coincidence, or was there a greater force at work than we realize? From what you shared earlier, you and Samantha have had quite an eventful day running around New Orleans in search of information. Get back on the computer and print a New Orleans city map. Then mark each place that your natural instinct led you to today. I think you may be surprised by the results."

"Okay, but I don't think we'll see anything special."

"Just try it. You might just learn something yet from this silly old man."

Zach printed the city map, as requested, and started to retrace the events of the day, marking the places he and Sam had visited: New Orleans Museum of Art in City Park, Saint Louis Cathedral in the French Quarter, Archdiocese of New Orleans in Gentilly, Saint Monica Church in Mid City, and the Notre Dame Seminary Uptown. Analyzing the markings around each location, Zach was astounded to find the geometric simplicity of his quest. The five points made by each exact location created a defined pattern on the map, and each point was equally distant from the last. Zach drew a straight line from one geographical location to the next, in the exact order in which he and Sam had traveled. He saw the easily identifiable symbol of five points of a six pointed star - *The Star of David*. Taking the existing measurements from the star and outlining the final location, he identified the sixth point as the Greenwood Cemetery in Lakeview: the exact location that Brother Guiden had confessed earlier was the site where Zach's family and other Royal Blood descendents were buried in a special, discreet tomb. Zach held the map up to reveal a perfect geometric Star of David, the holy symbol of the Jews.

Zach glanced over to the Brother to show him his astonishing discovery.

"You see, Zachary," Guiden said, "What I've lost in strength, I have gained in wisdom."

Once the touching moment passed, Brother Guiden continued. "There is another matter I would like to discuss with you, my son - one that I have put off way too long." Struggling as a parent and guardian in his search to find the right words, he said, "It would take a blind man to not notice how you light up in the presence of the angelic, but young, Ms. DelaCroix. You and I have never really had the occasion to discuss members of the opposite sex."

"Oh, no, this isn't my birds and the bees talk, is it?" Zach joked.

"No, it's not," a very serious Brother Guiden said. "It's about something far more intimate and powerful than you could ever imagine: a sacred and protected ritual that is almost two-thousand years old. Over the centuries, Royal Blood descendents have come to call it the Rite of Sacred Divinity."

"The Sacred Divinity? Sounds interesting."

"Interesting or not, my boy, the Sacred Divinity is one of the greatest powers a Royal Blood heir possesses. It is my understanding that when a pure descendent experiences the joy of consummation with a partner of his choosing, a direct portal or vortex to God is available to him to view and experience at the exact defining moment of orgasmic bliss."

"A direct window to God?" Zach asked.

"Well ... yes, I guess you could say that. A split-second of experiencing the divinity of God Himself, and of what He has created for all of us worthy of the heavenly union. I take it from your level of interest that you remain a virgin?"

"Yes, of course."

"Then the timing of our talk is appropriate. I will not preach to you about the moralistic virtues of manly desires. I, as a celibate Brother of the Sacred Heart, have chosen my path, however difficult it may be. I will only advise that you always respect the Sacred Feminine, and treat the human goddess with the love and affection that you, in return, will demand. Pleasures of the flesh are not sins. God has made the orgasmic journey for His followers primarily for procreation, but also for the intimate disclosures of feelings and emotions of one person to another. It is in the basic human design that all people want to be loved and needed. Without that, the human race would inevitably fall into a cruel and uncaring existence. Love would be replaced by chaos, which would surely cascade into the realm of an intolerable future. The only communication that the common person has with God is through the divine intervention of prayer. As a pure Royal Blood, you have the ability to command, however briefly, an audience with God Himself. Use this gift with the utmost respect and responsibility, for you, as the 'One,' are destined to become our future."

Zach, not feeling of divine essence, asked, "But Brother, why have I been chosen by God? I don't feel worthy of such a task."

"Patience, Zach. Rome wasn't built in a day. God has a master plan, and that plan will be revealed to you in good time. When you are spiritually ready, his revelations will become clear and your crucial role well-defined. When it is time, trust me, you will know," Brother Guiden answered.

As the two men shared a tender embrace, the fax machine aboard the Concorde's communication center came to life and started printing a multi-page fax correspondence. The private call letters indicated that it was from Sion headquarters. Brother Guiden promptly started reading page after page. His frown told Zach everything he needed to know.

"This isn't good. The Order of Sion has confirmed my worst fears. It appears that within the last twenty-four hours, the vast majority of Royal Blood descendents have been annihilated in some sort of genocidal plot orchestrated by the Illuminati and deftly carried out by their assassins, the Order of the Punarjanam."

"Why would the Illuminati want to murder the bloodline of Jesus Christ?" Zach asked.

"Zachary, the Illuminati have tried for centuries to gain control over the unique and special powers bestowed upon the Royal Blood descendents, but their attempts have failed. I fear that my speech earlier, which was televised to the Vatican, must have set off some kind of panic within the Illuminati hierarchy that led to today's events. Today's events were prophesied over seventeen hundred years ago by St. John the Divine. As I explained earlier, the Antichrist has already been reborn. It is now my personal opinion that the Illuminati have physical and mental control of this child, and no longer have a need to influence the Royal Blood descendents. When someone within the Illuminati witnessed my speech today, it was only a matter of time before this preconceived plan was to be executed, and their Royal Blood problem eliminated."

"Well, how many have been killed?" Zach asked.

"According to this report, unfortunately, nine out of ten," Brother Guiden answered.

"Do they have a list of survivors?"

"Not of survivors. Due to security protocol, all they have available are the Royal Bloods that have not been attacked by the Punarjanam assassins as of the last report."

"May I see the list, please?"

As Zach examined the list, he marked the remaining targets and current locations of Royal Bloods that could perhaps use their assistance. "Can you prepare for me the contact number for the assigned Priory of Sion guardian for each of the possible remaining targets that I have marked on this list?" he asked.

"I should be able to conjure that up without much tussle," Brother Guiden surmised.

"Good, then let's get to work."

#

In the interim, Zach contemplated the next verse of the riddle:

'This test does not allow lies,
So make sure you act smart.'

He then went to check on Sam in the forward cabin. Sam was asleep in one of the extended, black leather chairs. Zach was taken back to the observation Brother Guiden had made moments earlier about Zach's apparent feelings towards Sam. Just one look at her beautiful and serene face made Zach realize that the Brother was right. He was in love with his best friend. He always had been.

Knowing that they were in very real danger, Zach considered the idea of confining Sam to the plane once they reached the Vatican, but quickly realized that such a plan would not sit well with the strong-willed, intelligent, and head-strong young woman. He knew that his past track record in even the smallest of debates with her proved to be exercises in frustration. He leaned over, and kissed the top of her head oh so delicately, breathing in the citrus scent of her dark hair. Then he returned to the rear of the plane.

CHAPTER 20

Friday, 7:36 PM - Onboard The Concorde Jet

Brother Guiden split the Sion list, updated with contact phone numbers, in two. He handed one list to Zach, and they both began placing calls to the other Royal Blood protectors to gauge their current situations. Sam joined them in the communications center and sat down next to Zach, instinctively placing her hand in his. Zach was on the phone with Raphael, the Sion protector of a young doctor named Sofia Boudreaux in London. Raphael explained that there had been no suspicious activities, and certainly no attempts on Doctor Boudreaux's life in the last twenty-four hours. As Zach was requesting his present location, Raphael started to answer, then all Zach heard was a gargling of words and then what sounded like a struggle and Raphael's cell phone dropping to the floor. Within seconds, the phone was disconnected. Zach attempted repeatedly to call Raphael back, but with no response.

Zach knew something was wrong. Having learned from Brother Werner how to use the high-tech communication devices earlier, he was able to triangulate the last fixed position of Raphael's cell transmission. He was positioned outside the Royal London Hospital in England.

Obviously, this was where the doctor was employed. If the Punarjanam was able to get to Raphael, Sofia Boudreaux was in immediate danger herself. Using the computer phone book, Zach found the main phone number and called the hospital.

"Yes, operator, this is a matter of grave and utmost importance. I need to speak with Dr. Sofia Boudreaux right away."

As Zach waited impatiently, he listened to the uncanny hold button music: the instrumental abridged version to the Barry Manilow tune, "Could it Be Magic."

The phone was finally connected. "This is Doctor Boudreaux, how may I help you?" a soft and feminine voice asked.

"Sofia Boudreaux, my name is Zachary Dorsey, and what I have to say is of the utmost importance, so please hear me out before you speak or hang up the phone. Do you understand?"

"Why, yes, but what is this all about?" Sofia asked.

"You are in imminent danger. If you give me the opportunity, I'll explain everything. First of all, you and I are long-lost blood relatives. I know this because we both carry the family crest of the black and gold *fleur-de-lis* birthmark imprinted directly on our chest. I'm willing to bet that this mark magically appeared after your twenty-first birthday. Am I correct?"

Sofia responded, "Look, I don't know who you are, or how you found out about my tattoo, but I had that done while on holiday …"

"Sofia, it's okay. You and I are the same. Let me ask you another question. Are you an orphan who has experienced mysterious visions or night terrors? Are you a brilliant academic student who feels lost half of the time? Are you attractive but without social life? I already know the answers to these questions."

"What is your name again?"

"My name is Zach Dorsey. I'm from New Orleans, Louisiana, in the United States. I'm currently on a plane enroute to you in London, but I need to ask you to do something right now that you may not understand. You need to trust me. Your life is in grave danger."

"In danger, why?"

"That's a long and complicated story I am fully prepared to tell you on one condition - that you give me your cell phone number and promptly evacuate the hospital without telling anyone where you are going."

"I can't just leave. I'm on duty in the emergency room of a major hospital. I'm responsible for patients and have …"

Zach cut her off again. "Look, I suspect that within five minutes, a trained assassin will be entering the hospital with the sole mission to kill you and anyone else who gets in his way. This is serious business!"

"Kill me! Why would anyone want to kill me?"

"I'll tell you why after you are safely out of the hospital, and we're speaking on your cell phone."

Zach could sense that Sofia, now frightened, quickly weighed her options. "Look, I'll give you my cell phone number if you swear you'll call me back once outside and away from the hospital."

Sofia reluctantly agreed to take Zach's cell phone number.

"And, Sofia, this man who is coming for you at the hospital, he'll most probably be of Middle Eastern descent, and he'll know what you look like. So please, don't hesitate. Just leave the hospital and call me back in five minutes. Agreed?"

#

Sofia shook with fear in the confines of her office. She tried to replay the strange conversation in her head. With a break coming up anyway, she elected to get some fresh air outside and get to the bottom of this unfathomable notion that someone was out to kill her. She grabbed her purse and headed out to the nurse's desk to let Agnes know that she would be back shortly. As she looked up, Agnes was preoccupied with a visitor, dressed in black. She motioned back towards Sofia's office, and the man turned in her direction. He was a muscular Middle Eastern man. Their eyes locked upon one another. Sofia froze. The man started to walk towards her, quickening his pace. He reached into his pocket and pulled out the leather dog collar he removed from her loving dog, Max, and showed it to her.

Sofia, now realizing that the man on the phone was really her guardian angel, ran to the exit door at the end of the hall. The door led to the stairwell, and her only choice was to proceed up to a higher floor of the hospital. Sofia made it to the top of the second story ramp, when the alleged assassin entered the bottom of the stairwell. He pulled out a pistol with silencer, and took two shots at Sofia, missing twice. She came barreling out of the stairwell and crashed into the wall. Right there in front of her, she saw the fire alarm and pulled the lever. The alarm siren and flashing lights were instantly activated as the entire staff started to react. Sofia took a left down a corridor and hid.

She saw the assassin exit the stairwell and get caught up in the commotion from the fire alarm, but he continued to pursue her anyway. Sofia watched helplessly as he sliced his way through the staffers, and started indiscriminately firing his weapon in her direction, hitting many of her fellow workers who scrambled in the nearby halls. As she was told minutes earlier, this was no game. This man was out to kill her no matter what the collateral damage.

Sofia ducked into the pediatric ward that housed the infant-wellness center for newborns. The assassin slowed his pace and started checking door after door. Most of the staff had found safety, but the nurses behind the three-inch soundproof viewing glass area were unaware of the assassin. Although they saw the fire alarm's flashing lights, their duty was to stand down until a fire was confirmed by hospital security. Nine newborns occupied the ward that day. Sofia checked the hall and saw the assassin in his room-to-room search. Knowing that this was the worst possible place she could lead a stone cold killer, she devised a plan to retreat to the rear of the ward and make a break for it through another stairwell. She took a deep breath. One, Two, Three … Go. Sofia ran full-steam into the viewing area. The keen assassin caught the movement in his peripheral vision and turned to unload an entire thirteen round clip into the air. Broken glass showered down upon the infants in their open incubators. Several of the infants screamed from the splintering of their skin. Sofia, missed by the spray of bullets, reached the stairwell and turned to assess the damage. The assassin pulled his clip and reloaded. During the brief hiatus, a nurse made an attempt to reach the exposed infants. The radical movement again caught the eye of the assassin, and he rapidly fired three shots. This time, two of the three bullets pierced the upper body of the nurse, and she fell to the ground. It was in Sofia's inherent nature as a physician to render aid, but the immorality and disregard for human life apparent in the assassin caused her to lure him away before any other innocent souls were taken.

Sofia ran down the rear stairwell. Once on the main floor, Sofia saw hospital security forces headed her way. She directed them to the stairwell, and reported the assassin's location. The security team formed a perimeter around the stairwell and waited. Sofia took refuge in an office and watched through a small crack in the door. For sixty seconds nothing happened. The security team entered the stairwell, and the door closed. The sound of gunshots echoed in the cavernous enclosure, then silence. The door opened, and one of the security officers came crawling out, bleeding. The assassin stepped over him, and shot him in the back of the head. Sofia slammed the office door and locked it. Now trapped in a workspace with no window or means of escape, the assassin proceeded to shoot at anything that moved and continued his room-by-room search for Sofia.

#

Back on the Concord, Zach worried that he failed to convince Sofia of the imminent danger she faced. Fifteen minutes had passed since they spoke. Zach had already notified Brother Werner of the immediate course change to London. Was that all for naught? Did Sofia even want their assistance? Zach tried the hospital main number and got a busy signal multiple times. What the hell was going on?

#

The assassin came upon the office in which Sofia hid. He tried the door but it was locked. Two shots to the bolt and the door opened. The assassin scanned the commonplace office. There was nothing under the desk or in the closet, so, satisfied, he hastily moved on.

After ten minutes of silence, Sofia removed one of the ceiling panels and quietly lowered herself down onto the desk. Sofia had hidden undetected right above where the assassin was standing just minutes earlier. Checking one last moment for any sign of the assassin, Sofia slowly opened the door. The British police roamed the hallway. No one questioned Sofia with her white lab coat, and she calmly departed from the exit nearest to the employee's parking lot.

Once free of the hospital and miles away, Sofia sat in her vehicle taking deep breaths to calm her racing heart. She pulled the cell phone number of her newfound friend out of her coat pocket and dialed.

"Hello," Zach said.

"Zachary Dorsey?" Sofia asked.

"Yes, this is Zach."

"Oh, thank God. This is Sofia Boudreaux … and I am ready to hear you out."

"Are you safe, away from the hospital?"

"I am now. Where are you?"

"We should be landing in London in about thirty-five minutes. Can we meet?"

"All right. There is a little all-night café called the Knights Castle located about a kilometer in front of the London Eye. Meet me there in an hour, and sit by a window. I'll call your cell at that time to identify you. Please be prepared to tell me what the bloody hell is going on, and I don't want any hogwash. Your killer turned up at the hospital and promptly took out twenty harmless and innocent civilians."

"Sofia, he won't stop. Don't go back to the hospital or to your home. He'll know where you live."

"Why is he after me, Zach?"

"Like I said before, you and I are one of a kind from a very special family. We are known as Royal Blood descendents."

"Yes, I remember. But descended from whom?"

"I'll go into detail once we meet. Just lie low and don't speak to anyone until I get there. I believe you understand how serious this is now."

"Yes, I understand. I'll be waiting for you."

CHAPTER 21

Friday, 8:43 PM - Notre Dame Seminary, New Orleans

The New Orleans Fire Department had reduced the massive flames of the grand Notre Dame Seminary to a pile of smoldering rumble. The bombing and resulting fire destroyed over one hundred years of religious history and priceless writings and artifacts within hours. Appointed directly from the mayor's office, Homeland Security Superintendent, Nicky Triche, was in charge of the preliminary investigation. At the scene, Superintendent Triche met with the fire commander in charge of the incident, Chief Rossiere.

"Would you care to explain what the hell happened here?" Superintendent Triche asked.

"Well, sir, from the initial evidence we have been able to collect, I would surmise that the Seminary was under some form of military assault," Chief Rossiere answered.

"Military assault? On what evidence do you base your theory?"

"For starters, we've discovered that the assailants forced their way into the front entrance with at least two separate bazooka-style missile strikes. Recovered materials strongly suggest that the rockets were military grade, and apparently came from the black market stock pile of illegal weapons after the collapse of the Soviet Union. We couldn't identify any serial numbers because they appeared to have been manually filed off of each weapon. We also recovered several fragments from multiple hand grenades that were detonated within the premises."

"Any theories on why someone would use military grade force on a bunch of monks?"

"No, sir. We did recover several charred bodies, including one that I believe you should see."

Chief Rosiere walked Superintendent Triche over to a makeshift governmental triage station set up on the front lawn of the property. They approached an elongated body bag, and the Chief ordered the medic to uncover the body. It was the remains of Brother Martin. His body was severely burned. The Chief didn't need to point out to the Superintendent the readily apparent knife wounds on the corpse.

"Superintendent, what do you make of this?" Chief Rosiere asked.

The Superintendent knelt down to take a closer look at the distinctive handles on the knives, still piercing through the remaining flesh.

"Well, maybe some sort of gang or torture ritual," Superintendent Triche noted. "I count eight knives in all. He must have been targeted or possessed something these lunatics were seeking. Chief, make sure you have plenty of pictures of this man and send one of the knives to the FBI office downtown for analysis. Let's see if they can help determine who we are dealing with."

"Will do."

"Superintendent!" yelled one of the military police officers. "Over here. I think you will want to see this."

"Yes, what is it, Captain Fields?"

"We have recovered a standard police issued Glock 9mm hand-gun in one of the damaged rooms inside."

"Have you run the serial number through the database?"

"Yes. It comes back registered to a Mitchell Begg, a NOPD Detective out of the Mid City district."

"Has Detective Begg been located or accounted for?"

"Not that we can tell, but we have several unknown bodies. We'll have to wait on dental and DNA records to confirm positive identities. We've issued a summons for his detainment in case he's alive and kicking."

"Good. Bag the gun as evidence, and call police headquarters. I need to speak to Detective Begg's commanding officer at once and determine why a local cop is tied up in this fiasco."

#

On board the Vatican Concorde, Zach continued to input verses of the riddle into the computer for evaluation:

'Thirteen will be the key,

To fight the rising tide.'

CHAPTER 22

Friday, 9:02 PM - Metairie, Louisiana

Tiberius, the assigned assassin responsible for Zachary Dorsey, hailed a local taxi to the Louis Armstrong National Airport in Kenner. He wept quietly in the backseat because his failure would be considered a grave shame on the honorable reputation and vitality of his family back home. Knowing that failure was unacceptable to the militant Islamic Order of the Punarjanam, Tiberius changed his destination to the nearest holy site for Muslim prayer. The driver told him the nearest mosque was the Masjid Abu Bakr Mosque in Metairie. Along the way, Tiberius imagined his wife, Shilom, dressed in her traditional ivory robe with velvet trim and veil-thin hijab, and his only son Ahmad, a fine looking eight-year old boy whose pride in his father was immense. Tiberius put his head in his hands and realized that going home was no longer an option. A hero to his people, but the American version of a "soldier of fortune," he now regretted his decision to pursue monetary gain in such a radical organization.

Once at the mosque on David Drive, Tiberius paid the fee and expressed eternal blessings of Allah to the driver. Even past dusk, he was able to examine the exterior structure in the fading light. It was very different from the sanctimonious and holy shrine he was used to in his homeland. The structure was old and still reeking of the mildew from Hurricane Katrina. Tiberius could tell that a local mosque was not the original intention of the building, due to the square and boxy confines presented to him. No matter, he came here for one reason and one reason only.

With his traditional Punarjanam sword by his side, Tiberius knelt down in the parking lot, opened his small Koran and began to silently pray alone in the darkness. He wondered about the ambitious goal of his youth: to set an example to his people and try to unite the three main religions on the planet: Islam, Judaism, and Christianity. How had he strayed so far off course from the original teachings of his own father, an educator and man of remarkable faith and courage? The time had now come to pay for his misgivings. Even though he had brought death to dozens of men in his time, Tiberius was now scared of the unknown journey of his soul. He prayed to God that his wife and son would understand, and that he would be forgiven. Wiping the tears from his eyes, Tiberius closed his Koran, took out his sword, placed it before him, blade side up, and fell on it.

CHAPTER 23

Saturday, 3:10 AM - Vatican Suites, Rome

The Holy Seer, still anxiously awake, answered his door to find the beautiful, mysterious, middle-eastern woman, Cara Lesem, standing in the hall. Cara was the liaison warrior between the Holy Seer and the Punarjanam. A fierce competitor and undefeated in battle, but with the natural beauty of the goddess Isis, she focused her attention on the purpose of her late night visit.

"Your holiness, I'm here on behalf of all of the Punarjanam warriors today, to collect the first payment for the services rendered to your cause," Cara said, looking directly into his eyes as she handed him her report.

The Holy Seer donned his reading glasses and looked over the written report, showing the effects of *the operation* and its immediate results. "Tell your assassins that I am very impressed, but can't payment wait until the assignment is complete?" the Holy Seer asked.

"I'm afraid not, your Holiness." Cara stood at attention. "As you can imagine, I must pay my fees without delay. It's only good business practice."

"I understand." He handed the report back to her. "If you would be so kind as to wait here one moment, my dear." The Holy Seer walked over to a wall safe hidden behind an original Rembrandt landscape. He spent about thirty seconds going through the contents of the safe, and returned directly to Cara.

"Hold out your hand my child, and close your eyes."

Cara, with her eyebrow arched and eyes wide open, held out her hands. The Holy Seer gave her a bag overflowing with sparkling white and blue diamonds of all sizes.

"You know what they say: diamonds are a girl's best friend."

Cara, ever the business woman, was shocked at such a gesture. "With all due respect, sir. The deal was for cash payment for services rendered, not payment in blood diamonds that have been illegally acquired from the slavery of my own Islamic people." She held the diamonds up to him. "This is not acceptable."

The Holy Seer was taken back by the refusal of the very valuable and untraceable means of payment. "So you refuse my payment?"

"Your means of payment are a slap in my face and the faces of everyone I represent." She placed the diamonds on a nearby desk. "I will wait here until you have acquired the correct amount of payment in unmarked euros, as you promised."

"That will take some doing," the Holy Seer said.

"Must I remind you that the Punarjanam does not take deception lightly?" Cara pointed out.

"I will see what I can do," he relinquished. "Give me till the morning to contact the Vatican Bank and make suitable arrangements."

CHAPTER 24

Saturday, 1:32 AM - London, England

Zach looked out the window in awe at late night London's shimmering beauty. The nomadic glow of lights kept the city alive as a fine mist cascaded down from the heavens to chill the night air. The Vatican Concorde had landed safely at Heathrow International Airport, and Zach and his companions were speeding to meet Sofia Boudreaux at the all-night café, the Knights Castle. The Knights Castle was a modest, quaint café, situated directly across from the illuminated London Eye ferris wheel. A favorite among the locals, the café offered sixty-nine different flavors of coffee and tea.

Sofia arrived early and sat on a park bench adjacent to the café about seventy meters from the front entrance. Without her lab coat on, she was a fashion plate of London style. Her low-cut Channel blouse and short skirt enhanced her 5'7" petite figure. Her chic Prada flats, which performed so admirably in the hospital chase, were now a little scuffed and increasingly uncomfortable. One of the straps had ripped at the heel. Sofia was nervous, and she repeatedly checked the time on her cell phone. The phone had rung twice in the last ten minutes, both hang-ups. Unnervingly, caller ID showed both calls were blocked from the sender. She wondered to herself, how she became involved in something so surreal.

#

Zach directed the others to wait for him near the London Eye as he went to meet Sofia alone. He entered the café and was greeted by a delightful British server.

"Good morning, a table for one?" the young female server asked.

"I'll take a booth for two near one of the front windows," Zach answered.

She smiled at Zach. "Coffee or tea?"

"I'll have a double shot espresso with whipped cream please."

As Zach waited on his espresso, his cell phone rang. According to caller ID, the incoming call was placed by a local British phone number.

"This is Zach Dorsey."

"Zach, this is Sofia. I'm glad you could make it. Are you alone?"

"Yes. I've sent my companions to the London Eye to wait."

"Good. Now stand up and pretend to stretch so I know who you are."

Zach did as he was told, and Sofia saw his image through the window.

"I see you. I'll be there in a minute."

Sofia calmly stood up and walked over to the café entrance, joining Zach momentarily in his booth. The server brought Zach his espresso and took an order for herbal tea from Sofia then left them alone.

Sofia charmed Zach with her British accent as she began to speak, "Would you please tell me what the bloody hell is going on here?"

"It's a pleasure to meet you too, Sofia," he said with a cunning smirk on his face. "Now that all the pleasantries are dispensed, I'm more than happy to fill you in. I was en route from the United States to Rome when I learned of your particular circumstance. I'm here to offer you my assistance in any way."

"What circumstance?" Sofia demanded. "Why was that man trying to kill me? And what do you have to do with everything that is going on?"

"One question at a time," Zach said. "Here we go. In the simplest terms: before today, you and I were two of only several hundred of whom had been deemed, gee, how do I say this? Um … Royal Bloods. A Royal Blood is a direct descendent of Mary Magdalene and Jesus Christ…"

"A Royal what?" Sofia exclaimed.

Zach held his hand up. "Please, hold your questions as I explain." Sofia sat back and listened with wide eyes. "Today, a worldwide group of powerful traditionalists called the Illuminati have used an Islamic assassin order called the Punarjanam in an attempt to eradicate all of the Royal Bloods. The man at the hospital was one of these assassins." Zach leaned forward. "The only reason I became involved in your situation is because I, too, with the help of my colleagues, escaped from an assassination attempt earlier today. Afterwards, I sought out other Royal Bloods to warn them of this impending doom. Let me point out that over 95% of Royal Bloods were not as lucky as you and I were today. Hundreds have perished in the last twenty-four hours." Zach looked over his shoulder and then met Sofia's eye. "That is why

I'm here, Sofia. To help protect you, and to get to the bottom of this through the most powerful institution on Earth, the Vatican."

"How do I know that what you say is for real?" Sofia asked, still skeptical. "What proof can you offer me?"

Zach lifted the beige sweater that he acquired from the Concorde clothes closet. He revealed to Sofia the Royal Birthmark of the *fleur-de-lis* on his chest.

"Does this look familiar?"

"Oh!" Sofia brought her hand to her mouth and then slowly pulled aside her blouse to reveal an exact replica of the *fleur-de-lis* on her chest. "But how can this be?"

Zach reached out and ran his fingertips over her symbol. Her skin was warm and soft. He felt her warmth rush through him with the recognition that he had now found another like him. Sofia felt a mirroring warmth in her chest.

"I'm sure the answer has always been right in front of you." Zach slowly withdrew his hand. Do you know much about your family's heritage? Do you know the real names of your biological mother and father?"

"I know that my biological family was originally from Paris, France, and my mother's maiden name was Rothschild. It was also given to me as my middle name, Sofia Rothschild Boudreaux. Why?"

"Well, that would make perfect sense. My great-great grand-father, Dagobert de Longuory, and I presume, your great-great grandmother, Madeline Rothschild, both of Royal Blood, had a long romantic affair in the 1770s. This affair produced an offspring called Monica, a pure Royal Blood. Monica was known to have spent time in the New World as well as France. Somehow, we are both descended from that family tree."

"So, we are related."

"I believe so, but that is not important right now. We need to get you to safety."

"Do you have the gift as well?" Sofia asked, arching her left eyebrow.

"I have many talents. We can share details later when we are out of the public eye."

"With whom are you traveling?"

"I'm with my mentor, Brother Guiden, our Vatican escort, Brother Werner, a policeman named Mitchell Begg, and a friend of mine, Sam DelaCroix. The Concorde is currently refueling at Heathrow airport and should be ready to go by the time we get back."

Sofia squinted at Zach. "You must excuse me. As a single woman, I don't know how comfortable I am about accompanying a bunch of strangers on an intercontinental excursion in the middle of the night. Explain to me how you and this assassin both found me at the Royal London Hospital on a Friday night."

"For me, it was easy. I was able to triangulate the position of your protector, Raphael, his cell transponder... wait a minute." Zach paused, frowning. "Have you had any unknown calls to your cell tonight?"

"Why, yes. Around twenty minutes ago, I had two hang-ups. I was wondering who would be calling me this late, but I just figured it was a co-worker at the hospital looking for me after all of the commotion."

"Let me see your cell phone."

Zach looked at the blocked calls on the cell and then flipped it over and disconnected the SIM card. "Do you see here?" Zach asked. "SIM cards send out a constant small electronic impulse to the nearest cell tower to maintain a typical connection for incoming and outgoing transmissions and can be easily tracked in today's technological world. That's how I knew you were at the hospital. We have to get out of here, now."

Zach paid the bill, and he and Sofia moved towards the front door. Out of the corner of her eye, Sofia caught a glimpse of a man rounding the bend near the café.

"Oh, shit!" Sofia cried.

"What is it?" Zach looked briefly around.

"The man from the hospital - he's right outside."

CHAPTER 25

Saturday, 1:39 AM - London, England

"Okay, let's turn around slowly and head for the kitchen," Zach said. "There must be another way out."

Zach and Sofia proceeded behind the counter towards the kitchen while the assassin made his entrance. Sofia made the mistake of looking back at the man, and their eyes connected. The assassin, without pause, drew his weapon and fired at Sofia. Zach pushed Sofia through the revolving stainless steel kitchen doors, and ducked behind the counter. He drew his own weapon, which Brother Guiden gave him in preparation for such an event, and returned fire. This action froze the assassin as Sofia, terrified, continued through the kitchen towards the back exit. Zach eyed the assassin and fired a couple more shots, then pursued Sofia to the rear of the building. Once at the rear door, Zach flung open the exit and ordered Sofia to run along the tree line towards the London Eye. He assured her that he would catch up as soon as he could.

Now alone, Zach looked around for anything he could use to combat the assassin and conserve ammunition. By the door he spied a cleaning bucket, some liquid detergent and an old mop. Using his head, Zach temporarily secured the rear door with the mop's wooden handle. He then took the remaining liquid soap, spread it along the cobblestone exit, and sprayed it down with some water. The makeshift trap was set, but Zach knew it would only deter the assassin for a few extra moments, so he made haste towards the trees, in pursuit of Sofia.

#

The assassin made his way to the rear exit, and found that the door was held shut. With one heave of his shoulder, the wooden mop handle splintered and broke, and the assassin was free to exit. It took only two steps on the soapy cobblestones, and the assassin nearly did a complete one-eighty before he hit the ground with a thud. Cursing, the assassin regained his footing, vowing to make it a slow and painful death for his clever targets.

#

Sofia, now exhausted from running for the second time today, took a break behind some hedges in the park outlining the tourist area. She looked around, but saw and heard nothing except the pounding of her own heart. She placed her hand on the image of the *fleur-de-lis* and wanted to weep. Still scared, she stood up and continued towards the London Eye.

Zack saw Sofia, and quietly came up behind her. "Miss me?"

Unconsciously, Sofia let out a screeching yell that both the assassin and the rest of the Concord party must have heard. The assassin, now aware of the correct path, vigorously pursued. Zach, realizing his mistake, grabbed Sofia's hand, and they took off running straight towards the huge circular figure. They were directly within the assassin's line of vision, and he fired upon the couple, just barely missing them to the right.

#

Brother Guiden and Detective Begg heard the very distinct sound of the revolver with silencer firing, and rushed to the couple's aid, leaving Sam and Brother Werner near the base of the London Eye.

"Punarjanam, stop where you are," Brother Guiden yelled as he directed Begg left.

The Punarjanam stopped running and reviewed his surroundings. He could no longer see the couple or the man who had just spoken so defiantly. He yelled out, "No Westerner can stop the power of Jihad!"

"Is that what you assume this is, Jihad?" Brother Guiden shouted. "You think this is some sort of holy war between the Islamic people and the West? No one has to die tonight, my brother. This is the glorious time for rebirth, not death."

The assassin replied, "My rebirth *is through your death*."

#

Zach and Sofia made it to the main terminal at the base of the London Eye and hopped a rusty metal fence guarding the control booth of the ride. They broke the window for entry. Under the radiance of the Eye, the assassin could see them from the distance. He repeatedly rejected Brother Guiden's pleas for peace, and took off for the terminal. Brother Guiden and Detective Begg saw that the assassin was on a direct path to the London Eye.

"I'll take care of the killer, you get Zach and Sofia," Detective Begg yelled to Brother Guiden. The two of them gave chase after the assassin.

#

The assassin reached the terminal first and saw that Zach and Sofia had taken an observation pod towards the top of the tower. He chose to climb the rafters instead of waiting for the next pod. Detective Begg arrived about a minute later. Out of breath, he entered another pod from the ground level. Begg moved towards the summit in hot pursuit.

#

Zach and Sofia, now at the London Eye's pinnacle, perched on a maintenance landing overlooking the eminent city skyline, sought out alternatives to their current situation. Zach saw a maintenance hatch on the backside of the main crane's arm shaft, and opened it up. The small hatch was apparently used for storage of spare metal cable for the pulley system. Zach removed a bundle of loose cables and placed Sofia in the hatch to hide from the approaching assassin. He checked his gun but was out of ammunition. He then pulled out a large mechanical wrench, and crossed to the other side of the raised platform to wait. The swirling of the late-night, brisk wind whistled around the tower. Zach's heart hammered as he said a silent prayer to the heavens, and his primal fear was replaced with a peaceful tranquility. Was this the moment that Brother Guiden had spoken about that Zach was born to face?

The predatory sound of a man climbing upwards on the metal apparatus started to creep into Zach's consciousness. The assassin was near, and sought vindication. The faint sound of Sam screaming, "Watch out, Zach, he's coming," came from the distance. The thud of the assassin landing on the platform rang out, and Zach prepared for battle. Detective Begg stopped his pod, and began to climb with his weapon drawn. He slowly approached and probed the platform. The night air was eerily quiet at five-hundred feet, and the tension heightened. Zach, crouched in a dark corner on the other side of the platform, saw the assassin come up behind Begg.

"Watch out behind you!" Zach yelled to Detective Begg. It was too late. The assassin landed the first blow on the detective. Begg dropped to his knees. The assassin came around, and grabbed Begg's right wrist, still holding the weapon and bent it backwards. Zach heard the snap of the detective's wrist as he shrieked in pain. The assassin took the pistol, and held it up to Begg's temple. Without hesitation, Zach flung himself out of the darkness and hurled the huge wrench at the assassin, striking him on his left side. Stunned by the impact, the assassin dropped the pistol over the railing. Zach ran to the other side of the platform in order to draw the assassin away from Begg. He remembered the loose cables he removed from the hatch and dashed behind the elevator shaft. He reappeared swinging a piece of the metal cable above his head. Both the assassin and Zach were now in the middle of the concourse, face-to-face. Zach watched as the assassin approached, sensing that his opponent would not settle for a peaceful resolution. He swung the cable with more momentum and velocity, and heaved it at the assassin's legs. The impact of the metal cable, when it came into contact with the lower body of the assassin, caused it to curl around his left leg. Zach immediately pulled the cable back, and the assassin's falling body caused a loud metal ping on the grated platform. Zach charged the assassin, and jumped on top of him. He placed his hands tactically around his neck, cutting off his airflow. For the first time ever, a life was his to take. He heard another person reaching the platform, and the distraction gave the assassin a reprisal. As Brother Guiden entered the scene on the far side, the assassin fired back a series of right hooks to Zach's face, forcing him to loosen his grip. The assassin then used his powerful legs to launch Zach a full five feet towards the rear of the concourse.

#

Detective Begg, now partially recovered, shot a glance over to Zach as he remembered the words that Brother Martin had said to him: "*You cannot let the assassin get Zach, no matter what the cost!*"

Zach saw the detective, and Begg gave him an informal nod, like a subtle goodbye.

"May God forgive me," Begg mumbled.

With the assassin's attention now focused on Brother Guiden's arrival, the wounded detective launched himself in a full sprint of rage and determination at the assassin. The speed of the tackle carried both Detective Begg and the assassin over the flimsy metal railing system and into the ominous darkness below.

And then there was silence.

#

Detective Begg gave his life in exchange for safe passage to Zach, a man he had met just hours earlier.

Zach gathered himself with the aid of Brother Guiden, and together, they assisted Sofia out of the hatch. Along with Brother Werner and Sam, they blessed the dead body of Detective Begg at the bottom of the eye, and traveled back to the safe confines of the Vatican Concorde.

CHAPTER 26

Saturday, 3:27 AM - On Board The Concorde

Under the cover of night, the Vatican Concorde escaped London without complication. Zach sent a cryptic e-mail message to Interpol authorities and London police, notifying them about the bodies of Detective Begg and the assassin at the base of the London Eye. Sam and Sofia awkwardly sat across from one another in the main passenger area and attempted to make small talk. Sam was immediately struck by the natural beauty and intelligence of the young doctor. Even though she knew of the direct blood relationship between Zach and Sofia, Sam was concerned that somehow, this woman could be bad news to their possible future together.

"So Sofia, how well do you know Zachary?" Sam asked.

"I don't, really. He first contacted me just hours ago at the hospital with this unbelievable tale about an assassin. Then, sure enough, terrible things started happening, and before I knew it, I was here with you. Zach saved my life." She looked intently in Sam's eyes. "Maybe you can answer some of my questions, woman-to-woman."

"I don't think that's such a good idea," Zach said, walking in on the conversation and planting himself in the chair on Sam's right side. "I'm sure Sam will agree, she is as much in the dark about this whole matter as you are. If you want answers, Brother Guiden and I will try to supply them."

"Okay, then," Sofia switched her gaze to Zach. "First of all, where are we going?"

"Leonardo Da Vinci airport in Rome."

"Are you really going to the Vatican to meet with the Pope tonight?"

"Yes, we are," Zach confirmed. "What has reportedly happened today across every continent is of biblical proportions. I'm told by Brother Guiden that it's all been prophesied hundreds, even thousands of years ago. I'm afraid it's up to us to make sure that the Illuminati don't succeed in their quest for power and control over the billions of faithful in the Catholic Church."

Sofia scowled. "Wait. This is all too much for me. Are you telling me that we're currently involved in some foretold biblical story, in which the good guys, these Royal Bloods - which I am supposed to believe I am part of - are waging some kind of holy war against the bad guys, the Illuminati?"

"That is precisely what we are up against," Brother Guiden answered, now joining the group. "Young lady, close your eyes and search your heart, the truth is always found from within ourselves. If you cannot feel it from within that we speak the truth, then you are free to go when we reach Rome."

#

Sofia closed her eyes and concentrated. The feeling of her father's presence resonated within her. She could feel his steady hand guiding her to the path that lay ahead of her. His entity was clear, his meaning profound. Within thirty seconds, Sofia opened her eyes and said, "OK, I'm in."

"Excellent," Brother Guiden said. "It is probably time for me to fill you in on one more detail."

"What's that?"

"The family that raised you, is actually your adopted family."

"What?" Sofia furrowed her brow.

"You are actually Zach's twin sister. You were born in New Orleans to Evelyn and Holden Ratliffe the night they were assassinated. Evelyn saved you and Zach. The Order of Scion separated the two of you for safety. I raised Zach, and your adopted parents, members of The Order of Scion, raised you in London."

"Oh my goodness," Sofia said and blinked back tears of surprise.

"It's a lot to take in, I'm sure," Brother Guiden said warmly, placing his hand on her shoulder.

"That's putting it mildly. This whole night has been a lot to take in!"

"I thought you should know, so that you are clear and armed with all of the facts."

"Yes, I'd rather know everything. Somehow, I think I always sensed…something like this. It makes other things make more sense." She leaned back.

"So, this means I have a sister?" Zach aske Brother Guiden.

"Yes, slow poke," Sofia elbowed him. "Keep up!" She teased as if they had grown up together.

"It's just a lot to take in."

"Your telling me!"

He beamed at her. "I have a sister! This is amazing! I've always wanted a sibling. Family!"

Sofia laughed. "And I have a brother!" They embraced in a long hug, then looked at each other with more knowledgeable eyes, seeing the similarities in their features that they'd overlooked before.

"What do we do now?" Sofia asked.

"Get to know each other better, I guess."

Sofia smiled.

"We could start with you clarifying for me what you meant earlier at the café by *special abilities*."

"Sounds like a good start," Sofia said. "Ever since I was a little girl, I have been able to heal sick and dying beings, everything from plants and animals to humans. I don't understand how it works, but I think I was born with the ability. Would you like a small demonstration? Who has a small cut or scrape on their body?"

"I do, right here on my arm," Sam held out her arm, showing a small abrasion and cut she sustained from scraping against a tree limb in the park in London.

"That will do just fine."

Sofia positioned Sam's arm directly in front of her, and closed her eyes. She slowly began rubbing her hands together, and a small twinkling of brilliant light illuminated from her palms. She placed just one finger on the injured arm, and the abrasion magically disappeared.

"That is tremendous, Sofia," Zach said, studying Sam's arm. "Are there any limitations?"

"Yes. Each healing actually drains me of my own energy, and I need sufficient recovery time, so my powers are limited. These healing powers won't work on my own body, and, depending on what energy is exerted, it can take between several hours to a couple of days for recovery of full strength. Theoretically, I guess since we are blood related, you may have the same powers."

"Can you teach me your healing powers, please?"

"Sure, there's nothing to it. Just try to mentally empower yourself … "

#

Sam watched as Sofia and her trick mesmerized Zach. Letting the two of them have their moment as new siblings, Sam went to the forward cabin and sat down in silence. She saw that Father Dagobert's diary was there. She picked it up, and began to read. Brother Guiden joined her in the rear of the aircraft, and sat at the mini-conference table, where he pulled out a chart and a blank piece of paper. He started to scribble down sketches and notes, appearing to be hard at work.

Sam, now enthralled by the romance-driven diary, was smitten with the simple fact that Father Dagobert was truly in love with Madeline Ratcliffe. As she turned a page, an unopened letter fell out from a concealed pocket in a hidden back binder of the diary. Sam picked up the letter. The inscriptions were in French, but she noticed that the postmark was from Rennes-le-Chateau, France in 1781. The private letter was addressed to Father Dagobert, yet was never opened, presumably because of his death five years earlier in New Orleans. Sam turned the letter over and saw the all too familiar *fleur-de-lis* crest stamped in wax, sealing the letter closed. Should she open the two-hundred twenty-five year old letter? The perfectly preserved parcel proved to be too much of a temptation for Sam, so she used one of her nails to gently pry open the wax seal on the parchment.

Each letter was handwritten in a perfect, old calligraphy style. The content was in English, and signed apparently by Father Dagobert's friend, Father Bigou. The letter read:

My dear old friend,

Where has the time gone? It has been too long since we have conversed, for that I must apologize. A situation has arisen that requires reliable communication among all Blood Brothers. I have discovered that the sixth Grand Master of the Priory of Sion, Bertrand de Blanchefort, brought in dozens of German miners to construct a secret hiding place to conceal something near Rennes-le-Chateau in the 13th century. The prominent Hautpoul family member, Marie de Negre of Rennes-le-Chateau, having no one else to pass on her legacy to and on her unexpected death bed, entrusted this secret to me, her confessor. She directed me to a hiding place at what is now the remains of Saint Peter's Church. There, I found hidden deep in the rubble, four wooden tubes sealed in wax with several parchments bearing the title, "Litanies to Our Lady." They were the true Sangreal Documents that this old man's hands uncovered. Per Marie's request, and for the greater glory of God, I transcribed the information from the ancient parchments to scrolls, and carefully placed them in a special altar stone at Saint Mary Magdalene Church. Upon my death, please pass this knowledge on to our New World Brothers. May God grant you peace and tranquility forever.

Warmest regards,
Capuchin Bigou de Rennes-le-Château

Sam immediately retreated to the back of the plane to share with Zach her powerful new discovery.

#

After her exit, Brother Guiden was still hard at work, now analyzing the last lines of the CompuZen riddle:

'To find the three that you seek,
Blood and honor must be true,
Only the strong, not the weak,
Will the answer be awarded to.'

'For the singular task at hand,
Is to solve the end game,
The riddle will answer the land,
Lives will never be the same.'

'Stored up in the skies,
Is the beating of one's heart,
This test does not allow lies,
So make sure you act smart.'

'Thirteen will be the key,
To fight the rising tide,
To find the fishing three,
The answer will be your guide.'

He repeated each individual verse in succession. Then it all became crystal clear. The riddle was simple in nature but complex in thought. The perfect code. The words laid out the specific pieces to the puzzle taken directly from the Gospel of Mary Magdalene proverbs.

Brother Guiden frantically scribbled down word after word before erupting in a fit of excitement, slamming his hands repeatedly on the conference table. He pulled out the golden device Zach had presented him earlier from a small bag and entered three simple words on the small LCD screen. Verifying his notes one last time, he pressed enter. The CompuZen accepted the code and brought him to another information screen. Brother Guiden read intently before shouting, "I did it! I figured out the encoded puzzle."

Screaming toward the front of the aircraft, Guiden continued, "Brother Werner, you are not going to like this, but we have one more stop to make on our way to the Vatican. We have to go to the Royal Library of Alexandria in Egypt, and we must go right now!"

CHAPTER 27

Saturday, 3:44 a.m. - Back of the Concorde

Brother Guiden rushed to the back of the plane. Zach, Sam, and Sofia all looked up from the letter they were scouring as Brother Guiden flung back the curtain. He waved the CompuZen before the huddled group and exclaimed, "I've done it! I've solved the riddle."

"That's fantastic!" Zach said.

"We have to detour to Alexandria, Egypt!"

"Why, what's there?" asked Sam.

Brother Guiden explained how he had figured out the answer to the riddle, "it's in the phrases '*to find the three that you seek*.' and '*the fishing three*'... it's the Trinity or 'The Fisher Kings,' Jesus, Mary Magdalene, and their daughter Sarah..."

"Their daughter?" Sofia asked.

"Yes, my research has shown that there is much truth to the legend that Jesus and Mary Magdalene were secretly married the night before the crucifixion. On that night they conceived a daughter, Sarah, who later gave birth to three sons, Jesus' grandsons, were tutored by their grandmother, Mary Magdalene and each wrote a gospel. Legend tells that these three gospels were hidden in a secret vault for safety due to the exclusion and persecution of the Royal Blood."

"Right," Sam nodded, "I remember from your speech yesterday... wait, was that just yesterday?"

"I typed in The Fisher Kings to the CompuZen and it opened!" Brother Guiden continued. "The line '*the riddle will answer the land*' points to Alexandria where Mary Magdalene first fled and gave birth to her daughter. My hunch is that we will find the gospels of the Fisher Kings in Alexandria."

"So Sarah would be our ancestor?" Sofia asked Zach.

"Exactly!" Zach nodded. "When Sarah was still a young girl, Mary Magdalene moved with her to Gaul."

"Which is modern day France," Sofia connected the dots.

"I'll arrange to meet Brother Patrick O'Brien, a curator of the Christian documents at the Bibliotheca Alexandrina, the modern version of the Royal Library of Alexandria. He should help us find what we need to know." Brother Guiden made a move to the computer.

"Brother Guiden, wait just a moment. Sam has also made a discovery."

"Oh, you have?" Brother Guiden turned to Sam. "What is it dear?"

Sam handed him the ancient letter and quickly explained it's significance. Brother Guiden scanned the letter, then raised his eyes to meet theirs. "Astounding!" he exclaimed. "I've been looking for verification of this rumor for years, and all I've found is conjecture!" He reached out and hugged Sam to his chest, kissing the top of her head. "Bless you my child!"

Sam and Zach exchanged wide grins. Brother Guiden released her and Zach opened his arms for a hug. Sofia shook her head and plopped back in her seat.

"Everything okay?" Zach asked.

"Yes, it's all just moving so quickly," she met his concerned gaze. "I'm still processing what happened at the hospital as well as this new information about my family. But don't worry, I'm still in."

"Wonderful! I'll fill you in with more details about The Fisher Kings and our ancestry on the way." Sam felt the warmth of his arms leave her as he sat down beside Sofia. She sat across from them and listened as Zach explained the Royal Bloodline, and the rumor that within the gospels of the Fisher Kings was also hidden a gospel written by Jesus, himself, and in his own hand.

CHAPTER 28

Saturday, 5:33 a.m. - Bibliotheca Alexandrina

Sofia eagerly watched out the window as the Mediterranean Sea glinted blue and green under the first pink rays of sunrise. She had always wanted to visit Egypt with its pyramids and the statue of the Sphinx, the stories she grew up hearing of Alexander the Great and Cleopatra, the mysterious King Tut. As the city of Alexandria rose along the coastline, she imagined the ancient Lighthouse, now a ruin in the sea, once one of the seven wonders of the ancient world rising up to meet them. And nearby would be the ancient Great Royal Library, founded in 300 BC, once the greatest collection of information the world had ever seen when books were papyrus rolls. She imagined its halls and meeting rooms of scholars dressed in Egyptian togas debating philosophy or hovering over plans for the latest scientific inventions such as the Archimedes Screw, a pump for irrigating water, invented by Archimedes while studying at the library.

The ancient library had been partially burned by Julias Caesar in the Alexandrian War of 48 BC, and the library suffered a series of declines, ultimately most of its books were burned by the Muslim

Conquest in 642. Still the idea of Alexandria being the cultural center of the Ancient World fascinated her, especially now that she knew the story of Mary Magdalene fleeing there to raise her child. She looked forward to seeing the new, modern Bibliotheca Alexandrina. Built in honor of the ancient library, it was designed to look like a sundial facing the Mediterranean Sea and inaugurated in 2002.

As they approached the library, Brother Guiden pointed to the images and hieroglyphs, characters of myriad languages from 120 different scripts, engraved on the library's gray Aswan granite side. Although modern, Brother Guiden felt certain these markings would lead them to their next step. He reread the riddle outloud to Zach, challenging him to decipher the puzzle on the walls.

"It must have something to do with the number thirteen," Zach pondered out loud as they exited the taxi.

All four travelers studied the wall, and then as if communicating without words, Sofia translated some of the markings from her ancient study of Greek before medical school, "*stored up in the skies…*isn't that one of the phrases of the riddle?"

"Yes," Brother Guiden confirmed.

"Where on the wall is that phrase?" Zach asked. Sofia pointed out the letters about midway down and to the right on the wall.

"Help me count thirteen characters before and thirteen characters after," Zach directed.

"Thirteen before is in French," Sam said. "I can translate: '*the heart beats.*'"

"Thirteen after is some form of archaic German I think," Brother Guiden added, "*The beast that faces east.*"

"And thirteen after is Spanish," Sofia pointed, *"Angels of tomorrow."*

"And the last one is in Mandarin." Zach said. *"From the sea will arise."*

"Come on," Brother Guiden beckoned to the entrance. "We are due to meet Brother O'Brien."

The group jogged to the main entrance, where Brother O'Brien let them in, glanced furtively around, and then locked the door behind them. "I've already unarmed the building, but I'll have to arm it again in fifteen minutes or else an automatic security breach will be triggered."

"What are the art galleries displaying right now?" Brother Guiden asked.

Brother O'Brien began listing the names of artists, and Zach stopped him at Michelangelo.

"The Spanish," he said, *"Angels of tomorrow*, right?"

"Right!" Sofia agreed, for "Angelo."

"Take us there, please."

The brother led the way through the main reading hall capped with the glass ceiling that resembled a sundial on the outside. Sophia and Sam looked around with awe.

"It's even more marvelous in person," Sophia commented and Sam agreed. In the early morning light, the desks and rafters glinted with a golden hue.

Brother O'Brien opened the gallery door and ushered them in. Zach immediately noticed the painting of the sky on the ceiling, *"Stored up in Skies,"* he pointed up. They all studied the painting, focusing on the shapes of the clouds and then the negative space. Zach recited the riddle in his head, but couldn't figure out how the image related to the words.

"I'm not getting anything either," Sofia said at his side as if reading his mind.

"Maybe it's not the painting, but something else in the room," Zach said. "Everyone spread out and look around. Try to find something that relates."

After many false attempts at deciphering the riddle based on other sculptures and paintings in the room, Sam stopped in front of a statue of Venus, the goddess of love. The goddess stood with her hand at her heart and a dolphin at her feet.

"Zach, look at this," Sam called. "It reminds me of the Mandarin line - *"from the sea will arise...*"

Zach hustled over and examined the statue, "Yes, Venus was born of the sea… it must have something to do with…"

"Thirteen? Maybe?" Sofia asked. "I've been trying a different approach by counting the panels of the sky painting."

"That might be it!" They began looking under the thirteenth panel along the wall for anything hidden, but the wall was smooth - there were no buttons or levers, nothing to discover.

"Only five more minutes and I'll have to set the alarm again," Brother O'Brien warned.

"Maybe it's some other calculus with thirteen," Zach thought, studying the painting again, the shapes of the sky. He counted thirteen images of negative space, he added their sides, divided by thirteen, and got seven. He walked to the seventh panel. A small painting, a sketch really, hung on the wall beneath the seventh panel. He tilted the sketch and as he did, the statue of Venus also rotated, revealing a staircase beneath the floor. "Let's go!"

The pilgrims descended the stairs and traveled single file through a narrow passageway. The dark and cramped tunnel continued on and on. At a turn, the modern tunnel gave way to an ancient one of stone, and Brother O'Brien announced that he must return and set the alarm.

"If there isn't an exit at the end," he told Brother Guiden, "then come back to the museum, and I will try to figure out how to get you back in from the hidden stairway. You'll need to text me so that I can turn the alarm with its motion sensors off again."

Brother Guiden agreed. As they traveled on, the tunnel grew colder and began to drip with moisture.

"Zach," Sam implored. "Do you think it's safe to continue?" She wondered if perhaps they were under the Mediterranean Sea.

"Just a little farther," Zach said. "We have to find out where this leads!"

As they turned another corner, the tunnel opened into a round room lined with sarcophagi, stopping them in their tracks. Sam audibly sucked in her breath. They all began to search the room, feeling the tombs for levels, panels, anything that might reveal the next clue.

At a tomb in the corner, Sofia brushed away the dust and dirt and read the inscription in Greek. "Zach!" she called. Zach lifted a panel from the sarcophagus, and inside found a red earthenware jar. He shook the jar upside down, and out slid a roll of papyrus. He quickly read the Latin then handed the roll to Brother Guiden.

"Is it the gospels of the Fisher Kings?"

Brother Guiden examined the letters. "Yes, they appear to be authentic, based on the script. However, there are still a few pages missing. This roll ends mid-sentence."

"Where might the other pages be?" asked Zach.

"This might be a clue," Sofia called from a neighboring sarcophagus. She had opened its top panel and translating the Greek:

"If you've come this far,
You know there is more,
We would not leave you on this flooded floor.
To the South you'll find the riddle you seek,
In the rough beast that slouches toward
Bethlehem to be born.

Between morning and noon
The aperture appears;
Let Venus be Your guide as she has been here.

"What, prey tell, do you think it means?" asked Brother Guiden.

"I don't know, but I think those panels you opened may have triggered some kind of booby trap. It's beginning to flood." Sam pointed to the water starting to seep beneath the wall. Then it began to leak through the cracks in the ceiling.

"Good God!" Brother Guiden exclaimed. "We must find a way out. Memorize that riddle!"

"Already done!" Zach said. "Everyone take a wall, try to find another way out or else let's head back through the tunnel to the museum."

"Too late!" Sam said as they heard a loud rumble and turned to see giant boulders rolling down the tunnel, sealing the doorway. Water began to spill out through the cracks.

They all began to frantically feel along the walls and sarcophagi as the water pooled at their feet and climbed up their calves. Brother Guiden held the earthenware jar with the papyrus rolls above his head, as he searched with his other hand. Sam, being the shortest, started to tread water, and just as she did her hand knocked against something hard beneath the sarcophagus of a female child. She reached down, felt a lever and pulled back with all of her strength. Directly behind her she heard the creak of stone moving. She pushed and a window sized opening gave way just above the water's height revealing a stairway leading up. "I think I found the way out!"

The others cheered in joy as they waded and swam toward her.

Sam pulled herself through the opening and landed on the damp stairs. She led the way, climbing toward the bright morning.

CHAPTER 29

Saturday, 6:08 am - Alexandria

One by one the group emerged out into the ruins of an old bath house on the rocky beach of the Mediterranean Sea. Down the coastline, they could see the outline of the Bibliotecha's sundial shape in the distance. Zach called a taxi as they discussed the riddle.

"I think I know where to go," Sofia said.

"Bethlehem?" asked Sam.

"No, that's a red herring. The beast slouching toward Bethlehem is from the poem 'The Second Coming' by Yeats. It's a reference to the Sphinx, well at least the Sphinx is referenced earlier in the poem."

"You're right," Zach said, and quoted from the poem "A shape with a lion body and the head of a man/ a gaze blank and pitiless as the sun."

"And the German clue, "*the beast that faces east!*" Brother Guiden exclaimed. "The Sphinx is in Giza, just south of Alexandria."

"But that poem is modern," Sofia protested, "written about World War I, probably published in 1920..."

"The clue was probably included by a modern member of the Order of Scion," Brother Guiden said.

"Brother of Scion?"

"A secret society charged to protect the members of the Royal Blood. I'm sure that's who gave Zach the CompuZen in the first place."

"I see," Sofia put into place the new pieces of the puzzle.

Zach pointed to the taxi pulling up along the beach road. "Let's Go!"

#

From the Concorde, Zach made hotel reservations in Giza. They needed some sleep and wouldn't be able to explore the Sphinx with a bunch of tourists milling around. Brother Guiden had heard of secret passageways and rooms in the long right foot of the lion. He felt the poems and the number thirteen would help them find a way in. The protectors must have developed a coded way into the Sphinx to retrieve the missing pages of the gospel. They would rest and then they would try to find a passageway inside the iconic and mysterious monument.

#

Saturday, 4:18 p.m. - A Hotel in Giza

Zach's alarm woke him with a start. He looked around the dark hotel room, remembering the events from the night before. He had let himself sleep for a few hours, but set his alarm to wake before the others in order to read about the secret passages in the front foot of the Sphinx. He had a hint of how to get in. He hoped it would work, so that he wouldn't have to use his fallback plan, which was to ambush the guards.

"Thirteen will be the key/ to fight the rising tide," Zach repeated these lines of the riddle to himself. Did they apply to the flooded room they had just escaped? Or could they also apply to finding a way into the Sphinx? When reading the history of the monument, Zach kept pausing at how the Sphinx was buried in sand up to its shoulders for thousands of years, finally freed by an excavation in the 1930s and put on display. He thought if anyone had developed a secret passageway, it would have to be an entrance about the shoulder, and it would have been dug either before or during the 1930s excavation. He'd read a theory of a secret entrance behind the right ear, which he pondered, and of another entrance near the tail.

"Thirteen will be the key," he kept circling back to this phrase. Whoever wanted them to find the missing gospels, would most likely use thirteen again. Zach decided to try math. He tried out a few mathematical equations using the dimensions of the Sphinx. He thought about using years, but archeologists hadn't agreed on exactly when the Sphinx was erected and carved and by whom. It was shrouded in too much time, too much mystery.

"Think Zach, think!" He paced back and forth in his room. The hidden rooms, if they were there, had to have been erected from the beginning, or else, the structure wouldn't hold, but a modern passageway, someone who had hidden the gospels for safety there, would have to have been built later. How much later? Any time after 33 CE.

Then he thought of using coordinates. The latitude of the Sphinx was 45.171045, its longitude was -110.877996. After applying a few formulas, he thought he might have a location, and that location matched beneath the right ear, but much lower than he initially thought, just above ground level. Lower, however, would be easier. They wouldn't have to climb the ancient statues and cause more erosion. It was a hypothesis, but one he was willing to risk proving correct.

The group reconvened for dinner at the hotel restaurant. Over savory falafel and rice-stuffed vegetables and grape leaves, Zach told the others his hypothesis and how they might be able to get in. He worried, however, that it would take too much time to find the exact spot that would open the passage. They listened with concentrated interest. Sophia had also thought more about the poem she found and its possible clues. She relayed the story of *The Odyssey* in which the hero, Odysseus, answers the riddle of the Sphinx and is granted passage to Thebes. "What goes on four feet in the morning, two feet at noon, and three feet in the evening?"

"The answer is a human," Sofia explained, "morning is when the human crawls as a baby, noon is when they are an adult walking, and evening is old age, using a cane."

"But how does the Greek riddle relate to the Egyptian Monument?" Asked Zach.

"I think it points to the head, which is human, but then if you reconsider the last stanza of the poem we found in Alexandria:

Between morning and noon

The aperture appears;

let Venus be your guide as she has been here.

Then using the riddle, between morning and noon must be childhood or adolescence, which leads me back to crawling, so somewhere in the body of the lion."

"Which is where my calculations lead." Zach said.

"And what about Venus being the guide?" Asked Sam. "Are there any statues of Venus near the Sphinx? Or is there an Egyptian goddess who correlates?"

"I think they might mean the planet, Venus," Sofia said, "the Evening or Morning Star."

"Venus orbits the Sun faster than the Earth," Zach said, "so it will either appear in the sky in the West in the evening or rise before the Sun in the East. The face of the Sphinx faces east. So do they mean Venus in the evening or Venus in the morning?"

They all pondered the question.

"I don't know, Zach," shrugged Sofia. "My guess would be the east because the statue faces that direction?"

Zach began a search on his laptop. "Venus is seen in the evening between the end of March and through December. So, evening in the west. Tonight Venus will be in the thirteenth quadrant of the Constellation of Virgo. You may find it just right of Spica, the brightest star in Virgo. We should be able to see it a little after 8:00 p.m."

Zach looked up, and both women met his eyes. "Thirteen!" They all said in unison.

"The thirteenth quadrant can't be a coincidence!" Brother Guiden exclaimed. "Let's make a plan for tonight."

#

Saturday, 8:14 p.m. - The Great Sphinx

Zach peaked around the corner of the now closed and empty ticket office, and spied as the night watchman strolled from post to post down the walkway that encircled the Great Sphinx. Zach counted how long it took for the two guards to make each of their passes. They would have five minutes to make it to the Sphinx, find the passageway, and enter. Brother Guiden, being slower, would serve as lookout. When they returned, Brother Guiden would signal when it was clear to cross from the statue to the walkway.

After the guard passed, and they could no longer hear his footsteps, they lightly scurried across the sand to the statue's right side, and looked west. Sam quickly spotted Spica, the brightest star in the Constellation Virgo at the coordinates 13th quadrant. Near it to the right and just above rose Venus. Zach mirrored the coordinates on the statue with a ruler and pushed on the limestone. At first nothing happened. He made the measurements again and pushed. This time they heard what sounded like an ancient crank, and the stone gave way.

Elated they tried not to make any noise, and Sam even covered her mouth with her hand. Once inside, their flashlights began to pick up images along the walls of the tunnel. Sofia paused to investigate the markings and hieroglyphics, deciphering them to be mathematical formulas and equations, interspersed with architectural designs and sketches of the Sphinx as a whole and in parts.

Sofia could barely step forward, she was in such awe of seeing such ancient plans, the ancient minds at work so early on problems of such grand scale. The depth and range of human spirit and invention always swept her away. It was what she looked for and encouraged when a patient was fighting for their life or just to improve. She looked for that glint in their eyes, she listened to resolve in their voice, the attempt to squeeze her hand when she held their's. If she saw one of these signs, she became certain they would recover. These drawings and calculations moved her in much the same way, and she held her hand out, hovering over a graphic, tempted to touch it to make a concrete connection with history, yet keeping her hand at bay so as not to damage such venerable engineering. A little farther down the hall, she discovered the design and physics calculations for the great pyramids nearby. She marveled at the precision as she did the calculations in her head.

"Sofia," Zach interrupted from the end of the tunnel. "This way, hurry!"

She tore herself from the designs, and followed the sound of his voice. As she rounded the corner, the tunnel opened into a room with a long rectangular foyer crossed by a perpendicular opening, and then widening into an oval shaped room. Sofia's heart dropped to her stomach in awe, and she felt the deep sense of her father's presence. She didn't have the language for what she was seeing until Zach whispered at her side, "It's the Ankh Cross. The room is in the shape of an Ankh."

"Of course," Sofia replied with reverence, "the Egyptian symbol for life."

Sam had already entered the room and was searching for signs of irregularities in the walls. She walked to a stone podium in the center of the oval. Following her gut, she reached beneath the podium. Her sensitive fingers, now used to the impressions of stone and feeling for levers, felt a familiar give. She pressed down and a drawer opened at her waist. Inside she found more red earthenware containers. She motioned for Zach.

Zach quickly scanned the documents. "We'll have to show them to Father Guiden to be sure, but I believe these are the missing pages of the Gospels written by Sarah's children, the three grandsons of Jesus."

The three friends took a moment for this information to sink in, grasping each other's hands and feeling the sacredness of the space infuse them with peace and inspiration to continue their chosen path.

"Now, we've got to get back without the guards noticing," Sam broke the silence.

They quickly made for the exit. Although Sofia hated to leave the marvelous designs and calculations, she dutifully followed her companions. At the entrance they paused, listening for the guards' footsteps. Zach sent a text to Brother Guiden who sent back an all clear sign. Like gazelles, they ambled across the plain to the walkway and disappeared into the night, Venus rising above them.

CHAPTER 30

Saturday 8:46 p.m., Alexandria International Airport

Brother Guiden had a taxi waiting in the parking lot of the Sphinx, which whisked them to the Alexandria International Airport. Zach nodded to Brother Guiden that their foray had been successful, but waited to tell him the details once out of earshot of the taxi driver. As they waited on the tarmac to board the Concorde, he whispered in Brother Guiden's ear, "I believe it's what we've been looking for."

"I certainly hope so, son. With the Trinity Gospels, we can share the light of truth to the world. Bring harmony where there is division."

Once on the plane, Brother Guiden washed his hands in preparation to handle the ancient and fragile texts. When they were all seated, Zach reverently handed the red earthenware jar to Brother Guiden, who gently slid out the papers. At first glance he gasped and his hand shot up to his chest as if to cover his heart.

"These certainly look to be authentic!" He exclaimed.

Zach, Sam, and Sofia all looked on with awe and wonder as Brother Guiden perused the documents.

"What does it say? Can you translate?" asked Zach.

"Yes, give me a moment." Brother Guident inhaled deeply. "Here it says: *The Savior said, 'All natures, all formed things, all creatures exist in and with one another and will again be resolved into their own roots, because the nature of matter is dissolved into the roots of its nature alone. He who has ears to hear, let him hear.'*

The small group nodded and met each other's eyes.

Brother Guiden continued, "*Desire said, 'I did not see you descend; but now I see you rising. Why do you speak falsely, when you belong to me?' The soul answered and said, 'I saw you, but you did not see me or recognize me; I served you as a garment and you did not recognize me.' After it had said this, it went joyfully and gladly away. Again it came to the third power, Ignorance. This power questioned the soul: 'Whither are you going? You were bound in wickedness, you were bound indeed. Judge not'. And the soul said, 'Why do you judge me, when I judged not? I was bound, though I did not bind. I was not recognized, but I recognized that all will go free, things both earthly and heavenly.'*"

As the plane began to lift off and quickly gain altitude, Brother Guiden paused to let these words sink in.

"It's more mystical than the other Gospels," Sofia commented.

"It feels more like eastern philosophy or spirituality," Zach agreed.

Brother Guiden placed the scroll on his lap and raised his palms upward in thanks. Tears ran down his cheeks. His loyal student and friends all waited for him to break the silence.

"It's my life's work," he told them. "I am so thankful to have found it."

Zach rested his hand on the good Brother's shoulder. "Please sir," he said gently, "read us some more."

"After the soul had left the third power behind, it rose upward, and saw the fourth power, which had seven forms. The first form is darkness, the second desire, the third ignorance, the fourth the arousing of death, the fifth is the kingdom of the flesh, the sixth is the wisdom of the folly of the flesh, the seventh is wrathful wisdom. These are the seven participants in wrath. They ask the soul, 'Whence do you come, killer of men, or where are you going, conqueror of space?' The soul answered and said, 'What seizes me is killed; what turns me about is overcome; my desire has come to an end and ignorance is dead. In a world I was saved from a world, and in a "type," from a higher "type" and from the fetter of the impotence of knowledge, the existence of which is temporal. From this time I will reach rest in the time of the moment of the Aeon in silence.'"

"Why are the gospels all so different, yet similar?" Sam asked.

"They are inspired texts, but filtered through different consciousness, and passed down, often as oral teachings from Jesus' followers as only a few people could read and write. Some were written down earlier, some later," Brother Guiden said. "But only four were ratified by the early church as the true word of God."

"It would have been a lot simpler if they had just agreed upon one scribe," Sam said.

"History is never recorded by just one person," Zach said. "It's much messier than that."

"Yes, these gospels like the Gnostics are more esoteric, they focus more on the private teachings of Jesus to his apostles, not so much the public teaching with parables," Brother Guiden explained. "There is more about what it means to be human and how to see the divine reflected in the human. How to know God through knowing our true selves. It's more of a process of recognition."

"I find it interesting what Mary Magdalene seems to emphasize in hers...if each of them wrote down what meant the most to them, what would be most clearly impressed upon their memories, hers is the goodness of nature and the ease of balances, the wholeness of a person balancing their strengths and vices."

"Yes," Sam agreed. "It shows us a lot about her and what she values."

"I assume she passed that down to her daughter," Sofia said. "Brother Guiden, do you know what Sarah was like? As a person?"

"Not particulars really, in terms of personality, but there are many sources that point to her gift of healing, and that she ministered to the sick and poor where they settled in France."

Sofia nodded, enthralled.

"It is also said that animals tended to follow her, and she adopted many strays. Her healing worked on animals and plants as well, anything of the material world, she could connect to the radiant divine energy within."

Sofia felt a sharp pain of loss for her dog by the assassin. If only she had been there, she could have healed him. She thought of how she'd discovered her gifts as a child, healing plants, then birds, her childhood dog's leg when he got hit by a car. She recognized herself in Sarah and longed to know more of her - what her life was like, how she chose to live out her vast responsibilities, how she weathered her disappointments and supported her children and loved ones. She had ears and hoped to open them in the way the gospel meant, so she could hear the truth the way people saw light.

CHAPTER 31

Saturday, 10:35 a.m. - Vatican City

Cara Lesem sat in the Holy Seer's living room, watching Italy play Belgium in a football match. She leaned over with interest as the men on the screen passed, ran, and headed the ball. As a child, she'd dreamed of being able to play at this level - the world stage - but instead her athletic prowess got her recruited into the Punarjanam, well, more accurately her father conscripted her. She was never given the choice. One day, her father brought some important men to watch her midfield finesse, the next she was training in martial arts. She took to it immediately, and enjoyed not only pushing her body to feats she never dreamed, the high she got from flips and round kicks, the thrill from outwitting her opponent with gravity and balance, and later, the centering the practice gave her. She did not regret the long hours of training, the exciting life it gave her, but sometimes, something as banal as catching a glimpse of a match on the screen, filled her with raw nostalgia for just playing for the fun of it. The freedom she felt in her powerful body as a child, her body that always rose to the occasion when she asked. It was a gift.

But since then her gifted body had been abused and controlled by others. She was told where and when to perform, who to fight, who to protect, who to assassinate. Her current position was to serve as both the bodyguard for the Holy Seer, and as a liaison between him and her fellow assassins, members of the Punarjanam.

In the other room she heard the Holy Seer end one phone call and begin another. He had to take many secure steps to procure the Euros from the Vatican Bank. She began to pace, to rid herself of the unwelcome feeling of nostalgia. She knew that if she let such a feeling take hold, she would no longer be able to complete the tasks of her profession. Although it was chosen for her in the beginning, it was hers now: it was all she had. Without it, she would have probably been a young wife to an older man without any control over her decisions, and no prestige. In her position, she was still ruled by powerful men, but her talent and beauty let her say yes and no to some missions. And, she knew by the way most people observed her in battle, that she sometimes awed them and frightened them with her abilities. Just enough for them to mostly give her privacy and live in luxury.

When the pacing didn't rid her of the unwelcome emotion, she practiced back flips from a standing position. The feeling dissipated with the spring and skill she felt in her ability to fly through the air, watching the room turn upside down, and then landing exactly in the same position. After sticking her tenth flip, the Holy Seer reentered the room.

"My, what an agile creature you are," he flattered her, but she also saw the glint in his eye - that combination of awe and fear.

"Give me the update," she demanded.

"The courier will be here at noon," he replied, "with your unmarked Euros as requested."

She nodded.

"Shall we watch the game while we wait?" He gestured for her to have a seat on the couch.

With the energy of the flips coursing through her, Cara was able to sit and watch the game without the sneaking nostalgia worming it's way back in.

After a few changes in possession, the Holy Seer said, "There is another matter I was hoping to address with you."

Cara turned to him, arching one eyebrow. "And what might that be?" she asked with suspicion.

"The mission you passed over to be my bodyguard and envoy... do you know much of it?"

She faced the game again. "I am updated by necessity only."

"So the child is being trained?"

"Inoculated, I would call it, but yes, he is being trained as planned."

The Holy Seer nodded his approval and placed his palms together as if in prayer. "From your tone, I take it you don't agree with the method."

Before she was able to center herself and choose her words more wisely, Cara replied, "they are inundating a little boy with hate-training, 24/7. How can you agree with that?"

"But this is no ordinary boy, he's the fulfillment of prophecy..."

"I know, the anti-Christ... I've been informed."

"Then why such qualms?"

"Were you ever a child, sir?" she asked, realizing the flips hadn't rid her of the nostalgia after all.

"That is just his form, not his essence," the Holy Seer replied.

"Right," Cara replied, turning her attention back to the TV just in time to see a player make a stunning pass to another player who headed the ball just past the goalie into the net. The teammates all rushed and high fived and hugged the players. Such innocence, Cara thought, as she dug her nails into her arm to keep from saying anything more out loud.

"He will fulfill our goals."

She simply nodded in response.

A little while later the doorbell rang. Cara stood guard as the Holy Seer asked the courier for the password, then let him into the suite. Cara took the bundle from him herself and counted the Euros on the dining room table, ten million drawn from the Vatican Bank.

CHAPTER 32

Saturday, 10:20 p.m. - The Concorde en route to Vatican City

Back on the Concorde, the weary travelers reclined their seats to try to get some sleep before reaching the Vatican. Zach quickly fell asleep, but only caught a few hours of rest before experiencing a troubling dream. In the dream he wandered a serpentine course down dusty cobblestone streets through an unnamed city somewhere in the Middle East. Just as he turned one corner, he sensed that where he must go is farther yet, around the next turn. Ancient architecture of stone surrounded him, so that he couldn't see with any distance or perspective, only the walls to his sides, the passageway ahead, winding, winding. He grew hot and thirsty, yet he knew he must continue forward. He knew he was in pursuit, not being pursued. But what was he pursuing?

He turned a corner and a woman in a bright purple robe and scarf covering her face beckoned him to follow her. He did. She ducked behind multi-colored sheets of laundry, behind a door, down a hallway, then another door, and another. He was weary, confused, yet he followed.

Finally, she paused at a door and lifts a slot to peer inside. She pointed to Zach to look. Zach lifted the slot and peered inside. It was not so much what he saw, but how it made him feel that was so terrifying. What he saw was a young boy, being shown a series of videos of people from around the world, various cultures, ages, identities, communities, and being told vitriol about each image, hatred spewed from the mouths of soldiers. If the boy tried to contradict anything they say, he was slapped.

The scene was bad enough, but Zach felt something darker, something primordial, he couldn't tell if it was the boy or the soldiers or the room, but it was there, the feeling of pure evil. He backed away from the door to find that the woman in the purple robe was gone, but in her place raged a wall of fire, so bright and hot that he felt he was burning alive.

He searched for another way out, but everywhere he turned he confronted fire. Just as he was about to despair, a hand reached out to him through the wall of flames. His intuition told him to take the hand. The hand pulled him through the fire into another room which was immediately cooler, a vestibule of sorts with what appeared to be a baptismal font in the center. The person who had brought him there stood humbly nearby, offering him a cup of water. Zach took the water and drank, gradually feeling refreshed, but still wearing the deep evil like a cloak on his shoulders. He couldn't shake it, but was able to mumble thank you to the man, who now, mysteriously, seemed to glow with an other-worldly light.

Zach looked at him, a man with long brown hair and clear green eyes, dressed in a white toga with what appeared to be a brown quiver of arrows strapped to his back. Light and goodness emanated from him, and Zach could feel this energy confront the evil around his shoulders and at his back. It was as if a war was taking place, and his body was the conductor where these two forces met.

"Do not be afraid," the glowing being said, "you know me as the Archangel Michael. I bring good news to you."

Zach stood speechless. All he could think to do was hand the cup back to the man-angel.

"Thank you," he said. "I have something important to show you."

He took Zach to the font of water and waved his hand over its surface. Zach watched as a scene unfolded, this one of another boy in a small apartment in Brooklyn, NY. The boy played quietly with some construction paper and scissors, busy at his creative task. From another room nearby, perhaps the kitchen, he could hear a woman singing with a gentle yet vibrant voice. The singing calmed both Zach and the boy, and Zach began to feel the shroud of evil slip from his shoulders.

"This boy embodies the second coming of Christ," the Archangel Michael said.

Zach was filled with a deep sense of peace. "Why are you showing me this?" he asked.

"Because you must protect him. You must give him room to grow up to be the man he is meant to be."

"But how do I?"

"You will see the signs when it is time." Michael replied. He swiped his hand over the water font and the image of the boy disappeared. "Listen with your ears."

The Archangel Michael reached out and put his hands around each of Zach's ears. With his celestial touch, Zach awoke.

CHAPTER 33

Sunday, 12:38 a.m. - The Concorde as it lands at Leonardo da Vinci Airport

When Zach awoke, he felt disoriented. He still felt the calm of the Archangel Michael's parting words, but his mind kept trying to replay the entire dream to fully understand its significance. He shivered and realized that his shirt was drenched in sweat. He felt the plane begin to descend, and with the change in altitude, the other passengers began to awaken.

Sam yawned and looked his way. She smiled and he felt reassured. He returned her smile, uncertain what to tell her about the dream. He reached across the aisle for her hand, and she took it.

"My goodness, Zach, you're soaking wet. Are you ill?"

"No. I've had a terrible dream."

"Oh, I'm sorry." She squeezed his hand. "Do you want to tell me about it?"

"Yes, well, it wasn't all terrible. Just the first part. I think I should tell everyone at once."

She nodded.

Zach called out to Sofia and Brother Guiden. When all had gathered round, he told them of his dream.

"Oh, how frightening," Sofia said, touching her hand to her heart as if she, too, could feel the dark emotions that Zach had experienced in the dream. "What does it mean?"

"Unfortunately, I think it means exactly what the Archangel said," Brother Guiden answered. "The prophecy is coming true. We will soon see the rise of the Antichrist and the Second Coming of Jesus. As children, each's power is balanced by the other. But if as they grow, depending who tries to influence them, that power might shift. We must make sure that it doesn't shift to evil."

Sofia again had the vertiginous sensation that everything since last night was moving too quickly for her to process. She sat down.

"According to the dream, the wrong influences are already brainwashing the child I saw," Zach said.

"We'll need to act fast at the Vatican. We need to expose the cover up of the Royal Bloodline. That will be our first step to restoring the influence of the Second Coming."

Brother Guiden moved to the Communication Center to speak with Brother Werner as the pilot announced they would be landing in Rome in fifteen minutes. "Please buckle your seatbelts."

As Zach clicked his seatbelt, he said a little prayer for guidance. He felt instinctively that he would need it.

CHAPTER 34

Sunday, 12:56 a.m. - Leonardo da Vinci Airport, Rome

As the plane landed in Leonardo da Vinci Airport in Rome, Brother Werner picked up the phone to secure their credentials and lodging in Vatican City. Likewise, Brother Guiden called Brother Mollo and secured a visit to the Vatican Archives later that afternoon. Soon, an unmarked black car from the Vatican arrived at the airport. Brother Guiden gave the driver the passcode, and they all piled inside.

As the driver maneuvered through tiny streets in darkened Rome, Sofia marveled at the architecture, feeling again the same immensity of the human spirit that she felt in the pyramid as they traversed the old city. Intellectually, she was finding it hard to accept that all that had happened, but in her heart she felt interconnected to each of the steps, as if following her own constellation written in the sky.

She had always felt a profound connection to others that seemed both otherworldly and intensely personal when she healed people, and now, after hearing that her ancestor Sarah was also a healer, she felt as if finally her calling and discovery of her "special skills" made sense.

The mark on her chest seemed to throb with fire. She took deep slow breaths to try to calm her racing heart. With such a gift, with such a connection, she felt a growing responsibility to use it for the greater good, but with this acknowledgment also came anxiety. She glanced at Zach and wondered if he, too, felt this pressure.

"Zach," she said as they approached the Vatican Gate. "Do you feel it, too?" She placed her hand on her chest. He mirrored the action.

"I do," he said.

They locked eyes across Sam, who was sitting between them. As she looked back and forth at each of their twinned expressions and actions, Sam felt left out. A cringe of pain ran up her spine. Her heart plummeted. While they looked connected and filled with the same kind of Holy Spirit, Sam felt hollow. With Zach's new knowledge of who he truly was, would he really want to be with the likes of her? She felt like a mere mortal in a superhero comic book. She might as well have a bubble over her head that read "Drat!" or "Ouch!"

As they pulled up to their flats, a Vatican official met their car and passed them each an I.D and a key card to their apartments.

"Do not leave the premises," he instructed. "You are under the safety of the Vatican Guard as long as you are on site. We cannot guarantee your safety if you venture into the city.

They all nodded.

Zach squeezed Sam's hand as they got out of the car which made her feel a little better, but then Sofia touched his arm and said, "Can we talk in private for a moment?"

"Of course," he said.

"Once you get settled, come to our apartment." Sofia gave him the number.

Zach nodded, then turned to Sam. "Get some rest," he said.

"Zach…" Sam began, but she really didn't know what she wanted to say. She hadn't put into words yet what she was feeling.

"Yes?"

"Nevermind," she said.

"You sure?"

"Yes, I'll see you soon."

CHAPTER 35

Sunday, 1:33 a.m., The Holy Seer's Apartment, Vatican City

Cara slipped back into the Holy Seer's apartment after a brief visit with the local Punarjanam, where she paid those who had completed their assassinations of the members of the Royal Blood. The others she would get to in time - they were spread across the world in both large cities and small villages. For now, she needed to stay with the Holy Seer until the whereabouts of one Zach Dorsey had been confirmed.

Cara quietly opened the Holy Seer's door to check on him. He was asleep in bed, his chest rising and falling beneath the sheets. She shut the door and lay down on the couch to catch some sleep herself, when there was a quick rap on the door. Cara jumped up and stole across the room. When she peaked through the peephole, the same courier from before stood in the foyer. She asked him the password, then allowed him entrance.

"I have an urgent message for the Holy Seer."

"You may tell me, and I will convey it."

"Not possible. I have been instructed to tell him only."

"I'll wake him," Cara said.

A minute later the Holy Seer appeared in the main room. The courier explained to him how Zach Dorsey and Brother Guiden and two as yet unidentified females had snuck into the Vatican and were planning to meet with Brother Mollo in the Archives soon, possibly even as they spoke.

"I see," the Holy Seer said. "And do you know what they seek?"

"Negative."

"Thank you, you may go."

The Holy Seer then turned to Cara. "We must devise a plan. They cannot succeed in whatever information they plan to expose."

Cara nodded and they went to work.

CHAPTER 36

Sunday, 2:06 a.m. - Vatican Archives, Vatican City

Brother Werner led the way through a series of locked doors and passages to the Vatican Archives where Brother Mollo met them at the door. Zach and Brother Guiden had elected to let Sofia and Sam sleep for a few hours back at the Vatican Apartments.

Brother Mollo greeted each of them with a hug and kiss on the cheek. He was a portly older brother, with a deep sparkle of spirit in his eye and an amiable grin.

"So wonderful to see you, Brother Guiden. It's been too long. And it is an exquisite pleasure meeting you, Mr. Dorsey."

"Zach please, Brother," Zach said with a flush.

"Well, what is it that I can help you with that is so urgent?" Brother Mollo asked.

"It's time," Brother Guiden said. "We have the Trinity Gospels."

Brother Mollo's genial face turned grave. He nodded. "Follow me."

Brother Mollo led them through a series of rooms filled with shelves from the floor to the ceiling, all containing files. "We've been trying to digitize everything, but as you can see, it's a long process," he said, gesturing to the countless files. He turned a corner, entered another room, and walked about twenty feet until he found a specific row with a sliding ladder parked at the end. "Irenaeus of Lyons. Let's start here," he said. Brother Mollo pushed the sliding ladder down the row, then began to climb it. About halfway up he pulled down a file.

"Here is a copy of *Adversus Haereses*, or *Against Heresies* in English. Written in Greek around 180 C.E. by Irenaus, the Bishop of Lugdunum, now Lyon in France. In it, Irenaus distinguishes between orthodox Christian teaching and the teachings of the Gnostics. It's one of the first documents to establish Christian doctrine as the texts that became included in the New Testament such as the four Gospels of Matthew, Mark, Luke, and John. It was our best source on the Gnostic Gospels until the Library of Nag Hammadi was discovered in 1945."

Zach and Brother Guiden nodded. They had both studied this description of the teachings of Gnosticism and its claims about Jesus' private teachings to his disciples. The private teaching did not include as many parables as Jesus' public teaching. It stated more esoteric ideas such as that the Kingdom of God was not an event or place, but was within you and outside you, and when you know yourself, you will know God. For Brother Guiden, these Gnostic Gospels were meant to supplement the four in the New Testament, not replace them. But Ireneaus argued for their heresy in order to try to unify Christians around the world.

"You'll need it as evidence when you approach the Holy Father with the Trinity Gospels."

Brother Guiden took the file and explained, "Irenaus' primary goal was to attack cults that fell away from orthodox Christianity. He sought to disprove what he saw as incorrect interpretations of scripture. An unfortunate consequence was the tendency to think that all Gnostics were heresy by later scholars of scripture."

Zach nodded.

Brother Mollo led them down another row, locating another set of files. "These are the Gnostic texts found in 1945 in the Nag Hammadi Library," he said. "Here you'll find the Gospel according to Thomas where he suggests, when you come to know who you are on the level of the heart, you come to know God as the source of your being."

"These ideas and teachings don't strike me as that different from the New Testament Gospels," Zach said. "Why were they criticized as being so dangerous?"

"Turn to the forces of history and persecution for your answer," Brother Mollo suggested.

"I suppose if the early Christians were threatened with persecution, they would feel more safe if their beliefs were aligned in an official capacity," Zach said. "That pressure would have made them want to accord their people in all provinces and continents with one unifying thought even as early as Irenaus."

"Yes," Brother Mollo agreed. "We see that clearly in Constantine's vision for the council of Nicea in 325 which developed the Nicene Creed. Constantine needed to unify the people under the Holy Roman Empire, and so he brought together the bishops to draft a statement of orthodox faith; it's where they emphasized the doctrine of the Trinity in response to the teachings of Arius who thought that Jesus was created by God but not wholly divine. This controversy threatened the stability of the empire. The statement of belief affirms the Father as the "one God" and as Jesus Christ as the "Son of God" as begotten of "the essence of the Father" and therefore as "consubstantial with the Father" meaning "of the same substance."

"The teaching of Arius was of their utmost concern to declare a heresy to safeguard the republic, but as a consequence the Gnostics were also pushed out." Brother Guiden added, "Each successive authority continued to uphold official doctrine in order to maintain order, unity, and growth."

"It makes logical sense," Zach said.

"But it denies people the chance to know the full history and expression of their faith," Brother Guiden countered. "It's the same thinking and system that covered up the Royal Bloodline."

"Fear," Brother Mollo said. "It's what causes people to deny the truth. The full expression of mystery."

"We need all of the evidence you can muster," Brother Guiden said.

Brother Mollo led them to the documents on the Nicene Council.

"Can you think of anything else that might help our case?" asked Brother Guiden.

"Well, there is one more thing."

"What's that?"

"Follow me."

Brother Mollo led them through another series of rooms and hallways, finally turning down a hallway of all the portraits of the popes. He stopped in front of one, pushed it aside and typed in a code. At the end of the hall, a false door moved revealing a small dark closet. Brother Mollo motioned for them to follow as he entered the dark room and began to climb a ladder attached to the back wall.

One by one they followed him with Brother Werner taking up the rear. Third in line, Zach was impressed with how spry the portly Brother Mollo was as he scurried up the ladder like it was something he did every day. Brother Guiden, who was fit for his age, struggled to keep up. Behind him, Brother Werner, silent as ever, ascended the slowest. Just as Zach reached the opening of what appeared to be a turret, he saw Brother Guiden slip Brother Mollo the red earthenware tube. "Hide this for me," he whispered. Brother Mollo stealthily hid it in the folds of his robe. In exchange he unlocked a drawer and handed Brother Guiden a sealed envelope. Brother Guiden put the envelope in his robe pocket just before Brother Werner crested the opening of the ladderwell.

CHAPTER 37

2:17 a.m. - The Holy Seer's Apartment

Cara walked out to the balcony, her favorite place to be at the apartment, and scanned the green domes of Vatican city, lit dimly by streetlights. All was quiet. She breathed in the soft night air, knowing this would be the last peaceful moments she would have to herself in a while. The Holy Seer would call her in soon to give her his orders, and then who knew where the night would take her or how long she would have to complete her mission.

One lone car rolled slowly by the street below her. She checked it for malevolent intent, but the small Fiat seemed to contain just a late night worker, making his way home. She glanced at the rooftops out of instinct to make sure the Fiat wasn't a decoy. She heard nothing. Felt nothing in the air but a light cool breeze.

"There you are, my dear," the Holy Seer joined her on the balcony, placing his hands on her shoulders. He whispered an address into her ear and slipped a piece of paper into her pocket. "Find them and bring them to me, alive. Frightened is fine, but I want them unharmed. There is something I must discuss with them before the break of dawn."

"As you wish," she replied.

"The Swiss Guard will arrive soon. They will escort you and be at your command."

"Thank you, sir."

#

2:30 a.m. Vatican Apartments

Cara led the guard to the first doorway, motioning for them to stand back. She put her ear to the door, and then stealthily picked the lock. She nimbly crossed the living area and silently opened the first bedroom door where she found Sophia fast asleep. She tapped her on her shoulder, and when Sofia opened her sleepy eyes, and let out a cry of alarm, Cara quickly muffled her mouth with her left gloved hand and showed her gun with her right. "Don't make a sound. This will go easily if you just do what I say. Get dressed."

Sofia nodded, not knowing for sure if this woman was friend or foe. She dressed quickly, trying to mentally telepathize to Zach that she was in trouble. It seemed to have worked earlier in the car - communicating without speaking, but she didn't know if it could work without being in the same room. The *fleur-de-lis* on her chest throbbed. She hoped that Sam in the bedroom next door was unharmed. Flashbacks of the assassin in the hospital racked her with fear. Was this woman an assassin as well?

Cara escorted Sofia outside to the care of the Swiss Guard and then returned to the other bedroom. She opened the door quietly like before, but Sam, who was sleeping lightly and heard Sofia's earlier cry, was ready for her. Hiding behind the open door, Sam brandished a lamp. She swung at Cara's head, but Cara was too quick for her and intercepted the blow with her arm. Still, the American girl was scrappy, and put up a good fight - kicking with swift strong legs, and dodging Cara's attempts to hold her various times. Cara avoided using blows, to keep her promise to bring them in unharmed, but without force, this mighty scrambler might get away. "I don't want to hurt you," she seethed, as she dodged another kick to the face.

"Don't touch me!" Sam yelled. "Sofia! Are you all right?"

Cara ran to the bed for leverage and back flipped over Sam. Behind her now, Cara got hold of Sam's wrist and pulled it behind her back, finally able to restrain the feisty American.

"I don't want to hurt you," Cara hissed. "I'm just fulfilling orders. Please come peacefully."

"Where's Sofia?" Sam struggled.

"She's fine. Just outside."

"And Zach?"

"You will see Zach again in time."

Sam stomped on Cara's foot in a last attempt to flee. Cara grimaced in pain, but didn't cry out.

"Are you done?" she asked.

"I'll never go with you," Sam said.

With that, Cara pulled a syringe from her belt loop and swiftly plunged it into Sam's neck. Within seconds Sam went limp. Cara hoisted her sleeping frame over her shoulder and brought her to the care of the Swiss Guard.

Sofia shrieked when she saw them.

"Calm down," Cara commanded. "She's just tranquilized. No need to wake the entire building."

Cara directed two of the guards to take the women to the Holy Seer and the rest to follow her. They entered Zach and Brother Guiden's apartment who were still at the Vatican archives. They made themselves at home in the living area, awaiting the return of the brother and his protegee.

#

On the way home from the Vatican Archives, Brother Werner drove with Zach and Brother Guiden in the back. Zach felt the *fleur-de-lis* on his chest begin to ache. He placed the palm of his hand against it, and closed his eyes, concentrating to feel its message.

"What's wrong?" Brother Guiden asked.

"I think Sofia might be in danger."

"We better hurry!" He tapped Brother Werner on the shoulder.

Brother Werner nodded and pressed on the gas.

When they arrived, they stopped by the women's residence first. The door was locked and no matter how hard they pounded, no one answered. As Zach's anxiety rose, he heard footsteps running toward them. He spun around to see an attractive woman with dark hair and green eyes, dressed all in black; behind her stood soldiers dressed in blue doublets and blue berets.

He made to run, but soldiers approached from the other side. They were surrounded. The woman held up her right hand and the soldiers stopped at her command.

"Zach Dorsey?"

"Yes."

"I would like for you and Brother Guiden to come with me, peacefully. We already have your friends. The Holy Seer would like an audience with you."

"The Holy what?" Zach asked.

"Seer. A very important man here in the Vatican. He will explain."

Zach glanced at Brother Guiden who nodded his assent.

"We will go," Zach complied.

As the sky began to lighten with the approach of sunrise, Cara and the Swiss Guard escorted them to their holding cells.

"For your safety, we will have you wait here," Cara said as she typed in a code that opened a sliding door. Zach and Brother Guiden exchanged worried glances.

"It will only be a few minutes."

Warily, they entered the room. The door slid closed and locked behind them.

CHAPTER 38

Sunday, 7:03 a.m. - Vatican Apartments Commissary

Brother Mollo barely slept the night before, so he attended Prime in the chapel at six a.m., asking God for guidance during the prayers. Feeling more serene, he walked to the breakfast commissary. He joined the cafeteria line, accepting scrambled eggs, sausage, and grilled potatoes, smiling and nodding at the cooks and servers as was his usual practice. Walking to his table, he scanned the room of priests, brothers, and other Vatican officials and workers for Brother Guiden and Zach, but didn't see them anywhere. He felt a stab of worry, but quickly pushed it out of his mind. After their late night, they were probably still sleeping.

He found a quiet table and ate slowly, going over the night's events in his mind. He knew that there were people in the church, in its uppermost positions of power, who staunchly opposed revealing the truth about the Royal Bloodline and the Gnostic Gospels. He wasn't sure how dangerous such opposition could be, but if history had taught him anything, it was that when people felt strongly enough about a position, they would defend it with any means necessary.

A cold chill crept up Brother Mollo's spine, and he had the sensation that he was being watched. He looked up from his eggs to see a table of priests in the corner all staring at him as if he were prey. He returned their stare. They averted their eyes, talking as if they had not just been piercing him with their targeted gaze. He glanced around the room again. Everyone else seemed to be eating and chatting in self-contained groups, minding their own business.

He pulled out his phone and texted the number Brother Guiden had given him the night before: "Are you okay?"

He received no response. He ate more quickly.

When he finished his breakfast and still hadn't received an answer, he left the commissary and made his way to the archives to use his secure phone. It was time, he decided to place a call to the pontiff. He felt in his bones something was amiss. Someone needed to tell the Holy Father that the Trinity Gospels had been recovered. If Brother Guiden had gone missing, it was up to him.

Brother Guiden wasn't sure if Pope Aloysius was a member of the Illuminati or not, but Brother Mollo thought it was worth the risk of finding out. Back at the archives, he picked up the phone and dialed the office of the pope.

CHAPTER 39

Sunday, 7:33 a.m. - The Vatican Holding Cells

Sam's eyes fluttered open and she looked around at the cinder block walls. She slowly sat up, getting her bearings, beginning to remember the encounter with Cara. Her own adrenaline fueled actions. She blinked and saw Sofia across the room, staring out a small barred window.

"Sophia?" she called. Sofia turned and came to her side.

"Oh, good, you're awake!" she put her hand to Sam's forehead. "How do you feel?"

"Groggy," she said. "Like I have a hangover."

"It's the tranquilizer wearing off." Sofia said. "Here," she passed her a water bottle. "Drink some water."

Sam took it and drank it thankfully.

"I was hoping last night was just a dream," she said.

"Unfortunately, no," Sofia confirmed.

Sam nodded. "Have they told you anything? What do they want from us?"

"I don't know," Sofia said, but just as she was about to tell Sam what she suspected, they heard voices and then the beeping of the code being punched into the door. The door slid open to reveal Cara and two of her guards.

"Come with me," Cara commanded.

The women followed Cara down a hall of other holding cells to another locked room. Cara punched in the code and they entered the room. Seated at a table were Zach and Brother Guiden.

"Zach!" Sam exclaimed.

"Sam!" Zach jumped up and moved to go to her, but Cara held up her hand, stopping him from reaching her.

"Sit," she commanded. She motioned for the women to sit at the table on the other side from Zach and Brother Guiden.

"Are y'all both okay?" Zach asked across the table.

"Yes," they said and nodded.

"Wait in silence," Cara said.

A little while later the door opened and an older man with white hair, dressed in white robes and wearing a red Cardinal's beanie entered the chamber: The Holy Seer.

Cara motioned for them to stand for his entrance. She introduced him as the Senior Cardinal Lucien Villere, second in command of the Vatican Hierarchy.

Cardinal Villere motioned for them to sit. "Greetings, friends, you are friends are you not?"

The group nodded.

"It appears you are the guests of Brother Mollo, custodian of the archives?"

They nodded again.

The cardinal paced as he walked. "What I don't understand then, if you are friends, why would you steal from us?"

"What?" Asked Zach.

"From the archives, you have stolen documents. Cara's trusted soldiers found them on you this morning."

"We weren't stealing them, Cardinal Villere, sir, we were borrowing them," Brother Guiden began. "Just for our presentation today."

"There is no record of you checking them out. Those documents aren't even on the list of available documents to check out. They are too old and precious. Thus, theft. And theft will not be tolerated. I now pronounce you under arrest by order of Vatican City."

"With all respect sir, you can't do this. We have an audience later today, with the Pope himself."

"That will have to wait until after you stand trial for your transgression," the cardinal said.

CHAPTER 40
Sunday, 8:13 a.m. - Vatican Holding Cells

The Swiss Guard led the deflated group back to their holding cells. Along the way Zach kept a watchful eye on the guards and observed everything about the security system, from the location and angles of the cameras to the codes the guards punched in to unlock the doors. When they stopped at the door of the women's cell, Zach carefully watched the guard as he typed in the code at the door. An overhang protected the keypads from vision, but Zach was fairly certain he could figure out the code by watching the man's hand motions: six numbers up, down, right, up, left, down.

Both Sofia and Sam met Zach's eyes as they were directed back into their cell.

"We'll see you soon," Zach nodded.

"No talking," a guard directed.

After Zach and Brother Guiden were escorted to their cell, the next door down, the two friends began plotting their escape.

"There must be some way out," Brother Guiden paced. "It's of dire importance! Think, Zach."

"I'm thinking, I'm thinking…" Zach walked to the small window that overlooked a small alley.

"We don't have the might to do it, it's got to be by cunning."

"You could fake illness - a heart attack due to the stress. I could try to slip out."

"You may have to use force," Brother Guiden warned.

"I think I could do it for the cause. With your blessing."

"Yes, so many things we hope we do not have to do," Brother Guiden replied, "but they've forced our hand."

"Do you have any other ideas?" asked Zach.

"Short of a Trojan horse, no."

"We've got to try it then," Zach said. "Make sure you pass out in full view of the security camera," he motioned to the camera perched in the corner of the room.

Brother Guiden paced back and forth a few more times and then suddenly grabbed his right arm as if in pain. He pressed his hand to his chest and keeled over to the floor. Zach ran to his side. Then he ran to the door and pounded on its facade. He rang the intercom button and called for help.

Soon, two Swiss Guards entered the cell. One went immediately to Brother Guiden's side, the other stood in the doorway. Zach ran at the guard with all his might, knocking him out against the wall. As the sliding door closed, Zach was just able to wedge his foot into the gap, stopping the door from locking. When the guard at Brother Guiden's side turned to look, Brother Guiden jumped up and squeezed by him. He slipped out the door as Zach fought off this second guard, barely managing to thrust him away long enough to escape the cell. As the guard reached for the opening, the sliding door slid shut, locking both guards inside.

Once free, Brother Guiden and Zach ran down the hall to the women's cell. Zach typed in the perceived code, but it didn't work. He tried another, still no luck.

Brother Guiden glanced at the security camera. "Hurry Zach! They'll be on us in an instant!"

The third try worked, and as the door slid open the surprised women sprang to their feet when they saw Zach standing there instead of a guard. He motioned for them to follow him and soon all three were racing down the hall.

CHAPTER 41

Sunday, 8:25 a.m. - Vatican City

With some luck, the group managed to find an exit, but when they thrust open the door, an alarm sounded. Soon members of the Swiss Guard were pursuing them down the alley. They tried to turn right, but spotted guards exiting the building in that direction, so they turned left instead.

"Let's try to make it to the Passetto Di Borgo," Zach whispered. "It will lead us to the Castle Saint' Angelo."

They sprinted down the cobblestoned street, lined with dumpsters. Zach took the lead, and Sofia who ran regularly for exercise kept close behind him. Sam fell in third and Brother Guiden struggled to keep pace with her. Noting Brother Guiden's fatigue, Sam began trying doors, looking for a place to hide.

Ahead of them, Sofia and Zach turned a corner then entered a stairwell. Sam and Brother Guiden followed them and disappeared out of sight just as the Swiss Guard rounded the corner. The group climbed the stairs to the ancient Passetto Di Borgo, once used as an escape path for popes. In 1494 when Charles VIII invaded Rome, Pope Alexander crossed it to safety. Later Pope Clement VII escaped through its secret passage during the "Sack of Rome" in 1527 when troops of the Holy Roman Emperor, Charles V, fought and killed most of the Swiss Guard troops on the steps of St. Peter's Basilica. The Swiss Guard still kept a key to the secret passage for modern popes. It's upper level pathway was restored for tourists to walk across. The group took this elevated path, hoping to shake the Swiss Guard.

It worked for a moment, but then one member looked up and saw their figures sprinting across the pathway above. The chase began again. Luckily, even Sam and Brother Guiden had enough of a head start to make it to the landscaped gardens of the castle. They each found a hiding place in the dark shadows for a minute or two of rest. Zach observed the statues of the archangel Michael that lined the garrison and recalled the legend that Michael appeared at the top of the Castle sheathing his sword as a sign of the end of the Plague in 590, thus lending the Castle Sant'Angelo his name. Zach's dream of the archangel came back to him with a shiver. With renewed vigor and purpose he vowed to complete his mission.

His heart raced as the footsteps of the Swiss Guard approached and then passed him by. He squinted into the darkness to see if any of his companions would be discovered. The guard spread out to conduct a more thorough search. If they stayed put, Zach thought, they would surely be found. He raised his arm, motioning to the others to follow. One by one, they crouched amongst the manicured bushes and monuments, stealthily making their way to the ancient Ponte Sant'Angelo, built by the emperor Hadrien in 134 AD, over the Tiber River. The pedestrian bridge's travertine marble fascias glinted in the sunlight. Unfortunately, one of the Swiss Guard stood sentinel there.

"I'll distract him," Sofia said, picking up a rock and hurling it in the other direction. The guard shifted his view, looking alertly in the direction of the rock, while Zach sidled up behind him. Sofia threw another rock. The guard tood a few steps to investigate, giving Zach enough time to run up behind him and knock him in the back of his head, stunning him just enough for the others to pass onto the bridge.

The guard's call of pain, however, alerted his troop. Soon the Swiss Guard were all running towards the bridge, and once again in a footrace after Zach and his companions. With renewed adrenaline, Brother Guiden was able to keep pace as the group wove its way through the serpentine streets of old Rome. Pausing when they could to get their breath, Sam kept trying doors to find a place to hide.

They passed the Piazza Novena and its Fontana del Moro, splashing water on their faces before taking off again. They hid for a while behind the columns of the Pantheon, only to be flushed out by the flashlights of the guards. They came upon the Roman Forum and again spread out to avoid capture and find individual hiding places in the shadows of monuments in various levels of decay and restoration.

Brother Guiden motioned to Zach, "I can't go on," he said. "At this pace I'll have a real heart attack, not a fake one."

"I'll draw attention to myself, let them capture me. In the distraction, you and Sofia must make it free. Then make your way back to the Vatican. Tell the pontiff everything."

Zach hesitated, but then acquiesced. He hated to leave Brother Guiden, but knew for the good of their overall purpose, he must. He crouched through the shadows to where Sofia hid.

Meanwhile, Sam had made her way out of the Forum and was checking doors of surrounding buildings. In her persistence, she found the back door to a café someone had forgotten to lock for the night.

Noting where the Swiss Guard searched, she stealthily made her way back in the direction of Brother Guiden.

As she approached, however, Brother Guiden let out a loud yell as if he'd been hurt. The guard drew near and in the distance she saw Zach and Sofia scale the small hill and leave the Forum heading south. She flattened against the wall of the half-intact building where she hid. A guard found Brother Guiden, but yelled to the others to follow Zach and Sofia. "This one won't be a problem!" the guard explained.

When the rest of the Swiss Guard dispersed, Sam took off her sweater and quietly approached the man guarding Brother Guiden. As he lifted his radio to call in the arrest, Sam threw her sweater over his head and yanked him hard backwards. He hit his head on a rock, knocking him out cold. Sam grabbed her sweater, and she and Brother Guiden ran in the direction of the unlocked café. They closed the door behind them just as the stunned guard came to and began searching the area for the runaways.

As Sam and Brother Guiden crouched in the back utility closet, Sofia and Zach ran on through the winding streets of Rome.

CHAPTER 42

8:30 a.m. - The Holy Seer's Apartment

Cardinal Villere picked up the phone and answered, "Yes." He nodded and replied with a terse, "I see." After a pause he barked, "bring those two guards to me. I want to reprimand them personally."

He turned to Cara, perched on the couch.

"I can't trust anyone but you to do a job right and well. The prisoners have escaped and are fleeing through Rome. You must retrieve them."

Cara nodded, "Yes, of course."

"And Cara," he touched her shoulder, "I want them alive. Until those missing Gospels are found and destroyed, they must remain alive."

"Yes, sir." Cara spun on her heel and departed.

CHAPTER 43

9:35 a.m. - Near the Roman Forum

Sam helped Brother Guiden to a chair inside the café and then searched for water. She found two bottles in the refrigerator. She brought them to the table and sat across from Brother Guiden. They both drank from the bottles until they were empty.

"How are you feeling?" asked Sam.

"Better, my dear," Brother Guiden replied. "Thank you."

"I hope Zach and Sofia are alright."

"They are our only hope now," Brother Guiden replied, "unless…"

"Unless what?"

"Unless we can sneak back and find Brother Mollo. I gave him the Trinity Gospels for safekeeping."

"We can try. Let's see if we can find something to eat - get some fuel for energy," Sam said. She got up to look behind the counter, and when she did, she saw one of the Swiss Guard's spotlights shining in the windows down the street. "Get down!" she said.

Brother Guiden slid off the chair and crawled behind the counter with Sam. They sat in still silence as the spotlight swept through the cafe, illuminating the tables and chairs, the sign with specials, and the contents of the fridge. When it passed, she opened the fridge and pulled out a loaf of focaccia. She tore off a hunk and handed it to Brother Guiden. They shared the loaf, waiting with anticipation for the light to come back. When it didn't, they decided to make their move. They left the cafe in direction of the Colosseum, a landmark they could see rising above the lower shops and houses. They knew if they made it there, they could find their way back to Vatican City.

#

Meanwhile, Sofia and Zach managed to evade the Swiss Guard by ducking off the Appian Way and leaving the main piazzas of the city. They decided to hide out in the Catacombs of St. Callixtus for a much needed rest. They slipped behind the gate and descended into the dark, gloomy passageway greeted by the smell of dry decay: dust, minerals, and sulfur. Sofia's *fleur-de-lis* warmed in her chest as she felt the remnants of so many departed souls in one place. Soon they entered a chamber filled with loculi, niches in the walls that held the bones of the deceased.

They passed family tombs adorned with frescoes depicting the sacraments of Baptism and the Eucharist. Another wall depicted the story of the prophet Jonah and the whale. Zach and Sofia walked on, filled with awe at the dedication of these early Christians who honored their persecuted dead with signs and symbols, as the crypts were full of martyrs from the persecution of the emperor Nero and other Roman emperors through 300 A.D.

They turned a corner and entered the crypt of the popes, called "the little Vatican" to locals because of the nine popes interred there.

On three of the tombstones Sofia read the Greek abbreviation MPT for "Martyr." Zach read the names of the popes out loud: Pontianus, Antherus, Fabian, Lucius, and Eutichian. Sofia read the Greek inscription on the tomb in the front wall - Pope Sixtus II who was beheaded by the emperor Valerian.

"So many people have suffered such atrocities for their faith," Sofia said.

Zach came to stand beside her and they both prayed for the souls of the martyred.

"Seems a small thing to ask for - to have the freedom to believe, no matter what your religion," Zach commented.

"Let's see what's in here, I feel drawn to this room."

They entered the crypt of St. Cecilia, patron saint of musicians, also a martyr. A sculpture of the saint by Stefano Maderno in 1599 now lay where her body was first entombed. The statue shows her sleeping peacefully.

"I've read about St. Cecilia," Sofia told Zach. "Her husband and brother were martyred before her. She was a noble woman, and in response she gave away all her possessions to the poor. This action enraged the prefect who ordered her to be burned, yet her body would not burn, so he had her beheaded. According to legend, at the beginning of the 9th century, Pope Paschal I discovered her incorrupt body and moved her relics to Rome to Trastevere, in the basilica named for her."

"Let's sit here and rest for a while," Zach gestured to a bench across from the venerated statue. They sat in silence, observing the other images in the room. An ancient painting of St. Cecilia adorned a wall near the statue. In the fresco, St. Cecilia kneels in prayer. Lower down they viewed another fresco depicting Jesus holding a Gospel. Nearby hung three paintings of martyrs.

They leaned back and rested their weary eyes. Little did they know that the Swiss Guard had radioed the coordinates of their last sighting to Cara, who was now on her way with her fresh troops.

CHAPTER 44

Sunday, 10:03 a.m. - The Holy Seer's Apartment

As the Holy Seer awaited word from Cara about her search, he paced the living room floor, pondering the most recent events. All signs pointed back to the curator of the Vatican Archives, Brother Mollo. He must have helped the fugitives. The Holy Seer decided to make a call to confirm.

He scrolled through his contacts and slowly lifted the phone to his ear.

"Were you with them at the archives?"

Pause.

"Tell me a summary of events."

"I see. No, I know what I need to do." He hung up the phone, then called the guard stationed outside his door.

"Call your superior," he commanded. "Have Brother Mollo arrested."

CHAPTER 45

Sunday, 10:43 a.m. - The Roman Colosseum

Sam peeked out the front door, glancing left and right. When she
didn't see the Swiss Guard, she motioned to Brother Guiden, and they
hastened down the street. They turned into the first alley they saw, and
stayed in the alleys and courtyards as they followed the ruins of the
Colosseum in the skyline above.

The Colosseum's ruins rose before them, ancient and imposing
amongst the modern city streets and buildings. A hovering shadow of
past glory, past battles, and past torture and atrocities. Sam and Brother
Guiden scurried across the green space. They reached its edge and Sam
couldn't help but be amazed at its architectural precision, its arcade
of symmetrical arches and ionic, doric, and corinthian columns still
bearing weight. They rested in a shadow against the wall, then began
to follow the elliptical path around the structure, darting in and out of
shade. As they left the shadow of one column for another, Sam spotted
a blue uniform poke out from a side street across the road and disap-
pear just as quickly.

"Wait!" she stuck her hand out to stop Brother Guiden behind her. They flattened against the wall.

They braved one more sprint, but as they ran, Cara and the Swiss Guards darted out from the side street and pursued them. Sam and Brother Guiden ducked through an arch inside the Colosseum entrance and joined a tour heading to the arena floor and underground chambers that were used to house gladiators and lions alike. They tried to blend in, but Cara and her troops were close behind. They left the group and hid behind an old cell, and then moved through the maze of structures until they found another hiding space.

"Spread out and find them!" Cara commanded.

Sam put her finger to her lips and they crouched lower, trying to slow and quiet their breath as they felt the steps of the guard approach. Sam imagined what the waiting gladiators must have felt like, waiting below the floor of the arena to challenge themselves to the heights of their mental and physical abilities, their hearts longing for the glory of victory. She was just about to dart to a new hiding space when she felt a hand on her shoulder.

She spun out of its grasp, but another guard sprang from behind a wall, blocking her path. He charged her, she ducked his blow and dodged left, only to be yanked from behind. She kicked and fought with her fists, but soon she was surrounded. Meanwhile, Cara had captured Brother Guiden with her martial arts skills, delivering him to two guards for holding. Once the guards had her hands behind her back, Sam looked up to see Cara striding pompously toward her.

"Glad to see you still have your fighting spirit," Cara smirked.

Sam stood unable to move, panting as Cara leaned in closely, invading her personal space.

"I have a soft spot for scrappy Americans, but you will never be a match for the ancient arts of combat," she smiled and backed away.

Sam glanced at Brother Guiden who gave her a disappointed look, but also whispered, "don't give up."

"Now," Cara turned from Sam to Brother Guiden. "Which of you can tell me where your friends have run off to?"

Neither Sam nor Brother Guiden spoke.

CHAPTER 46

Sunday, 10:30 a.m. - St. Callixtus Catacombs

Sofia's eyes fluttered open. She turned to Zach who, sensing her movement, opened his eyes. She brought her hand to her chest, and Zach mirrored her movement.

"Do you feel rested?"

"Physically, yes," she replied, "mentally, I'm not so sure."

Zach nodded. "Take another minute."

Sofia looked around her. She stood up and approached the statue of St. Cecilia.

"I've felt a lot of fear the last few days," Sofia began, "fear for myself, my own safety, and fear for the people of the world."

"Yes, I'm sure it's been quite a shock, quite difficult for you."

"And then we came down here, and we're surrounded by evidence of fear and violent death, for what reason? So one group can stay in power over another?" She turned to face Zach. "What does it matter now, so many years later?"

"It may seem like ancient history, but Sofia, it's not," he took a step towards her. "These martyrs, these popes who tried to make good decisions for the early church, they're significant. Their lives and choices still matter even if they lost the worldly fight to disbelief or corruption." He spread his hands to the tombstones, "They may represent battles lost, but they also represent the battle that goes on, the one we need to continue to fight."

Sofia dropped her eyes.

"We're a part of this long arc of history as people who choose to fight the good fight, but also by our bloodline, something we didn't choose. You can think of it as a terrible burden that you can't accept, or you can think of it as an amazing opportunity, a chance to live to your fullest, to accept the challenge and responsibility. I'm not saying it's easy. Trust me, I've only lived a few more hours with this knowledge than you, but if you can think of it as a gift, then we can go together, stronger together," he touched the *fleur-de-lis* beneath his shirt. "We'll make it, I know we will."

Sofia touched her *fleur-de-lis* in response. Her gesture encouraged him.

"We need to go back, figure out how to get back into Vatican City. Find Brother Mollo and present those missing Gospels to the pope. It's the only way."

"Zach, I can't imagine going back above ground right now." She turned from him, "I'm afraid. I feel safe here amongst the saints and martyrs."

"Sofia, do you know what is more powerful than fear?"

She turned back. He took her hands in his.

"Hope." He said. "Hope is more powerful than fear." He squeezed her hands and she squeezed back.

"Yes," she said after a moment. "I do believe that."

Zach smiled. "In our darkest hour, if we can tap into hope, we can find strength."

Sofia took a deep breath. "It hasn't all been fear and darkness, you know. I've also felt purpose. A deeper sense of purpose and direction than ever before."

Zach nodded.

"Being here," she gestured to the tombs and loculi, "makes it even more significant. I see it from your perspective now. All of these people before us fought for the right to believe, lived out their faith, and struggled to live righteous lives. We can't let them down."

"Are you ready?" Zach asked.

"Yes, but how are we going to get back undetected?"

"We'll have to figure out a disguise. I've been thinking. I think we can find what we need on the way back."

"Let's go!" she said with renewed conviction. They wandered the dark passageways back to the entrance, climbing the stairs into the light.

CHAPTER 47

Sunday, 11:03 a.m. - The Roman Colosseum

Zach and Sofia emerged from the dark entrance of the St. Callixtus Catacombs and blinked into the bright sunlight. After a few minutes they hailed a taxi. On the ride, they looked up costume stores and found one located near the ancient Roman Colosseum. Zach directed the driver to make a stop there before delivering them back to Vatican City.

As they pulled up in front of the store, Sofia grabbed Zach's arm. "Zach, look!" She pointed out her side window. Zach leaned over and they both watched as Cara and a group of Swiss Guard soldiers emerged from the arches of the Colosseum. Handcuffed in their custody were Sam and Brother Guiden. They watched as the soldiers escorted their friends to a Swiss Guard van, placing them inside and driving away.

"Zach! We have to do something!" Sofia exclaimed.

"I know," Zach said. He pointed to the costume shop. "Let's look in here and see if we can find something to help us sneak back into the Vatican holding cells."

CHAPTER 48

Sunday, 11:02 a.m. - Costume Shop

Sofia and Zach rummaged through the costume shop in search of anything to help them gain entrance to the secure area in the Vatican that housed the holding cells. Sofia searched through the racks and held up various suggestions: a delivery person for Zach or a cleaning lady for her? Zach shook his head. She held up a white nurse's costume. He shrugged.

"I could try convincing them someone needed medical assistance? I'm good with medical jargon."

"Maybe…"

Sofia sifted through a few more outfits on the rack. "Oh wait. What about this?" She held out a black long-sleeved dress and matching habit with white trim. Zach studied it.

"A nun's outfit? Now that, I think, might work."

Sofia grinned.

"You'll have to talk your way in - say you have official business or something. Then come around to the alley door we used and let me in. Do you think you can do it?"

Sofia nodded. "There was that older gentleman in the room next to ours who looked so sad. I will say I've been called to minister to him."

"Oh, yes, I noted his name - Father Basil."

"What? How did you get his name?"

"I was watching the guards closely at first to learn anything I could about security. It's how I figured out the code to yours and Sam's room. His name was on a list one of the guard's was holding."

"One of your gifts?" Sofia teased.

"Yes, the photographic memory - it's mostly a gift, sometimes a curse."

"Depends on the images, right?"

Zach nodded. "Once you let me in, we may have to use force to get a guard to open a door. I'm sure they've scrambled the security codes after our breach. It won't be the same code."

"Oh," Sofia placed her hand to her chest. "I don't think I could..."

"I'll take care of anything physical if needed. Just try to stay alert. I don't want you to get hurt."

Sofia agreed. They paid for the nun's outfit and jumped into their waiting taxi.

CHAPTER 49

Sunday, 11:05 a.m. - Vatican Holding Cells

At the sound of the door sliding open, Brother Mollo looked up to see the guards ushering in Sam and Brother Guiden. He rose to greet the Brother and meet his young friend. Brother Guiden embraced Brother Mollo.

"I didn't know what happened to you," Brother Mollo said, pulling back but still holding onto Brother Guiden's shoulders. "I am happy to see you are well, but unhappy to see you in this cell with me."

"And I am surprised to see you here. What happened?"

Brother Mollo described his arrest, and in turn, Brother Guiden introduced Sam and summarized their recent adventures and arrest in the Colosseum.

"Do you think they are listening or can we speak frankly?" Brother Guiden glanced at the security camera in the corner.

Brother Mollo shrugged, "I wouldn't risk it."

Just then the door opened and a guard announced they would be transported for questioning. The three exchanged quizzical glances and they dutifully followed the guards down the hall to the questioning room.

CHAPTER 50

Sunday, 11:20 a.m. - Vatican Holding Cells

Dressed in the nun's dress, habit, and sensible black shoes, Sofia took a deep breath and strode purposefully across the courtyard to the door of the Vatican Holding Cells. She rang the doorbell quickly before she lost her nerve. As she waited for admittance, she remembered the nuns who taught her in Catholic school, modeling her character's personality after their self-assured confidence, their exacting command of language and authoritative delivery of instructions.

When the door opened, she thrust her chin up. A young novitiate stood in the doorway, "May I help you?" he asked.

"Yes, you may," Sofia began, studying his round baby-face, his clear blue eyes. "I am Sister Mary Jacinta, Ph.D. in psychology, here to minister to Father Basil in room 402. He is in need of spiritual counseling, and I am an expert in the field." She took a few steps forward as she talked, hoping her body language would convince the young priest of her authenticity.

"Wait, ma'am," he said. "I don't have you down on the list of official visitors."

"That's because I was just called by the Cardinal. It's a dire matter, a mental health emergency you see. No time to put it on the list, but I assure you this man needs me." She brushed past him.

"Wait!" The young priest said as he shut the door and started after her.

"Just point me in the direction of his room, and I'll do all of the rest." Imagining the nun who taught her third grade, she marched smartly down the hall.

"I can't let you go back there!"

She spun on her heel. "And why not? Have they not given you the power to ascertain important decisions? Are you just simply a follower? Use your own brain, lad. What is more important - a man who is in deep spiritual pain, so much so that he's in psychological danger? Or for you to simply follow procedure?"

The young novitiate paused, "Well, when you put it that way…" He looked around as if hoping someone else with more authority would appear to make the decision.

"I'll be sure to write up my report in a timely fashion and mention how thoughtful and accommodating you have been," Sofia said, smiling sweetly.

The young man blushed. "Oh, thank you ma'am," he answered.

"Now, I think I know the way, so you may resume your post."

The young man nodded, and Sofia performed an about face and marched swiftly down the hall to the holding rooms.

She passed Father Basil in room 402 and kept going, remembering the path they ran when they escaped. It was quiet in the hall. As her steps clicked on the tile, she glanced through the small door windows, trying to catch a glimpse of her friends, but besides Father Basil, she only saw a few other prisoners - people she didn't recognize. Little did she know that just minutes before her friends had been escorted down this same hall to be questioned by the Holy Seer. She turned the corner and quickened her step. One more turn and she would be at the alley door.

She made the turn and to her surprise came face to face with a Swiss guard, standing in front of the back door. There hadn't been a guard there before, so they must have decided to station one after their previous escape. The guard stared at her. She took a step back. "Oh my, I must have made a wrong turn," she said.

He nodded, "Yes ma'am," he said. "This is the alley door."

"Oh, I see. Could you be so kind as to direct me back to the main entrance?"

As the guard began giving her directions, Sofia dropped her pocket book. The chivalrous guard bent to retrieve it. When he did so, he collided with her swift uppercut, knocking him out.

"Well, would you look at that!" Sofia said, shaking her fist. She quickly opened the door. Zach, who had been hiding behind a dumpster, ran up the stairs and through the door. When he saw the guard splayed out on the tile, he gave Sofia a surprised look. "And I thought you were the pacifist!"

Sofia shrugged. "I'm just wondering why the alarm didn't sound!"

"I'm guessing they're still in the process of refiguring the door codes - maybe they had to turn off the power to the alarm system. That's good news for us. It might be easier to spring Sam and Brother Guiden!"

Zach started jogging down the hall.

"Wait, Zach, I didn't see them in any of the rooms when I passed."

"Maybe they are holding them somewhere else?"

"Or interrogating them?" Sofia asked.

"Do you remember where they took us for questioning?"

She nodded. "I think it's this way." She pointed to a stairwell. "I remember they took us

To the tenth floor."

Sofia and Zach climbed the stairs quickly. When they reached the tenth floor, Zach put his ear to the door, then opened it slowly and peered left and right down the hall. He motioned to Sofia, and she followed him quietly down the hall. Zach peered around the corner, then flattened himself against the wall.

"They're right there!" he whispered, thumbing to the connected hall.

Sofia nodded. Her eyes widened as she heard the heavy steps of the guards approaching.

In a moment, two guards rounded the corner escorting Sam, Brother Guiden, and Brother Mollo. Without time to plan, Zach stuck out his foot and tripped one of the guards. He fought the other guard while Sofia yelled, "follow me!" to the prisoners. She took off in the direction of the stairwell. Just as she reached the door, Cara and a group of guards entered the hallway from the other direction and ran their way.

Sofia flung open the door to the stairwell, and began taking stairs two at a time. Sam ran close behind her, then the two Brothers, but the guards were quickly upon them. They swiftly secured the two Brothers, and grabbed Sam just as she was about to reach the ground floor.

"Sam!" Sofia turned to help her friend.

"Don't worry about me! Go and get some help!" Sam yelled.

Sofia nodded, spun around, and fled through the exit.

At the same time, Cara and the remaining guards quickly surrounded Zach on the tenth floor. He fought valiantly, but so outnumbered, was quickly apprehended.

CHAPTER 51

Sunday, 11:40 a.m. - Vatican Holding Cells

Once she had secured Zach and the other three prisoners in holding cells, Cara checked in with Cardinal Villere.

"Excellent!" he texted back. "Now I need you to coerce them to give us the missing Gospels."

"Exactly how?" she asked.

"If they won't tell you, then the one with Royal Blood should suffer as Christ did. It's only fitting."

"Which one has Royal Blood?"

"Zach."

"I'll see that it's done," was Cara's reply.

#

The door to the holding cell slid open and a guard called for Zach to follow him. The friends all looked up in trepidation. A few minutes later, the security camera began to play footage of Zach in another

230

cell being asked a series of questions about the missing Gospels. Zach explained what the Gospels were, but when asked where they were, he refused to tell.

Brother Guiden, Sam, and Brother Mollo all look on with fear in their eyes and hearts. After a few minutes, Cara entered the screen and talked directly to the group.

"Since no one will tell us where these texts are hidden, we will begin coercion." She looked directly into the camera. "You have the power to stop it at any time. Simply push the intercom button in your room and tell us you are ready to give us the Gospels."

"Oh, my Goodness," Sam said, her hand flying to her mouth. "They're about to hurt Zach!"

Brother Guiden placed a hand on her shoulder to comfort her.

On the screen, a guard ordered Zach to turn around and press his palms against the wall. He pulled out a whip and with a flick of his wrist sent the whip stinging across Zach's back. Zach flinched but didn't cry out.

"No!" Sam screamed. "Brother Guiden, we have to do something!"

"Wait, my child. Zach is strong."

"No! This is horrible!" she darted toward the intercom. Brother Guiden tried to hold her back, but she was too quick and nimble for him.

She pressed the button and spoke into the receiver, "Stop this! Stop it right now!"

On the screen Cara held up her hand, signaling the guard to stop. Zach leaned against the wall in pain, catching his breath.

Cara's voice filtered through the intercom. "Are you ready to tell us where the Gospels are?"

"Yes," Sam said.

After a pause, Cara replied, "We're waiting. Where are they?"

"I would tell you if...if I knew." She looked to the Brothers. "Where are they?" she asked.

The Brothers hesitated, exchanging a glance.

"Do you want me to tell them?" Brother Mollo asked.

Before Brother Guiden could reply, Zach looked over his shoulder and spoke into the screen. "Don't do it, Brother Guiden. I'm okay. Sam, it's important that we don't tell them."

"I can't let them do this to you!" Sam replied.

Zach turned his sweating face towards the camera in his room. "I know, and I so appreciate how much you care for me, but this is bigger than us or me. Trust me."

"Zach!" she implored.

"Let it happen," Zach said. "I have faith."

"Last chance," Cara spoke. "Where are the Gospels?"

When no one answered she signaled for the guard to begin again. Sam crumpled to the floor, her face in her hands.

CHAPTER 52

Sunday, 11:46 a.m. - St. Peter's Square

After running down the alley and out into the street, Sofia ditched the habit, and crouched in a sheltered doorway to get her breath. She didn't know if they were looking for her or what had happened to Zach. She assumed that he was also captured just as Sam and the two Brothers.

She pondered trying to sneak back in, but how could she? And even if she did find a way in, how could she alone free her friends? No, she had to think of another way, one that didn't rely on might or luck.

Pretty soon, people started to pass her, moving in the direction of St. Peter's square. At first she thought they were just tourists, visiting the area, but then she remembered: the pope held an audience with his people every Sunday at noon. Sofia contemplated her chances, then decided she had to try to speak to the pope. She joined the crowd of people walking towards St. Peter's Square.

CHAPTER 53

Sunday, 11:54 - The Vatican Holding Cells

Cara held up her hand and the guard stopped his flogging of Zach. Zach almost collapsed, but pressed himself up with his hands against the wall. Cara walked to him and spoke into his ear, Zach shook his head no.

"He still refuses to tell us," Cara said. "Wait for my order."

She sent a text and then left the room. She turned down the hall and entered another room a few doors down. Inside this room, the Holy Seer rose to greet her. She gave him a report on the prisoners and they began to discuss their next steps.

CHAPTER 54

Sunday, Noon - St. Peter's Square

Sofia followed an older couple in front of her as they approached St. Peter's Square. Once in the square, the crowd fanned out, most people pressing to get as close as possible to where the pope would speak. At first Sofia followed along, but soon she started scouting out a place where she could get closer to the pontiff when he rode by in his popemobile. She saw that people were starting to line the route where he would pass. She quickly secured a spot on the curb, as close as the guards would let her stand.

As she stood in the crowd, she began to feel hot all over. A sensation of pain flicked along her back and legs. The *fleur-de-lis* pulsed in her chest. When she raised her hand to her mark and closed her eyes, she knew in her heart that the pain she was feeling was being inflicted ten-fold on Zach. She was only feeling a shadow of the sensation. She took a deep breath and prayed deeply for Zach, for God to send him the strength he needed to withstand his trial. After feeling some relief from the sensation, she opened her eyes. The popemobile was heading directly toward her. She felt a deep sense of purpose and peace. She knew what she had to do.

When the popemobile arrived, Sofia took a step towards it. She raised her hand and projected the throbbing of the *fleur-de-lis* into the feeling in her eyes. She caught the pontiff's open gaze and held it.

"I must speak with you," she implored.

The pope turned and waved at someone else as the driver continued on, but soon he looked back at Sofia. Sofia continued trying to communicate her urgent request to him.

The pope looked away and then met her gaze a third time. He brought his hand to his chest and leaned forward and spoke to his driver and guards. The driver stopped and the procession came to a halt. A guard approached Sofia, "Pope Aloysius would like you to join him," he said. He briefly searched her and escorted her into the popemobile.

Sofia bent to kiss his ring, then sat beside the pontiff in the small vehicle enclosed by bullet-proof glass. The pope smiled at her, then continued waving to his people. Once at the podium, Sofia was escorted inside the building to wait until the pope had finished his speech.

CHAPTER 55

Sunday, 12:17 - The Vatican Holding Cells/ Vatican Necropolis Dungeon

Zach stood facing the wall. His hands, placed against the rough surface, helped him to stand. He let his weary head fall, pressing his forehead against the cold cinder block. He concentrated on his breath to take his mind off the searing pain, an electric sizzling feeling, that ran down his back and legs. *Breathe in, hold it, breathe out,* he thought, *in....out....in....out.*

The door opened and Cara strode in. She looked Zach over, then approached.

"We will ask you once more," Cara warned, "Where are the hidden Gospels?"

Zach lifted his head and turned to meet her gaze. "I will not tell you," he said.

"Oh, you won't? That's your final answer?"

He nodded.

"We'll see about that," she spun on her heel and motioned to the guards.

Two guards grabbed Zach by the arms and led him behind Cara. They marched down the hall and took the elevator to the lowest floor. They took a few more halls and turns, eventually entering a stairwell. Before them was the exit door, but Cara turned to the left to what appeared to be a wall. She reached up behind the illuminated exit sign and felt for a switch. She flipped the switch and then pressed on the wall which slid open revealing more stairs leading downward. "Follow me," she said to the guards on either side of Zach.

Down they went into darkness. A small glow from a generator light on a landing below guided their way. Zach began to notice condensation on the walls, and then steam rising up from below, it was as if they were walking down into the pits of hell.

Once at the bottom of the stairwell, they entered a catacomb tunnel with rows of bones and skeletons on either side. They marched forward taking twists and turns deeper into the ancient burial ground, but this time instead of feeling inspired by the Christian martyrs who had given their lives for their faith, Zach felt a simmering ominous dread. They walked on, and Zach felt they must be beneath St. Peter's Basilica, and were in fact very close to St. Peter's tomb.

Cara stopped in front of an iron wrought gate with spikes lining its top. She pulled an ancient set of keys from her pocket and unlocked the gate. They traveled through a tunnel, stopping at another gate, and then a third gate. At the third gate, Zach lifted his eyes to see the spikes lining the top were actually in the shape of the center piston of iron-wrought fleurs-de-lis, like he had seen innumerable times lining the streets and houses of New Orleans. He blinked, not sure he trusted his tired eyes. Cara fished for the right key and turned the ancient bolt. The gate swung open with a loud and rusty creak.

When Zach stepped into the room, he realized it was an ancient dungeon. Chains were bolted into the stone walls, at various intervals; steam rose in eerie patterns from the crevices. He suddenly felt hot.

Cara nodded at the team of guards who stripped Zach of his shirt and began fitting chains to his wrists and ankles. Once done they hoisted him so that he was suspended, just above the ground, face down, the chains pulling him in four different directions. He struggled, but that only made it harder to breathe.

The guards laughed at his attempts to free himself. "Look at the Royal Blood," they mocked. "Look how mighty he is now!"

Zach breathed in deeply, tried to relax into the position and make himself as comfortable as possible, but his body tensed, waiting for what pain and agony would be demanded of it. The creak of the wrought iron fence told him more people had entered the chamber.

"Oh, my God!" he heard Sam's voice and turned his head in the direction.

More Swiss guards escorted Sam, Brother Guiden, and Brother Mollo into the dungeon. At Cara's command, they began securing them with chains around the room; each with a good view of Zach.

A guard brought forth four whips and handed one to each of the guards who had chained Zach. Each took a whip and returned to his position, so that at each of Zach's hands and feet stood a guard with a whip. Cara nodded and they each took turns cracking the whip across the air and flogging Zach's back. Like the flagrums used to flog Jesus, the whips had three thongs, each ending with two lead balls. The balls added weight to the whipping, but also tore the flesh.

Zach, unable to help himself, began to cry out in agony. Sam closed her eyes, she couldn't stand to watch, but there was no way for her to close her ears and be rid of the horrible sounds of the cracking whips, their searing contact with flesh. Her lips moved in prayer as she tried not to hear or invision the torture.

Cara raised her hand and the guards stilled their whips. She approached Zach, "Are you ready to tell us where the hidden Gospels are?"

"No," Zach said between gasps of breath.

Cara rolled her eyes. "Perhaps you'd like to heal yourself, then? Since you're of *Royal Blood*?" She enunciated each syllable of Royal Blood in an exaggerated haughty tone.

"No ma'am," Zach replied. Red streams of blood flowed down his back and began pooling on the ground.

Cara spun on her heel and eyed the guards, making them her accomplices. "The inheritor of *Royal Blood* is supposed to possess certain abilities...gifts...isn't that right?"

The guards nodded. "So the legend says," one replied.

"And out of these abilities, isn't healing one of them? Aren't members of this family line supposed to be able to heal the sick? The wounded? The mentally downtrodden?"

"Yes," the guards all replied, nodding at each other. "We've all heard that tale."

"Then why don't you heal yourself?" Cara turned her attention back to Zach. "If you're so special, so capable, it seems like an easy and small task."

"Yes, why don't you?" one guard said.

"Yes, go on, show us your powers," another said, snapping his whip so that it hit the ground near Zach, but not on him. Zach flinched.

"Heal yourself!" The chorus of guards chimed in with mocking tones.

"Make yourself feel better."

"Heal yourself, oh royal one!"

"If you're so special, show us!"

"Show us! Heal yourself! Show us!"

The guards all picked up the chant, taunting Zach, asking him to heal himself, to prove his membership in the Royal Blood lineage. They leaned near his face, chanting; they circled around him, threatening more violence. They cracked their whips near his head and ears.

"If only we had a crown of thorns for his precious head!" One said.

"Are you thirsty?" another asked. When Zach nodded, the man pulled out a flask of wine and dipped it in a sponge holding it up to Zach's mouth. "Drink this!" he laughed.

Sam opened her eyes, "Brother Guiden," she called across the way to where Brother Guidend was chained. "Can you please stop them?"

Brother Guiden shook his head in sorrow.

"Stop!" Cara commanded. "That symbol on his chest might hold the source of his power. See if it's glowing or something."

One guard dropped to his knees and looked up at Zach's chest. He shook his head. "I think it's just a regular old tattoo. Evidence of some night of Royal Blood debauchery!" He laughed.

Cara approached Zach. "So interesting, this symbol," she reached down beneath Zach's chest and traced her finger across its pattern. To think it represents so much over time, and now seems to have even taken on a new life in your home city after such a devastating hurricane and loss of life. Is this the source of your power? Why doesn't it shine with heavenly light?"

The image throbbed in Zach's chest, but he didn't flinch. He refused to give Cara any satisfaction for her taunt.

"If I touch it will I get powers, too? Is this how you heal others?" She placed her palm across the symbol.

"Maybe he can only heal others but not himself!" A guard mocked.

"Yes, that's probably it. These Christian weaklings... always going on and on about helping others. If their kind Jesus couldn't help himself, why would we expect his progeny to do so?"

Zach closed his eyes. He fought against the impulse of the *fleur-de-lis*, as he could feel its power beating in his chest. He could feel it wanting to help him, to soothe his wounds and restore his energy, to calm his mind. *Breathe*, he told himself. *Breath in...and out...*

Brother Guiden spoke, "Don't do it, Zach!"

Zach tried to raise his head to meet the eyes of his old friend through the steam, but he didn't have the strength. "Hope," Zach said in a weak voice. "Hope is stronger than fear."

"That's right, dear boy!" Brother Guiden encouraged.

"Silence!" Cara commanded. "You may only talk if it is to tell us where the Gospels are."

Zach hung his head. It was getting harder and harder for him to think clearly. He was exhausted, physically, emotionally, spiritually.... and as he closed his eyes, he saw a warm glow that widened into a vision. Soon, he saw a figure walking toward him through the glow. He recognized the cloak, sword, and wings of the Archangel Michael.

"Peace, be with you," the Archangel said.

"And also with you," Zach replied, he lifted his head to meet Michael's eyes.

"I am sorry that you are suffering," Michael said. "I can release you from your human pain if you so desire."

Zach looked into the Archangel's kind blue eyes. He wanted nothing more than to be set free. He took a deep breath. "Let me think for a minute." He shut his eyes and thought of Sam and Brother Guiden watching him; he thought of Brother Mollo and what might happen to him; he thought of Sofia and their previous conversation. He wondered if she was safe. He thought of the generations of people fighting to know the truth and to do the right thing before him, and he felt a reservoir of strength begin to well up within him.

"Thank you, Michael," Zach said. "I appreciate your offer of mercy, but I must decline. I must go on."

"Then I will pray for your strength and safe passage." The Archangel touched him on the shoulder, bowed, and vanished into the steam.

Zach opened his eyes. With renewed courage he said, "I will not heal myself. I will not tell you where the Gospels are."

"As you wish!" Cara exclaimed. She motioned for the guards to turn him around and resume their flogging.

CHAPTER 56

Sunday, 1:07 p.m. - Vatican Necropolis Dungeon

Cara held up her hand and the guards stopped their whips. She walked to Zach's side and examined his still and quiet face. She reached under and felt his chest.

"He's passed out," she told the guards. "Leave him and follow me."

The guards all followed Cara, leaving two to stand guard at the wrought iron fence adorned with fleur-de-lis spikes.

"Oh, Zach," Sam broke into tears. She pulled futilely against her chains, rattling them weakly.

The steam rose up around the friends, chained to their respective walls, so that they could barely see each other. Father Guiden finished a prayer of blessing over Zach, raised his head, and began to sing. His rich and layered voice rose permeated the steam with a warm timbre that moved smoothly from note to note. Sam soon recognized the song as "Danny Boy." She had no idea that it was a song Brother Guiden sang to Zach whenever he was sick or in need of comfort as a boy. She prayed quietly that it would soothe him now. She looked from Brother Guiden to Brother Mollo, and, through the gaps in the steam, they exchanged awed glances at the poignant beauty of Father Guiden's rendition of the old Irish classic. For the first time all day, Sam felt her own chest rise with hope. "Choose hope, Sam," she told herself. "Hope is stronger than fear." She repeated the mantra over and over as she listened to Father Guiden sing.

CHAPTER 57

Sunday, 1:30 p.m. - The Vatican Holding Cells

Cara joined Cardinal Villere in the conference room. She recounted her failure to get Zach to confess.

"It's alright, I saw it all," Cardinal Villere motioned to the camera whose screen revealed the scene of Zach suspended in the dungeon.

"What do we do now?"

"Let's see what other ammunition we have...he won't save himself, but his altruism might make a different choice for others."

"Do you have his phone?"

Cara pulled Zach's phone from her pocket and handed it to his outstretched palm. The Holy Seer scrolled through the contacts and decided to call the last number in Zach's recently missed calls.

After two rings an exuberant voice answered, "Zach! Thank God!"

"Hello, dear," the Holy Seer replied with his sinister calm.

"Zach?" Sofia questioned, then said, "Oh, no, who is this?"

"Cardinal Villere."

"Where's Zach?"

"He's here with me. Well, not in the same room right now, but in the same building."

"Is he alright? What's going on?"

"He'll recover," Cardinal Villere said. "I think."

"Why? What have you done to him?"

"Let's just say we had to apply a little pressure."

Sofia gasped.

"And now, we have to apply a little more."

"He must be unharmed," the anxiety in Sofia's voice rose. "You have no idea how important he is."

"Oh, I have a quite clear idea, my dear," the Holy Seer replied. "I am also suspecting the same idea as you."

"I don't know what you're talking about."

"If Zach is so important to you, I'm sure you wouldn't mind being of some assistance to me, now would you?"

Sofia paused before she answered, "What do you want?"

"I would like for you to join us here, at the Vatican. All of your friends are here but you," he taunted. "You're missing all of the fun."

"No, thank you."

"But you see, my dear, I'm afraid it isn't an invitation," his tone changed from friendly to authoritarian, "but a command."

"I said, no." Sofia asserted.

"When was the last time you saw Zach?" The Holy Seer tried a different tactic.

"This morning."

"Well, I hope you took a good long look, as that will be the last time you see him alive, unless…."

"Unless I turn myself in?"

"You are such a smart young lady," the Holy Seer returned to his faux friendly, slightly mocking tone.

Sofia paused and the Holy Seer waited. "Where should I meet you?"

The Holy Seer smiled a knowing smile at Cara. He instructed Sofia to turn herself in to Father Rose in the Vatican Gardens.

CHAPTER 58

Sunday, 1:45 p.m. - Vatican Gardens

Sofia hung up the phone and pondered what to do. Just before the Cardinal called, she had left her audience with the pope and was crossing St. Peter's Square. The pontiff had listened to her story and promised to hold a meeting with Cardinal Villere and to check on her friends, but first he had a scheduled meeting with some "heads of state" that he couldn't miss. She'd been escorted back outside to St. Peter's square. If only Cardinal Villere had called while she was in the same room with the pope! That would have given the pontiff even more evidence.

Now she contemplated going back and begging the guards to grant her entrance again. But if the pope was in an important meeting, she would have to wait her turn to hope to see him again. She felt very lucky to have gotten her first audience; it would be pressing her luck to expect a second. She decided to return to the holding cells and see how she could help Zach and the others. She had felt so many phantom pains on her back and legs, that she knew Zach had been hurt. She wasn't sure the Holy Seer's threat was real, but she also didn't want to risk it. She already felt the blood of the people in the hospital on her hands as well as her own beloved dog. She had no desire to risk the lives of Zach, Sam, Brother Guiden, and Brother Mollo. Plus, she felt confident the pope would intervene on their behalf soon. After she surrendered, she would not be in captivity long.

Sofia recalculated how to get to the gardens. As she walked, she mentally prepared herself for the difficulty that lay ahead. She entered the gardens and found a priest watering a grove of trees. He introduced himself as Father Rose and asked her to follow him. As she walked with him through the gardens, she breathed in the fresh scents of roses, rosemary, and hyacinths, enjoying her last moments of nature before being locked back behind the walls.

Father Rose led her back to the holding cells, but instead of riding the elevator up to the tenth floor, he guided her to a secret passageway at the bottom of the stairwell. Reaching behind the illuminated exit sign, he opened a hidden door in an adjacent wall. He led her down the dark stairwell to the catacombs. They followed the same journey taken earlier by Zach. When he unlocked the third iron wrought gate, Sofia also noticed the fleur-de-lis spikes adoring the top. He escorted her into the steaming dungeon. When she saw Zach suspended in his chains, she cried out.

Brother Guiden, Sam, and Brother Mollo all looked up at her with wide, sad eyes. Disappointment filled their faces as they had been holding out hope that Sofia would find a way to free them.

"Sofia!" Sam broke the stunned silence. "Are you alright? Did they hurt you?"

"No, I'm fine," she called back, but her eyes were riveted on Zach, sizing up his injuries, his closed eyes, his slow and shallow breaths.

Father Rose led her to a wall near where Zach hung; he took her wrist and fastened it with a chain that hung from the stone wall. She grimaced. "Is this absolutely necessary, dear father?" she asked sweetly. Could you leave my feet free at least?"

"I have to follow orders."

"One hand?"

He shook his head no and secured her other hand, then her feet tightly with shackles. "What will become of us?" she asked.

"You'll hear from Cardinal Villere soon," Father Rose replied. He took his leave, nodding to the guards as the fence.

Once he was gone, Sofia whispered, "If I can reach him, I can help him." Sam, Brother Guiden, and Brother Mollo all nodded and encouraged her as she reached first with one hand and then the next, but she couldn't reach Zach's suspended body. She turned her own body and stepped sideways toward Zach's extended leg. Leaning over on her tiptoes, she extended her arm until she could just barely reach Zach's foot.

"Yes!" Sam cheered.

Sofia dropped her hand and stood in prayer. She pressed her hands together and asked for the gift of healing to manifest one more time. Then she leaned over onto her tiptoes, letting the chains support her weight. With her feet almost leaving the ground, she could just barely touch the tip of Zach's toe, but it was enough. She felt the warmth of the healing power imbue Zach's skin.

#

The Holy Seer and Cara watched the screen as Sofia placed her fingertip on Zach's injured body. They observed her words of comfort and prayer and how the others looked on in respectful reverence.

"Perhaps we were wrong," said Cardinal Villere, "it seems she is the one with healing powers. Maybe he doesn't have the ability at all."

"Perhaps she's the one we need," Cara agreed.

A knock on the door interrupted them. Cara opened it with caution to find Brother Werner there. She escorted him to the Holy Seer.

"Ahh, Brother Werner," Cardinal Villere said, reaching out his hands. Brother Werner bowed slightly and took the Cardinal's hands in his. "So wonderful to see you again and to welcome you back after your long journey undercover."

"Thank you, sir," Brother Werner replied.

"Excellent job. You provided us with the most exceptional intelligence. Without you, we never would have apprehended Zach Dorsey."

"And now you have Sofia, I see," he nodded at the screen.

"Yes, what can you tell us about her?"

Brother Werner began to fill them in. He confirmed that Sofia, too, was of the Royal Blood lineage.

CHAPTER 59

Sunday, 2:33 p.m. - The Vatican Necropolis Dungeon

The iron wrought gate opened with a foreboding creak, and Brother Guiden, Sam, Brother Mollow, and Sofia all looked up from their respective chains as a group of Swiss guards entered the room. Zach, now awake, tensed in his suspended chains as he listened to the guards' footsteps and their announcement: "The Holy Seer would like to speak with you."

To save his energy, Zach kept his face down, but he wiggled his fingers and toes to make sure the blood was circulating everywhere. Sofia's healing powers had sealed and scabbed his wounds and relieved much of the pain, but he still felt the exhaustion and humiliation of four people recently scourging him.

Behind the guards' uniform footsteps, he made out The Holy Seer's heavy tread and Cara's ninja light steps as they entered the dungeon. Surrounded by steam, they appeared to be spectral beings, more menacing than usual. Cara's dark eyes flicked over Zach, assessing his condition. Her sharp gaze roved over the other prisoners, catching a particular venomous stare from Sam. She smiled back with baleful eyes.

The Holy Seer circled Zach peering at his half-healed wounds. "Cara and I have been discussing the best way to reason with you," he proclaimed as he walked. "We now recognize your importance and the significant influence you might have on others."

Cardinal Villere stopped at his prisoner's head, and Zach raised his weary eyes to meet the cardinal's, wondering what this new temptation would be.

"We have decided to grant freedom to two of you," he put his hand on Zach's bare shoulder and Zach flinched, rattling his chains.

"Brother Guiden," Cara announced, "and Samantha." She turned her wry smile on Sam.

Sam gasped in surprise.

"With one condition," the Holy Seer continued, "that Zach renounces Jesus and pledges his allegiance to the Illuminati."

Zach lowered his head. The request was impossible. He heard Sofia groan nearby. Each of Zach's friends all made sounds of protest, murmuring, "never!" and "don't even think about it, Zach."

"What?" Zach looked from Brother Guiden to Sam to Sofia.

"That is my price. Your loyalty for Brother Guiden and Sam's freedom."

"No," Zach shook his head. "Impossible."

"He'd never consider it!" Sam said.

"He's too true. He'd never sell out," Sofia added.

"And why shouldn't he think about it?" The Holy Seer picked up on the chatter. "The Illuminati have been seekers of the truth for hundreds of years...isn't that what you are, Zach? A seeker of truth?

Isn't that why you want to expose these hidden, so-called, Gospels?" He began to walk around Zach's hanging prone body again, speaking in a logical tone that increased with rousing emphasis as he made his points like a lawyer building his case.

"What exactly do you want to achieve by sharing this presumed truth with the world? You could achieve this kind of power quickly and easily by simply joining the Illuminati - we have people in power positions all over the world influencing policy decisions, creating revolution when needed and squelching revolution when needed. We have influenced the French Revolution, the Founding Fathers of America, the American Civil War, Napoleon Bonaparte, Adolf Hitler, the list goes on and on. Where there is a power struggle, we are there... We are the true movers and shakers in the world...Your exposure will just be a flash in the pan, a light on an old controversy, it won't change anything, certainly not the corruption and atrocities of the past. Join us, and your ideas, your goals will be made manifest."

The Holy Seer stopped again at Zach's head and bent down to see the suffering man's eyes. Zach only stared straight ahead at the floor. He blinked.

"Everything you could possibly want would be at your fingertips," the Holy Seer continued. "Anything that wealth and power can buy... the latest technology, the finest house in any city of the world, the freedom to travel anywhere, a trip to space, the most exquisite food and wine, and of course the most beautiful and exotic women...nothing," he paused, "nothing would be out of the question. Nothing and no one would be denied to you. Joining us would give you pleasures and freedom you've never known, couldn't even imagine."

"Just worldly pleasures," Zach whispered.

"Yes, besides the pleasures, the prestige! This is something that cannot be bought. You would be known for your Royal Blood." He paused. "You would be honored for such." He paused again. "You would be treated by the masses like more than a king," the Holy Seer spoke slowly and emphasized each word, "but the descendant of the son of man himself. No one on earth can match that position. No one else would have such power."

He leaned in to speak directly into Zach's ears. "Imagine, your ideas, opinions, decisions all put forth into action. Think of all the *good* you could do." The Holy Seer's voice rose with his own building emotion suggesting that he, too, had once been convinced by this argument. "Your influence would be global. There is no better life!"

Zach shook his head. *For you probably, but that's not how I define goodness, the good life.* The words rang in his skull. He felt hot all over and unbearably weary. Sweat poured from his skin.

The Holy Seer backed away and began circling Zach again. "And not only you, but your most treasured friends," he gestured to Brother Guiden and Sam as he walked by, "would lead free lives, safe from any harm. The Illuminati would protect them and give them anything they ever needed. They would no longer suffer or want for anything."

The Holy Seer paused until he'd circled back to Zach's head. "Truly, this is something you want, Zach, for your friends?"

"I do want that for them," Zach managed to say between labored breaths. "But not in this way."

"Think about it for a little while." The Holy Seer pressed his fingertips together in front of his chest. "Think of all the good you could accomplish. Think of the safety and happiness of your loved ones."

The group waited…All eyes watched Zach hanging forlornly in his chains.

Finally, Zach broke the silence. "I might consider it, if…."

"If what?" asked the Holy Seer.

"If you also guarantee Brother Mollo and Sofia's freedom." When Zach spoke the chains rattled in eerie rhythm with his heavy breaths. "If you promise that no one will ever be accosted or troubled again in their free lives."

The Holy Seer lifted his left eyebrow and clasped his hands together in contemplation. "It is an interesting proposition and worth our consideration." He motioned to Cara and they moved near the gate to consult.

"Zach," Sofia whispered. "You can't. You can't betray your beliefs."

"She's right, Zach," Sam agreed. "We'll be alright. Don't negotiate."

"Please, Zach," the friends all echoed each other. "Please don't."

A long time seemed to pass. Zach had to wiggle his toes and fingers to keep the blood circulating. He felt as if he might pass out at any moment. If only they would take him down from the chains - then he could think more clearly. Then he would be able to figure out how to respond, what to do.

The Holy Seer and Cara returned to stand beside Zach. "We have considered, and we reject the offer," the Holy Seer said.

The group of friends exchanged glances with each other.

"Brother Mollo must do time for his betrayal, and Sofia, well, since she, too, is of Royal Blood, we need to keep an eye on her. She may not be released."

CHAPTER 60

Sunday, 2:56 p.m. - Vatican Necropolis Dungeon

The friends searched each other's eyes across Zach's hanging body through the steam from their chained stations. They tried to communicate, to figure out a way to lighten Zach's burden, as his body now sagged from not just his physical weight, but the heavy spiritual darkness of feeling abandoned.

Sam sent imploring eye signals to Sofia who sadly shook her head and shrugged her shoulders, "I've done all that I can do," she said. Weary from her effort to restore Zach's physical health, she leaned back against the stone and the steam engulfed her.

Sam set her gaze on Brother Guiden who was thinking deeply, but returned her beseeching look with a nod.

After a few moments, Brother Guiden began speaking in Aramaic, a language he assumed only he and Zach could understand. Sam watched Zach closely as the unfamiliar sounds of the language floated over her. She knew whatever Brother Guiden was saying was vital to Zach's decision, and she offered her own prayer that he wouldn't make a deal. Zach lifted his head and cocked it in the direction of Brother Guiden to show that he was listening.

In Arabic, Brother Guiden reminded Zach of the immense power of "The One Star Rising." He asked Zach to look inside and find that power. He explained how as a member of the Royal Blood family, Zach could tap into this power, his lineage going back to Christ, and find all the strength, hope, and wisdom he needed to carry on. He countered all of the Holy Seer's temptations to power and influence with points of his own, with the light of the truth, with the purity of purpose. Although the Holy Seer promised worldly power, by following the light of spirit and truth, Zach's influence would be even far greater, even if he never saw it in the time of the world. He urged Zach not to broker a deal. He told him he would be the light of the days to come - that the current people, his descendents, and the generations to come would always look to him for inspiration. He told him that he could call on the community of his Royal Blood family for help.

The Holy Seer and Cara exchanged impatient gazes. "Enough!" Cara commanded, stepping toward Brother Guiden as if to silence him.

"Search your heart for that power, Zach," Brother Guiden continued in Aramaic. Zach lifted his head to meet Brother Guiden's gaze. "Wield it. The time has come. Search within all your heart Zachary. Call on your fellow Brothers and Sisters."

Cara motioned to a guard who approached Brother Guiden. Brother Guiden flinched in fear of being struck, but the guard only bent to unlock his handcuffs. Then the guard walked to Sam and unlocked hers as well. Sam immediately dropped to her knees to get on eye level with Zach. He saw her and gave her a weary smile. She placed her hands on her heart and then held them out to Zach. He nodded.

The guard jerked Sam up from her knees and motioned for her to stand next to Brother Guiden against the wall near the iron wrought gate.

"Now, Zach," the Holy Seer said. "These two may leave and have their freedom, as soon as you swear your allegiance to the Illuminati. If you do not honor the deal, they will remain."

As the Holy Seer finished his sentence, Brother Guiden lunged from his place on the wall and rushed the cardinal. Following his lead, Sam ran to jump Cara from behind. Cara spun around at the last second, and Sam punched her in the face. The force sent Cara sprawling to the ground. As Sam turned to help Brother Guiden, Cara swiftly recovered. She pulled her weapon, and shot Sam in the back.

Gripping her back, Sam cried out in anguish. She stumbled forward, clutching the air, then fell to her knees in agony.

"Sam!" Zach cried out.

Sam pivoted toward Zach and crawled a few paces in his direction before falling to the ground at his side. Bleeding profusely, she called his name weakly, "Zach!"

Zach struggled in his chains, trying with all his might to break free, to help his beloved. But he was stuck, suspended just a few feet from where she lay bleeding. "Hang on, Sam! Just hang on!"

Sam reached out one hand to Zach, but all she could reach was the space between them.

She collapsed to the ground.

Zach rattled his chains in rage and despair, but he couldn't reach her.

Meanwhile, Brother Guiden continued to struggle with the Holy Seer. Brother Guiden seemed to have the upper hand, holding the cardinal inert in a headlock from behind. But in a swift, clandestine move, the Holy Seer freed his right hand and reached into the thick layers of his robe. He pulled out what appeared to be a crucifix, but was actually a concealed knife. He stabbed Brother Guiden in the side. Brother Guiden tried to keep his hold, but the pain was too great. He released the cardinal, grabbed his wound, and backed away, holding his other arm up to ward off more blows. The Holy Seer followed brandishing the crucifixion knife, his blue eyes glinting with a manic evil light. A red bloom blossomed across Brother Guiden's white cloak, and the Holy Seer nodded with satisfaction, his rapacious eyes glinted, and he turned to assess the room.

"Brother Guiden!" Zach yelled. Horrified, he and Sofia watched helplessly as Brother Guiden, clutching his bleeding side, fell to his knees near Sam.

"Sam, Brother Guiden, come to me," Sofia called. "Try to make it to me!"

Brother Guiden crawled a few steps, then paused to try to get his breath. Sam lifted her head but was no longer able to move.

Zach looked from Brother Guiden to Sam. Sam raised her eyes to Zach and mouthed

"I love you!" before closing her eyes for the last time.

CHAPTER 61

Sunday, 3:11 p.m. - The Vatican Necropolis Dungeon

Zach uttered an otherworldly sound of anguish. His chains rattled. He looked from the lifeless Sam to the bleeding Brother Guiden. He shut his eyes and searched inside, feeling for the power of the "One Start Rising" that Brother Guiden promised he would find. He remembered Brother Guiden's words in Aramaic, especially the ones about calling on his Brothers and Sisters, the other members of the Royal Blood Family. He concentrated so hard that his face turned red and blood started to exit his ears and roll slowly down his cheeks.

Sofia froze and stared at Zach. She, too, closed her eyes and concentrated. She clapped her hands together and began to rub them back and forth. Across the globe, every Royal Blood heard the call and instantly stopped whatever they were doing. In unison they clapped their hands together and began to rub them back and forth. Each individual life force joined together with Zach and Sofia, thousands of Royal Bloods in perfect harmony with one another. Golden light began to emanate from their hands. Together as one, the Royal Bloods all faced their palms outward. The continuous golden strains swiftly flew away, traveling to Zach at the speed of light from all around the globe in a worldly display of community, power, and strength. Across the continents these whimsical golden trails traveled to Rome until they united with Zach's light. Zach held out his handcuffed hands, and the metal broke in half, crashing to the ground. Zach's body began to rise higher and higher, then it turned upright and he levitated in a standing position off the ground.

Brother Guiden looked up with a reverent smile and his eyes shined with the light of truth.

Cara advanced to control Zach, but he resisted, smacking her gun to the ground and kicking it out of the way. A lengthy battle ensued. At first Cara gained the upper hand, swiftly attacking with kicks and strikes, but Zach, with his new otherworldly confidence, didn't back down. He deflected her strikes and kicks, landing a few blows of his own. He advanced on her, forcing her back with his fists, feeling the life-giving energy of his family coursing through him. Cara back-flipped out of his way and then returned with a round kick in the air. Zach deflected the kick with such force that Cara couldn't regain her balance, landing on her neck. She died instantly.

Once the Holy Seer realized Cara would probably lose her fight, he rushed to Sofia's side and unlocked her from her chains. He pressed his crucifixion knife into her back and hissed, "you're coming with me." He pushed her before him in the direction of the iron wrought gate.

CHAPTER 62

Sunday, 3:36 p.m. - The Vatican Necropolis Dungeon

Weary from sending her light to Zach, Sofia had no recourse but to comply. She felt the jab of the knife and quickened her steps towards the exit. But just as the Holy Seer and Sofia were about to escape, the gate swung open with its loud creak to reveal Pope Aloysius. He entered the room with a bevy of Swiss Guards, two of whom stood close to his side. The pope looked swiftly around the room, taking in the scene of carnage.

"What is going on here?" he demanded.

Everyone froze for an instant, and Sofia's heart sprang with hope, but the Holy Seer quickly recovered and spun a lie: "These prisoners were arrested for a possibly assasination attempt on your life, pontiff," he said. "When we brought them here for questioning they attacked us. As you see, the head of my command lies dead," he gestured to Cara on the ground.

"What?" the pope tried to make sense of this fabrication.

"This one I'm taking with me," The Holy Seer grabbed Sofia's arm and made a move to slip past the pope and his guards.

"No, I recognize her," the pope said. The guards blocked the path. "She came to see me earlier today. She's part of the Royal Blood family. She can't possibly be tangled up in an assasitnation plot."

"She can and she is," the Holy Seer claimed. "I must get her away from you at once."

Even though the pieces of this puzzle didn't make sense to him yet, Pope Aloysius knew letting the cardinal leave with Sofia was a mistake. He felt it deeply. Thinking quickly to change the course of events he said, "No, let her be. It is I who will go with you."

"No!" Sofia exclaimed. "This man is very dangerous. He will hurt you!"

"And will he not hurt you if I allow him to leave with you?"

The Holy Seer looked from the pope to Sofia to the group of guards in the hallway. Although he hated to release Sofia, he realized Pope Aloysius was giving him his only way out. "I accept that offer," the Holy Seer said. "I will leave Sofia here and take you, pontiff, instead."

Pope Aloysius nodded, and the incredulous guards stood by as passed through the gate with the Holy Seer.

CHAPTER 63

Sunday, 3:45 p.m. - The Vatican Necropolis Dungeon

As the heavy gate clanged closed behind the pope and Cardinal Villere, Zach flew to Brother Guiden's side. Kneeling beside him, Zach grasped the Brother's cold and shaking hand; he searched Brother Guiden's fluttering eyes.

"I'm dying," Brother Guiden said.

"No!" Zach shook his head. "I need you.."

"You'll be fine." Brother Guiden gave Zach's hand a gentle squeeze. "You've become all I ever dreamed for you."

"Please don't leave me." Zach said.

"Dear boy, you have all you need inside," Brother Guiden assured him.

Zach shook his head, he pressed Brother's Guiden's robe against his wound. As the robe filled with blood, he called to Sofia, "Please come and help Brother Guiden!"

Sofia made her way over and knelt at the other side of Brother Guiden's prone figure; she held her hands out and pressed them together. Brother Guiden shook his head. "No, my dear. Don't waste your healing energy on me." He turned his face to Zach. Tears brimmed in his eyes as he said, "It's my time to die. I've fulfilled my calling. I am at peace."

"No, Brother Guiden," Zach shook his head, and tears rolled down his cheeks.

Brother Guiden clasped his hand harder. "Zach, you must let me go. You must also fulfill your destiny!" His eyes shined. "Form a new church and call it Chritianology. Teach the way of your ancestors." Brother Guiden's eyes closed briefly, then opened again with intensity. "Pray with me."

Zach bowed his head in prayer. Time seemed to freeze for a minute as they prayed.

Brother Guiden began to sing one more lullaby for Zach who kept his head bowed, holding his friend and mentor's hand. The lyrics spoke of bringing his body home. Even in his weakened state, Brother Guiden's voice maintained its rich timbre. As he sang, his voice softened, lessening in volume until he finished the song and relinquished his spirit.

CHAPTER 64

Sunday, 3:55 p.m. - Vatican Holding Cells

Zach wept at his beloved mentor's side, pressing his head to Brother Guiden's chest. He felt as if his heart was shredding into bits. He held the good Brother's body in his arms and fought to catch his breath. Brother Guiden had been more than a mentor, he'd been a father figure. He'd raised Zach at the orphanage as if he were his own son. Zach could still hear his tender voice singing in his ears.

"Zach," Sofia put her hand on his shoulder and the warmth ran down his arm. "There will be time to mourn," she said, "but for now we need to…"

Zach forced himself to raise his weary head, "I know." He kissed Brother Guiden's forehead and moved to Sam's lifeless body laying nearby.

"It may have been Brother Guiden's time, but I'm not sure it's Sam's," he said to Sofia. "Is it possible? Can you heal her?"

Sofia joined Zach, kneeling at Sam's side. "I can try," she said.

Sofia raised her eyes upward and pressed her palms together. She said a silent prayer. She gently rolled Sam on her side and placed her hands on Sam's wounded back. A radiant light emanated from her hands and climbed skyward. This beam filled the room with a golden hue, and all were transfixed by it. The remaining guards all watched with amazement as Sofia's healing powers imbued breath back into Sam.

Sam coughed gently at first, then more robustly. She opened her eyes and looked around in confusion. Both Sofia and Zach smiled at her.

"You're going to be alright," Sofia soothed. "Just take it easy. Breathe slowly."

Zach reached for Sam's hand and kissed it. She smiled.

Sofia leaned back against the stone wall, resting her head and eyes.

"Are you alright?" Zach asked her.

"Yes, I'll be fine. Just exhausted at the moment. I need to rest. I'll stay here with Sam. You go and help the pope."

Zach looked nervously up at the Swiss guard, not sure where they stood on matters, but they all seemed to have been converted by first Zach's breaking of his chains then Sofia's display of healing. One stepped forward, "Go with peace," he said. "We will make sure no harm comes to them," he gestured to Sofia and Sam, both now resting against the wall.

"Thank you," Zach nodded. He climbed to his feet and ran out the door.

CHAPTER 65

Sunday, 4:07 p.m. - St. Peter's Square

Zach ran through the halls of the old building, looking for signs of the pope and the cardinal. He fled down the stairwell towards St. Peter's Square where he spotted them, vaguely disguised in dark cloaks, beginning to cross the square.

"Stop!" Zach called out. "Freeze!"

The Holy Seer and the pope turned to see Zach in pursuit. Before heading to the exit, the Holy Seer had brought the pope to his office where he grabbed the cloaks and a gun. Instead of freezing, he drew a gun on Zach and fired. From instinct, Zach raised his hands. He immediately felt the power from his family, and as he concentrated, the bullets slowed down, stopped, and dropped to the ground. It all happened in an instant. All three of them, Zach, the cardinal, and the pope were amazed. The Holy Seer couldn't believe his eyes. He realized his only leverage was the pope. With a swift motion, he stabbed Pope Aloysius in the chest with his crucifixion knife and let him fall to the ground. Zach ran to the pope, and in the ensuing melee, Cardinal Villere darted into the crowd of St. Peter's Square.

Zach kneeled by the pope's side. He removed the cloak and different veils and garments to find the wound. "Help me, my son," the pope said, raising his eyes.

Zach removed the last garment and sat back in stunned disbelief. Gracing the right side of the pope's chest, exactly where it resided on Zach, blazed the mark of the *fleur-de-lis*.

The pope began asking for forgiveness for his sins. Zach quickly regained his composure. He couldn't let the pontiff die, especially now that he knew the pope was also a member of the Royal Blood. He needed his help to present the lost Gospels and to begin the Church of Christianology. Zach bundled up a veil and applied pressure to the wound.

"Stay with me, your holiness," Zach said, but the pope's eyelids began to flutter and his breath slowed.

Zach thought of his lessons with Sofia and of her most recent display of healing power. Mimicking her, he took a deep breath, said a silent prayer, and pressed his palms open on the pontiff's chest. He felt a surge of warmth fill his hands, and when he opened his eyes, he saw a rainbow of light emanating from his hands across the surface of the pope's chest. The wound began to close, and the pope's breath returned to normal. The pontiff's eyes fluttered open and made contact with Zach's.

Zach breathed a deep sigh of relief. "You're alright!" he exclaimed. "Thank God!" He raised his eyes to heaven. "Thank you," he said sincerely.

The pope coughed and tried to sit up. "Wait, I'll support you." Zach moved so that the pope could rest his head in his lap. Curious onlookers who had scattered and hid at the first sound of gunfire began to peek out and approach the site. Zach looked up to see Sofia and Sam leaving the Vatican and crossing the square to join him. He looked around for the Holy Seer, but the cardinal had escaped.

CHAPTER 66

Monday, 8:17 a.m. - The Vatican Apartments

Zach woke up after a much needed long night of sleep. The night before, Pope Aloysius invited the group to be his guests at the Vatican. Zach shook his head as memories of the last few days flooded his mind. He went to the window and drews back the heavy curtains, taking in the view of St. Peter's Square and the green gold domes and orange rooftops of Vatican City. He marveled at how so much history had brought him to this moment. A welling emotion bubbled up inside him - he couldn't put an exact name to it, but it was a mixture of joy, grief, amazement, and reverence followed by a strong urge to see Sam. He needed to find out how she was feeling, to talk to her about...all of it....what it meant to them.

He dressed quickly and walked down the hall to Sam's room.

Sam opened the door dressed in a short silk robe, her long dark hair still wet from the shower. She smiled at Zach and invited him in.

Zach pulled her to him in a hug. "Well, what do you think we should do for our next date?" he joked.

Sam laughed. "A simple romantic dinner for two out in New Orleans will suffice."

"Turn it down just a notch?" Zach held her tight.

"Just a smidge less excitement," Sam joked, hugging him back.

Zach held her another moment. "Or we could see where these feelings are leading us," he said. "I think it's leading to the Sacred Divinity." He explained to her what Brother Guiden had taught him about this sacred act. "It's the long line of love between people that first put the *One Star Rising* in the sky. Brother Guiden explained that it's my turn to step into my position in that chain. I'd like you to step there with me."

"I've felt this way for you for a long time," Sam said, "but I didn't think you felt that way about me….you were always so busy with your studies and your projects with Brother Guiden."

"Well, I may not have known it at school, but I know it for certain now," Zach said. "I love you, Samantha DelaCroix. I think we're right together. With you by my side, nothing can stop us."

He kissed her.

"Do you want to take it to the next level?" Zach asked shyly, running his hand up and down her back. "If so, I'd like to share the physical love God made for us." He ducked his head and then met her gaze. "What do you think?"

Sam smiled and agreed. They kissed passionately and fell into bed in a loving embrace.

CHAPTER 67

Thursday, Noon - Vatican City Press Conference

For the next three days, Zach and Pope Aloysius worked day and night to develop the plan for the Church of Christianology. Sam assisted steadfastly by Zach's side. Their love for each other grew stronger day by day.

Pope Aloysius announced a special prelature for Christianology with Zach as its organizational leader. A worldwide press conference was called to announce the organization.

Just before the cameras started rolling, Sam whispered into Zach's ear, "You're the chosen person for this moment in history. You've got this!" She kissed him and squeezed his hand.

The press conference began with an overview of Christianology and its tenets. Zach also explained the significance of the lost Gospels, reiterating the speech Brother Guiden had given so many days ago in New Orleans. He told the press how they had found the Gospel of Mary Magdalene and reminded them of how it was to Mary Magdalene that Jesus bore witness and gave instruction to, not Peter. How apart from the Virgin Mary, Mary Magdalene was the only woman reported, specifically by her individual name, in all recorded gospels, and her significant value is suggested by the fact that, almost without exception, her name comes first whenever a list is given of Jesus' female followers, ahead of even the Mother Mary. How she was present at the Anointing, Crucifixion and Resurrection. He relayed how the church initially recognized her utmost importance to Jesus by granting her the title in the religious hierarchy of *Apostola Apostolorum* or the Apostle to the Apostles / The First Apostle.

He reminded the audience that the early Church suffered many power struggles, and the only way for the early Roman Church to restrain the heirs of Jesus and Mary Magdalene was to discredit Mary herself and deny any marital relationship with Jesus. Mary was then portrayed unjustly as a whore and sinner in history. For her own safety after the crucifixion, Joseph of Arimathea, James who was presumed to be Jesus' brother, and John brought Mary Magdalene, now pregnant, to Alexandria, Egypt. There they settled in a nondescript, growing Jewish community and planned for the future, passing the true message of God down through the divine blood generations. Zach stressed that the wisdom in the lost Gospels would change the world for the better.

Next, Zach appointed Sofia the first Cardinal of Christianology and announced that she would be the leader of the European sector. He also explained there would be special memorials for Brother Rodney Martin, Detective Mitchell Begg, and Brother Jeremiah Guiden who all died in the fight for the cause. He explained how Brother Guiden, particularly, helped develop the inspired ideas for the organization. Finally, he named Brother Guiden the first saint of Christianology.

After a round of applause Zach gave a riveting and thought-provoking speech on "The Potential Greatness of Humankind."

CHAPTER 68

Two Years Later - United Nations Headquarters

Zach, Sam, and Sofia are all seated at a conference table with many other world leaders and heads of religious organizations. They have gathered for a universal televised peace conference. Zach beams brightly into the camera as he discusses the many acts of justice and peace since the development of Chritianology. The world leaders discuss their current and future programs and their plans to maintain and promote peace. The hearty meeting is full of goodwill, uplifted spirits, smiles, and pats on the back.

Meanwhile, in a nondescript home, a two-and-a-half year old boy sits on a couch in front of a television, watching the live coverage of the peace conference. He watches with a passive face, but alert, investigative eyes. On the back of his neck rests a small mark. If one looks closely they might easily make out the number, "666," the number of the Beast. It is the AntiChrist taking note.

TO BE CONTINUED....